I0609585

HOME SWEET WITCH

BETTINA M JOHNSON

AQUA RAVEN PUBLISHING

Home Sweet Witch

Copyright © 2020 by Bettina Johnson

ISBN: 978-1-7350692-0-3 (paperback version)

Cover Art by StunningBookCovers.com

For my husband, Larry, who reminded me I could do anything I set my mind to

ACKNOWLEDGMENTS

I want to thank the people on my team who all work to make my books shine.

To my editor, Janie Mills, the minutiae queen, thank you. She corrects the errors I overlook (or had no idea I was even making).

To my amazingly talented cover artist Daniela Colleo. Oh, how I enjoy our collaborations. All your hard work makes my covers stand out and shine.

To Michelle Lynn MacQueen, formatter extraordinaire, you do a stellar job of getting my books readable and fixing everything, so it isn't off to one side or lopsided. And doing so over and over, graciously, due to a plethora of my minor errors!

To the men at Benchmark Automotive in Gainesville, Georgia, for helping me with anything and everything to do with auto service and repair, I don't know the difference between a differential or a dipstick, so their gentle correction to my auto mechanic faux pas is invaluable!

I mainly want to thank my husband, Larry. He is the one who has to put up with me. When I go into a writing frenzy, his home-cooked meals go on the back burner, and he has to be satisfied making do with a bowl of Raisin Bran instead. I'm thankful he has not opted to strangle me and toss me into a chipper-shredder! It is a testament that I chose the best person in the entire world to spend my life with. I love him more than I can decently express with words—ironic considering I write books and use vocabulary daily—and I am so grateful he said "okay" when I told him we were getting married.

Finally, to you, Dear Reader, for embracing the beloved characters who run amok in my head, waiting for me to tell their stories. Without you, none of this would be possible, and I am truly grateful.

– Bettina

PROLOGUE

*W*ill they come for her? That thought danced around the fogginess one experiences before fully awakening and it causes me to shiver as I realize I don't have that answer.

I'm tired. Even looking around the room makes me ache in ways most people wouldn't understand. Not the nurses. Never the doctors. Certainly not my Lily. *My* Lily—like she's something I possess. No one can possess that child.

Not that she is a child any longer.

I can see the sadness in her eyes when she looks at me. Oh, how I hate that look. Like I'm already dead and she is about to have her entire world turned upside down. Maybe it is better this way. With my death, her freedom begins—if they don't find her. When the Lord closes a door...

I don't even know how I feel about an afterlife. Part of me wants utter darkness, nothingness, the release of the soul to oblivion. I will finally have the peace I've sought ever since running away from home, dragging Lily with me. Home. Will she go? Will she heed my instructions and seek out what she has been forever asking of me? Who our people are?

Where she came from? And the most pressing in her mind—who her father is?

Perhaps I've made a mistake. But it's too late now to try and rectify it. What is done is done, as they say. What will she think of me when the truth is revealed? Do I even care? I do. I do care, but I'm tired.

I feel Death coming for me. I'm ready for her embrace. Perhaps I will get the life I wanted—only in death. After all, this might be the start of a new adventure. And that is all I have ever wished for.

A grand adventure.

Here it comes.

CHAPTER 1

"*G*irl, your face looks like a bug that just spied an oncoming car windshield.

Are you ever going to open that thing?"

I looked up from staring at the package in question as my co-worker and friend Molly came over to the booth where I was taking my mid-afternoon break and sat down across from me.

"I'm not sure. The last time I spoke with my mother, she never mentioned an estate, an inheritance, or that she even had a lawyer. Then she took a turn for the worse and died, leaving behind all this secrecy and intrigue." I slid to one side of the bench, stretching my legs up onto the vinyl seat, and looked at Molly with a lopsided grin, trying to disguise my sadness with a cavalier attitude. "We butted heads my entire life, and I have only been close to her these last two years while I helped care for her, but I never genuinely knew my mother or the particulars of her personal affairs."

My name is Lily Sweet, wannabe artist and cafe worker—I dare not call myself a barista—and all-around nice person. I tried my best to be pleasant, loved animals, preferred the mountains over the ocean. Although if I could afford to live in a mountainous area that overlooked the sea, I'd be in heaven. I'm an avid reader and could be bribed with black Jelly Belly jellybeans. My only fault, that I could see anyway, was my inability to get along with the woman who gave birth to me. I didn't mean to sound flip, because I loved my mother. But we had a classic love-hate relationship.

It was only recently that the woman I had known my entire life as someone who regarded me as an inconvenient nuisance became this serene, tender sweetheart—at least to the nurses who cared for her. She still complained to anyone within earshot how much of a burden being a single mom was and how traumatic it was to have a grown daughter see her become a skeleton. Yeah, nice one, Mom.

Jessica Croy Sweet was peculiar. No, not the *she collects garden gnomes and has velvet Elvis art on her walls* weird. No, *my* mother believed in every conspiracy theory known to man, and if we ever spent more than four years in any one place, it was a miracle. Her paranoia defined her. Insomniac extraordinaire, she listened to obscure radio programs in the wee hours when most people were sleeping. The host would converse with questionable "expert" guests nightly. Every episode had someone warning the listeners of impending doom coming from *Them*, and she would always expound to me the dangers of ever staying anywhere very long because, "*They* might find us."

She never could tell me who they were.

Mom spent her days peeking out of heavily blanketed windows until she became too weak to remain home and went into hospice. While there, the peace that had been evasive her entire life finally gave her respite from her never-ending fear. Unfortunately, it was short-lived, and she died within a year.

"We had an unusual relationship," I glanced up at Molly. "I

think she waited until her death to give me this package because she knew it would freak me out." I bit my lip.

Molly started shaking her head while regarding me as I stared askance at the unassuming parcel. Her Southern came to the forefront, and she guffawed loudly faced with my obvious discomfort.

"Hon, you can say that again. Never have I seen two women more ill-suited to be mother and daughter than you two. She wanted to hide in a cave, while you just want to be a recluse artist that never has to speak to a client." She looked at me pointedly then sighed. "Maybe you were too alike? Anyway. Hon, you look plumb afraid of a wee bit of cardboard and packing tape. It's not as if the darn thing is going to jump up and bite you like a chigger in a blackberry patch! Open it."

I looked back and forth from the tiny package to my friend then just shook my head with frustrated angst. She knew I had miles of baggage to crawl through to even remotely start accepting the death of my mother and how to feel about all my emotions. Molly Hogan was the type of person who loved socializing, deciding in five minutes flat after meeting you if she was going to give you the time of day or keep you at arms distance. Since I'd started my job at the coffee shop and met her, we'd grown closer and closer as the weeks and months passed. Why she decided I passed muster was beyond me.

Molly reached out to touch me lightly on my arm. "Ever since you started working here, I've taken you under my wing, even though you're standoffish at the best of times."

Who, me? I was downright friendly, the life of the party. When I was ten, at least I think ten, I once, well…okay…so… no, not particularly gregarious.

I lifted my head to protest, but Molly held her hand up to stop me.

"Just wait and listen. You know you are. You've said so yourself that you tend to be an introvert who loathes having to be out in the real world and would rather spend hours making art. Hon, the first time I gave you a hug, you stiffened up like a surfboard. All I am saying is you have spent the better part of the last two years doing nothing but taking care of a woman who spent your life being distracted and distant toward you at her best. At her worst, she just ignored your existence and worried at shadows. Never mean to you, don't give me that look, but with a begrudging love that makes me wonder what her life was like before you came along. I think the real reason you keep putting off opening this bundle is fear of finding out who she was and what your relationship truly meant to her."

I felt my eyes misting and looked across the coffee shop out to the parking lot as Molly's word rang true. I agreed with the assessment that I didn't know much about my mother or why it had to be the two of us against the world. In the last few years of her life, I knew we had grown closer, even if it was strained. Tension existed because she would never tell me about our family, especially my father, or where we came from and why we were alone. But I knew that I wouldn't have traded those last two years for anything. Now, I was afraid of finally getting answers to questions I had been asking since I could remember...which was why I kept putting this off.

Sighing, I placed my hands on the table and swung my legs back to the floor, pulling the package forward.

"Well, you are right about one thing." I smiled as Molly looked at me inquisitively. "I am private enough to know I won't be opening this here, at work, but maybe later while I am scrounging for dinner and going over more bills I can't pay, I will. I hope there's something in there that can help!"

Molly smiled at me and pointed a finger in my direction.

"Lily Sweet, only you could get this worked up over something your mama left you." Standing up, she started to head back to her station, but not before finishing her thought, "For your sake, I hope it is something that puts a smile on your face, and all your fears were over nothing."

* * *

LATER THAT EVENING, I did indeed manage to put together a meal of the remaining two eggs that were still in date, barely, along with some questionable asparagus, and made an omelet. The bills were in a pile waiting for me to worry over them. I succeeded circumventing my impatient landlord, Leo, yet again by slipping through the neighbors' yard and over the fence, going in the back door to my tiny bungalow. I was a ninja, slinking quietly through the dark, silent, deadly. I didn't even scream when I ran through a humongous spiderweb. Yep, the spider was front and center, not a sound out of me. Boss.

Groaning a little, I stared at the package, knowing I had to get over this unreasonable dread and just open it already.

I mean, how bad could it be? I'm now on my own, cut away from family I hardly remember, living like a monk, and just barely making ends meet. It couldn't be worse than this. Right?

"Okay, here goes nothing," I mumble.

Hands trembling a little, I reached for the butter knife.

As I slit open the tape then opened the flaps, I peered inside the box and pulled out a manila envelope. Sliding the contents out, I began organizing the items on the table in front of me. A small, careworn, leather-bound book, a thin black box, a letter from the lawyer, and a photo. So far so good.

I picked up the photograph first and saw it was a way

younger version of Mom, standing next to a pleasant-looking man holding a baby. I turned it over, noting the date. My birthday. My second. The inscription was in my mother's perfect cursive:

Before everything fell apart: Charles and Lily, last of The Dolce Family Dynasty.

Dolce family? My last name is Sweet!

Wait. That *means* sweet in some other language. Italian? It must be since I knew I had Italian in me. I just never questioned it—or my surname, for that matter. Why would I? Could it be that my father's family changed their names at some point when they emigrated to the United States? Not unheard of, but odd that Mom chose to write that inscription. Last of a dynasty.

Flipping the photo back around, I scrutinized the man who must be my father. Whoa. I looked a lot like him. I didn't remember him. I knew nothing of him other than he died when I was not much older than the toddler in his arms. He was medium stature, slim, and rather dashing looking with dark espresso brown hair like my own. One time, a beautician told me it was the darkest shade of brown you could have before she would classify it as black. Of course, the same beautician had felt like experimenting with color and had added two purple streaks in my hair on a whim, which I kept up ever since, because I thought it made me look kicky.

On the sporadic instances my mother spoke of him, she told me I had his molten, cognac-brown eyes. Mom, in comparison, was almost the same height as her spouse, but where he was dark, she was all red-haired Scottish and eyes a cornflower blue. I looked nothing like her except we shared a pale skin tone, hers dappled with freckles. On me? Let's just say when I went through my goth period, I didn't need to whiten my skin with powder; and there are no freckles. I did have one beauty mark near my shoulder, though, and it stood out whenever I had a swimsuit on. Oh, and while Mom burned even thinking about the sun, I could kept my pale skin tinted a light golden-brown shade without much effort...that Italian blood I mentioned coming in handy! I was golden most of the year and only faded in the dead of winter.

Setting the photo aside, I reached for the next item, the letter from the attorney. It was rather short and to the point:

"Miss Sweet. Enclosed you will find items your late mother entrusted me to pass on to you upon her death. After you have time to go over them, I will be at your disposal to move forward with your decision on how to proceed. Please contact me when you are ready to meet at my office. —J.L.P."

Decision? Well, that certainly brought some intrigue to the table, adding ambiguity to what so far remained unremarkable objects. Reaching for the leather-bound book next, I began reading the contents, trying to make sense of what I found.

A genealogy of sorts in Mother's handwriting, listing grandparents and great-grandparents on both sides as well as my mom and dad, ending with me in the bottom space. My paternal great-grandparents were listed as Dolce, so that was one mystery solved. A glaring oddity was a space next to my father that registered a name but was scribbled out with a permanent marker, making the name impossible to see. How odd. Another spouse? Was my father married before and my own mother, a second wife?

Turning the pages, I saw names listed that meant nothing other than I now recognized we were related: Dolce, Sweet,

Croy, Fortune, and several more that made my head spin. A town in Georgia called Sweet Briar with notes about a family compound. Georgia, did I come from there? The name didn't ring any bells. I sat back and pondered every bit of what I could remember my reticent mother telling me about anything that smacked of family, which added up to a great, fat, heap of nothing.

I barely recalled playing with who I assume were cousins and sitting at a table having lunch with another woman, an aunt maybe, but they could have just as well been neighbors, so distant were my recollections. My memories, flotsam drifting in and out of my mind, like a stone tossed in a lazy river, rings spreading out then dissipating until they were gone. Why did I never pester Mother harder for these answers? Well, because she became upset, and it was definitely more comfortable not going there, ever. In truth, Mother spent so much time in a melancholy funk, looking with caution out the windows for zombies or whatever, that I was afraid of the answers I'd hear if I persevered.

The final page had a pocket with my birth certificate and baptism document, a lock of baby hair, a little Pisces charm for my birth month, and sure enough, Sweet Briar, Georgia, was listed as my birthplace. Another mystery solved. I allowed my finger to run across the charm and felt a pang of loss. I remembered this charm—I think. I thought it lost, or...no. My thoughts became foggy, so I turned to the paper. There was a photo of a young lady holding me as an infant paper-clipped to this page, and when I unfastened it and turned it over, there was an inscription on it as well:

Adelaide and Lily.

The young woman appeared to be about seventeen or eighteen, with a lighter shade of red hair than my mother's.

She was looking down at baby me with a slight smile on her face. Yet, somehow, the entire photo gave off a sense of sorrow that made me react the same. I wondered at her identity.

Setting it all aside, I reached for the final item, the black box that had seen better days. It took a moment to figure out how to open the filigreed clasp. Lifting the lid, I found myself staring at an ornate key with a moss green satin ribbon tied at the end of it. Folded inside the lid of the box was a simple note from mother:

"Lily, should you choose to accept your fate, take this key to open doors. The home is yours. Go in secret to Sweet Briar to claim your birthright. If you decide against this task, burn the package and everything in it, destroy the key, and walk away from your name. My attorney will help you gain a new identity. The road ahead will be arduous, and you may be in danger. I'm sorry I was never the mother you hoped I'd be. I did my best. Always remember these words: Sometimes a little Wicked makes everything good. Always be wary. They have eyes everywhere, watching. With love, Mom."

What the heck? I turned the key over and over in my hand and reread the note, then one more time for good measure. Home? Birthright? Wicked in capital letters like it's a proper noun? Danger? *Them,* again, Mom, seriously? Who are they, and what could they possibly do to me and why? How could I travel to Sweet Briar when I couldn't even afford to go food shopping, let alone pay the rent this month?

That thought barely left my mind when I was startled by a loud pounding at the front door, and the angry voice of my landlord began yelling.

"I know you are in there, Miss Sweet. You're not fooling me with the lights out and curtains closed!" The pounding got louder, and I sighed, getting to my feet. I knew no manner of persuading was going to get me out of not having the rent money to pay the man. Sweeping everything back into the box, I squared my shoulders. I headed for the front door, knowing by this time tomorrow I'd have more answers or, at the very least, could throw myself at the mercy of Mother's attorney, since I had a sneaking suspicion I was about to get my eviction notice.

* * *

THAT'S IT, then. Not only was I correct in assuming the worst —eviction—I also found I had no legal grounds to fight it. My wonderful mother, before her death, apparently signed a piece of paper stating that, once she passed, I would also agree to leave the rental home within two weeks of the sad event.

After spending a few moments cursing the heavens, throwing a few pillows, kicking the coffee table, and injuring my big toe in the process, I stumbled around hopping on one foot then fell in a miserable heap on the sofa and began to cry. What? This conundrum I faced was due to my own mother doing me in from the Great Beyond. I was allowed a pity party!

It made absolutely zero sense. But the facts were the facts, and the evidence was right before me with my mother's signature on the paperwork from my landlord. All nice, legal, and notarized. Perfect. It looked like she was forcing my hand and making the decision an easy one for me now that I had nowhere to live. I guessed I was heading to Georgia. How I was going to afford to go, well, that's another story.

Leo had to add insult to injury when he declared we were a nuisance.

"Two nutty women all holed up in here all the time, alone,

and half the neighbors convinced you're up to no good. Your mother was crazy. Did you know that? Covering the windows with blankets. Who knows what you were doing in here?" He looked around, wide-eyed and suspicious, like he expected monsters to jump out from behind the pantry door. Oh wait, the door fell off last week. *Oops!*

Hitching up his pants, he all but spit on me when he cried, "Good riddance to bad rubbish!" Then he stormed out, voice fading as he headed to his car, professing all the way that I had to be gone by noon the next day. *Or else.*

Issues much, Leo?

Why did she do this? We had our differences: fights, bad words between us, the usual BS some mothers and daughters went through. But to leave me without a place to live so soon after she died? I mean, I knew I could not go on living here on my salary with no benefits coming in now that she was gone. But I could have stayed another three months once the last check hit our post office box in a few days. I guess she didn't want me to grow moss dithering over my decision, forcing me to choose this crazy road trip. Yet one more occurrence to make me retreat into self-pity and put a wall up on my emotions, and it started like this between mom and me a long, long time ago.

I assumed I would get more answers from her attorney tomorrow. I'd call him first thing and set up an appointment to meet.

CHAPTER 2

I spent that night throwing my stuff in a suitcase and packing a few boxes. It's not as if the task took a long time to accomplish; we didn't own much of anything. The sum total of my possessions would easily fit in my vehicle. My thoughts kept going back to what Leo said earlier that evening.

So, we were bad rubbish and up to no good—evil wretches to be shunned and chased out of town. I supposed my landlord and a majority of the neighbors thought keeping to oneself and being poor meant we were bad news. I mean, we eventually managed to have the rent money even though we were almost always a few days late!

I don't recall any neighbors acting weird around us. We waved when we saw them, even talking from time to time with Mrs. Riley across the street. Maybe she was a bad example, however, since she thought Elvis was still alive, lived above the hardware store in town, and played Santa at the town's VFW post every Christmas. She even showed me a photo taken of her sitting on his lap. How come *we* were being talked about and painted as some evil, crazy villains? I certainly never did anything even remotely wicked since... well. There was this one time.

I did remember an occurrence from my past, probably because it was so traumatic. Everything else from my childhood had always been strangely fuzzy, and I was always jealous of people who seemed to remember every detail of their lives with aplomb.

Because I couldn't remember my father, I had no emotions for dealing with the type of tragedy a young child felt upon losing a parent. My relationship with my mother was forever rocky, which led to a bit of a rebellious streak in my teen years. Lack of money or the wherewithal to leave and start out on my own in life never came about. I had hopes and dreams, but every time I thought about it enough, started planning anything, all the energy seemed to seep out of me, and I'd find myself still selling coffee and working on my art projects with no end in sight.

But this one memory had stayed with me over the years and was troubling in light of what Leo inferred people were saying. Funny that I thought about it now when it was too late to try and convince my mom to finally let me know what happened that day. Because in the past, when I asked her about it, she would clam up. It *must* have occurred just before we left Georgia for New York State.

* * *

FOR AS LONG AS she could remember, Lily wanted a kitten. Not just any kitten, but one that looked just like the Halloween cat on her plastic pumpkin that she got to carry that October, her very first time going trick-or-treating with her mommy. Lily was dressed up as a witch, pointy hat, cape, and a miniature broom and all, and on the pumpkin that was to hold her candy loot, a little black cat

15

with green eyes smiled while wearing its own pointy hat. She had little earrings on that matched—tiny black cat heads with green eyes. It had hurt when Mommy pierced her ears, but it was worth it to always have those kitties on. She didn't know who gave her those earrings, but she knew they were a gift, because the box they came in was wrapped in cute Halloween paper with a tiny, shiny black bow!

Upon returning to what she assumed was her home, Lily remembered her mother had gone through the candy, sorting out anything she said looked old or too difficult for "your growing teeth," as she put it, to handle. Lily didn't mind as she gazed at her pumpkin and happily munched on a piece of chocolate, swinging her legs in contentment. Her night had been perfect. Which was why a few days later, when she saw the little kitten at the gas station when her mommy pulled in to fill up for what she called "the long journey ahead," Lily pressed her face up to the window and cried out, "Oh, Mommy, look…a kitty!"

Her mother was distracted and seemed sad as well, so she didn't respond. Mommy rushed out of the house that morning, suitcases in hand, and urged her to be quiet and swift, that a new grand adventure was happening that very day, and she was to be a big brave girl and not fret. She almost left Lily's favorite Pisces charm necklace on a side table, but Lily grabbed it before they rushed out, slipping it over her head. Having never had a grand adventure before, Lily was quite excited. They never went on any kind of journeys, so she decided this day, despite her hurried departure, was going to be awesome.

Her mother's name was Jessica, although she got scolded just last week for calling her that and not "Mommy." She would get confused at times and go back and forth, saying "Mommy" sometimes, "Jessica" on other occasions. She didn't understand what all the fuss was about, because her mommy's name *was* Jessica, after all!

Jessica never went anywhere except to shop once a week. They had no friends except a lady who would call on the phone late at night and ask questions like, "How much longer will the both of you stay here? You need to go hide." Or, "You know they will find her eventually." *Find who?* she always wondered. But her Mommy would shush the lady and say, "Little ears mustn't hear." Then she'd whisper into the phone, making sure Lily couldn't eavesdrop. Lily would shrug and go back to whatever it was she'd been doing before the lady had called. Every so often, she could almost remember other people that she was certain meant something to her, but everything seemed fuzzy, and Lily's head would hurt if she tried too hard to recall their names. She sighed. That was the life she knew, so she decided this day must be extraordinary!

Lily knew she was supposed to be in her car seat; she was little, not big enough yet to ride without one. However, she reached down and managed to push open the clasp.

"Mommy?"

Lily looked to where her mother seemed to be fighting with her credit card and the gas pump. She knew she should just stay in the car, and it would not only be terrible to get out on her own but also to walk to where the small black fluff ball was crouched; but something compelled Lily to quietly open the door and hop out.

Knowing better than to just run over and pick up the kitten, Lily stopped and looked both ways. Mommy taught her to be aware of everything going on around her and be a safe, smart girl. After checking the parking lot and seeing no cars about, Lily crept to where the kitten was gnawing away at a bit of sausage.

"Hey there, little one. I don't want to scare you, pretty kitty. Are you hungry?"

The little kitten stopped what it was doing and arched its back, green eyes wide. *Oh! Just like on my plastic bucket and earrings!* she thought. This must be a sign that *this* kitten was meant to be hers. Just as she was reaching out her hand and making soft, kissy noises she hoped would win the little cat's trust, a shadow loomed behind her. The kitten hissed and ran under the big, square trash can.

"That's not your cat, it's mine!" said a rather nasty, mean voice.

When Lily stood and turned, she found a much taller boy standing there smirking, peering around her toward where the little cat had run.

"No, it's not; she's all alone and hungry, and if it was yours, why is she at a gas station?"

Lily wasn't afraid to stand up to this bully, not when she knew her mommy wasn't too far away, anyway.

"Because I said it was mine, you baby. We just got here, and Momma promised me something, so I'd stop bothering her. This is it. Now get out of my way before I push you down," he stated then began to laugh in a disturbing way, kind of like one of those hyenas Lily heard on the animal shows on television.

The boy flung himself past her in a flash and, dropping to his knees, reached under the trash can and came up holding the squirming kitten by its scruff. The poor animal was spitting and mewing at the same time.

"Stop! You're hurting her! You put her down!"

The boy sneered at Lily and, with a horrible glint in his mean gray eyes, reached his other hand up and began to choke the kitten.

"I will not. It's mine, and I can do anything I want to the stupid thing, even kill it."

Horrified, Lily began to tremble her eyes wide, and she reached her hands out toward the evil boy.

"Please, no, stop!" she pleaded.

"Or what? You'll cry, baby? You gonna cry baby tears? Or are you going to make me stop?"

Laughing a nasty chortle, the boy raised the kitten high in the air and was about to break its tiny neck when Lily balled one hand into a fist, grabbing his arm with the other, glaring at him.

"No, I won't cry, and yes, I will stop you. Now give me back my kitten."

The boy suddenly howled with incredulity as something painful slammed into the back of his head. Darkness took hold of Lily in the pit of her stomach, crept up, and sparkled menacingly through her eyes. She fastened them to the confused boy—never once blinking or looking away—and began to pull him toward her as if by some unknown force. She placed both hands on his chest and felt a strange electric current running through them.

"Stop it! What are you doing?"

He shrieked as he felt the most intense pressure in his chest, and a void of sound began to fill his head and dull his senses. Dropping the kitten, he broke away from Lily's touch and fell to the ground. He began to keen in a highly unnatural voice. Lily reached out with one hand and touched the distraught boys chin tilting his head up. His now-bloodshot gray eyes met hers; Lily's eyes turned coal black.

"I think it's time for you to go to a bad place where cruel people who hurt my kitten ought to go, and never...ever... come back."

Guttural, anguished sounds were spilling out of the boy's open mouth as he clutched at his neck, his shoulders heaving forward as if he was about to vomit. Just as Lily went to rest her forehead against his in a freakish embrace, a voice shattered her concentration.

"Oh my God...what are you doing to my son?"

Footsteps pounded behind her as more shouts and calls of distress broke the spell that came over her, leaving a perplexed little girl and a whimpering boy blinking up at a hysterical woman.

"What have you done to him? Get away!"

In the ensuing melee, Lily heard her own mother's voice filter through the chaos around her. "Oh, Lily...no. Please, she didn't mean anything. It's a misunderstanding."

"Misunderstanding?" shrieked the boy's mother as she clutched her dazed and still choking son to her, reaching out and snagging the collar of Lily's jacket before her mother could pull her safely into her embrace.

"Look at my son! What did she do to him? Is she some kind of *deranged* witch? She ought to be locked away in a looney bin! She's insane!"

"No, it's a misunderstanding. She just...look, please, she isn't feeling well. I thought we were friends. I promise this won't happen again. We're leaving today."

"Oh, you are so right about that," cried the other woman, standing straight and furious and pointing a finger directly towards Jessica's face. "You had better leave before I call the police or worse. I ought to report you to our Council. They should know about this wicked child. No wonder you have bad people looking for her!"

Clutching Lily and backing up slowly, Jessica kept shaking her head back and forth, tears running down her face.

"No, please, I *told* you we are leaving."

They were almost to their car, but the woman kept yelling.

"Stop her! Someone, help! She is trying to get away with that evil child! She needs to be reported!"

Jessica turned and ran to her open driver's door and all but tossed Lily in, but not before ripping her prized necklace from her throat. "That's the last time she wears any of *that* jewelry, you can believe me!" Jessica scrambled into the driver's seat and slammed the door. Before she knew what was happening next, Lily found herself thrown backwards then plunging forward onto the floor of the passenger side of their old car as her mom careened out of the parking lot and into traffic without so much as a glance to see if it was safe. As she floored the gas pedal and frantically glanced in her rearview mirror, Jessica sobbed as she uttered a heartfelt plea. "Not now, please. She won't do it again. I won't let her do it again. They can't find her. We're leaving this place— leaving the darkness behind."

As the road noises and vibration surrounded her body, Lily remained curled up on the floorboard, in shock, frightened and confused. But she also had emotions running through her that were alien, yet at the same time, it gave her a small sense of comfort.

I am not sorry, and I will never apologize to that boy, she thought. *He will get what he deserves someday if it's the last thing I ever do. He is evil, not me. I wanted to save the kitty, and he was hurting it. That makes me right.* Just as those thoughts crossed her mind, the little girl's eyes widened at the sight of two tiny eyes peering at her from under the passenger seat. The kitten!

A calm came over her, a small smile played at the corners of her mouth, and a delightful wicked gleam danced in her big brown eyes. The little cat looked back at her, solemnly for a moment, until it too had a glint of some otherworldly mirth flitter across its bewitching green eyes. Then it blinked once, yawned, and stretched. Then turning around twice, it curled up into a pint-sized, black, perfect ball and promptly went to sleep. Lily thought that this was indeed turning into a grand adventure now that she had her kitten.

* * *

AND THERE YOU HAVE IT. I came back from those memories with a renewed sense of confusion. I still didn't understand what happened that day, all that talk of evil. It made no sense, and I was still convinced my mind was playing tricks on me and made more of what must have happened. I didn't even get to keep that kitten. Sadly, I remembered my mother leaving it in the yard of a big fancy-painted home with promises it would be able to fend for itself. Despite my pleading to keep it, my tears had zero effect, and we drove away with me staring at the house as if I could memorize its every detail.

Yep. Definitely one of the first of many barriers that came up between mother and daughter. And an incident I tried to forget but one of the only memories that managed to stay with me. I reached out and lifted the Pisces charm to my hand and felt a tear run down my face. And now this last one, where apparently, despite our getting closer than we'd ever been at the end of her life, she seemed set on wanting me to do her bidding without any real choice. Jessica wanted me to leave everything I knew here in New York State and head out on another journey, back to a place she ran away from oh so many years ago—and do so running blindly into the unknown.

CHAPTER 3

*T*here was nothing that compared to waking up with a sense of urgency, knowing I had to gather all my worldly possessions and move out of where I'd lived for the last three years and having it take only about one hour with minimal sweat. It was a sobering moment to realize just how little I possessed.

With everything hurriedly shoved in my truck—a very old Ford that was a heaping pile of rust and faded blue paint with the words *Scramble Carpentry* painted in white on the side by a previous owner—I gave one last wistful look at our rental home and headed into town.

I wandered over to the only neighbor I cared about, Mrs. Riley, last night to give her the news, and she seemed to already know I'd been given the boot. Did all the neighbors know my fate? And Molly wondered why I was so standoffish!

Turning down the main road into town, I followed the directions I had hastily scribbled after looking up the address of Mom's attorney. Pulling up to a stately brick mansion, I found myself outside the offices of one J. Landing Pearce,

Esquire. I hated people who had an initial before their middle name; it always had me assuming the worst. Joffrey? Jedediah? Josiah? How bad of a J name could it possibly be to want to *not* use it? Worse, I always jumped to the conclusion that it was being used for the snob factor, like, "Look at me, I'm too cool to even use my first name!" *Sigh.*

There was no escaping the fact that I was handed my walking papers and already begged a sofa for the night from Molly, who graciously acquiesced, telling me I could stay as long as I liked. *Ha!* Little did she know. This mystery business with my mother's estate had to be settled, and I most assuredly knew a road trip might be in the cards.

I sat there for a bit, gnawing on my thumbnail as I was wont to do when nervous. Then I managed to bite the nail right off, and much to my chagrin, as I opened the window to spit it out, a man walked by and caught me. Giving me a wide berth, he shook his head and kept going down the street. *Yeah, haven't you heard? I'm the town nutcase, bud!*

I sighed dramatically again, then flipping down the visor, staring at myself for a long minute. This was ridiculous. It wasn't like I'd done anything wrong or was in trouble much, so I needed to get in there already! Plus, my belly was grumbling, and I was going to be late getting back to work, so no time to grab a bite for lunch—not that I had any money to spare for any such luxury. Complain much, me? That handful of the last of my black jellybeans was not going to suffice.

Setting all this newfound snark aside, I hopped out onto the pavement and gave a worried glance back at my vehicle. It wasn't very secure; not many pickups in its condition were, what with the back window stuck open, and everything I owned there for all to see on the rear bench. I would have to believe in fate and the fact that it would be pretty brazen for someone to walk up to my vehicle in broad daylight, in front of an attorney's office no less. It's on a busy street in the center of town, across from a police station. Trust me, they'd be disillusioned once they had the time to go through what they filched!

The only item I had safely locked in a hidden compartment under the passenger seat was the urn holding my mother's ashes. Something had stopped me from having her interred, and now, with it looking more and more likely that I'd be heading to Georgia in the near future, I thought maybe she would have preferred to go home. I hoped that's what she would have wanted, anyway.

I headed to the entrance and told myself to remain cool, calm, and collected, no matter what I discovered. Walking into the attorney's office was like stepping back in time. The music being piped through the hidden speakers was pure big band, Tommy Dorsey or Glen Miller, and everything in the waiting room reception area could have come from circa 1940. It didn't stop there, though; the receptionist was a woman who, from the top of her bleached blond bob all the way down to her sensible pumps, could have been playing a role in a crime drama starring Humphrey Bogart. She even had cat eyeglasses on with a chain. Okay, they were rather fetching, I'd admit.

"May I help you?" The receptionist had a no-nonsense stare and gave me a once over, which gave me pause.

"Um, I am here to see Mr. Pearce. I am Jessica Sweet's daughter, and I am here about her final papers. I called earlier?" Ugh. I hated that I squeaked that out like a small mouse in front of a big, mean cat, but this woman's demeanor had me feeling like I had been sent to the principal's office. Seriously. She peered at me with such intensity, I almost flinched. Then she blinked as if coming out of some reverie, and smirked.

"Please have a seat, and I will let Mr. Pearce know you have arrived."

I sat down and glanced around the room, admiring the taste of whoever decorated it, yet I couldn't enjoy it fully because I was too jittery. I nervously touched my ears, finding comfort in those tiny cat earrings from my childhood. Yeah, I still wore them.

The cat heads were made of obsidian, with eyes of peridot. I found that out once I was older and curiously asked Mom about them. I never took them off, another weird request from her. Mom begged me to always keep them on, and toward the end of her life, it became a plea. I was sure she had yet another conspiracy theory associated with them.

I groaned and began perusing the reading material spread out on the table in front of me, knowing I could never stay mad at Mom for long. Hate was not something I was comfortable with. Choosing a magazine about things to see and do in the area, I settled in my seat and started to read. I barely had time to glance at a few articles before the attorney walked out to greet me.

"My dear, please come back to my office. Barbara, would you fetch us some, what? Tea? Coffee?"

"Coffee, please, but you don't have to go through the trouble, really."

I heard Barbara make a barely imperceptible snort behind me and instantly decided to not like her. I judge. However, I was not in any position to turn down any offering of food and drink, so I shyly agreed to refreshments and was ever so grateful to see an assortment of cookies on the tray that Babs brought in with her. Okay, maybe she wasn't so bad. Mr. Pearce smiled as I surreptitiously grabbed a few, all the while denying I was hungry when asked, yet my stomach gave me away when it chose that moment to betray me with a loud protest. Bad stomach.

Barbara gave me a knowing look as she parted, and I had

to control the urge to stick my tongue out at her receding back.

I sat in what could only be described as The. Most. Comfortable. Arm. Chair. Ever. So soft and welcoming, I may have whimpered a little as I sat. Between that and just about drooling over the cookies, my plan to appear cool and confident wasn't fooling anyone. It certainly didn't fool Barbara of the bleached blond hair and beguiling spectacles.

The entire office was one of understated luxury, albeit one that screamed old money. Very masculine in dark jewel tones, it immediately put my mind at ease, and I spent a moment gazing at the man I hoped could answer the list of questions that had been growing since I opened that package. In truth, I was hoping he'd adopt me and let me live in this cozy room. I was small, a tad over five foot three inches and one hundred and eighteen pounds soaking wet. I could curl up on this chair. He'd never even notice I was there. Just keep the coffee and cookies coming, please! No trouble at all.

I met him briefly before, at the humble service I'd arranged when Mother passed. A pitiful one, really, since we had very little acquaintances and kept to ourselves. Hence the suspicion among the nosy neighbors. Mr. Pearce had come, and dear Mrs. Riley, like us, apparently, a bit on the crazy side and two steps away from being out on the street herself. She had wept openly, much to my embarrassment, since I still had yet to shed a tear for Mom. Didn't I feel a ton of guilt about *that* actuality?

Molly and her boyfriend Ted came, although I had a feeling he was dragged there since he looked sullen, resentful, and uncomfortable the entire ceremony. He spent much of the time staring at me like he wanted to ask me something or knew something. It gave me the willies, and I was glad he's not a live-in boyfriend. That would have been awkward with me on the sofa for the time being. Lastly were three of the nurses who were with my mom at the hospice center. That was the sum total of mourners, and wasn't that just sad?

The most comforting presence that day had been Mr. Pearce. I had found him solid and kindly. He patted my shoulder and said a few words about Mom, stepping in when I froze. He informed me that the funeral cost and having her cremains put in an urn were already paid for and not to stress over any of it. Although I was in a fog that day and for a few days after, it didn't connect with me that he had introduced himself as my mother's attorney and handed me the package after everyone had left.

That realization came later when I had a moment to think, with nothing but time on my hands in the days following her funeral. I spent way too much of it in a fog. Until yesterday, when I noticed the box on the table in the kitchen where I had placed it and brought it to show Molly, starting this mess. Now he was sitting here giving me the space I needed to collect myself, all the while smiling in encouragement with a kind face. Okay, I forgave him using the J in front of his middle name.

He looked a bit the old-time dandy with his bow tie askew and his suit from another era, reinforcing my first impression that this office might feel at home as an old movie set from the Golden Age of Hollywood. His hair was a soft white, and he had the bushiest eyebrows I had ever seen on a man. In fact, he reminded me of the actor that played the Wizard of Oz from the classic film. He could be a close relation! This revelation put me further at ease, and I settled in, ready to get some answers.

* * *

"FIFTY THOUSAND DOLLARS?"

Molly squinted, looking askance at my pale white face.

"Fifty thousand dollars," I verified and met my friend's eyes, which were now wide open.

"I don't believe it!"

"Believe it. You know I wouldn't joke about money. I don't joke about not having any myself. Heck, I don't even joke about *other* people's lack of funds, so why would I joke about being handed a wad of cash?"

"But...but that's...but *why*? I mean, why would your mom have that kind of cash yet keep the two of you one step away from being tossed on the street? And now you *are* out on the street, and it's too late to make up with your landlord, who probably already has a fat little family lined up for your rental!"

"It gets better."

I reached for the coffee Molly had plunked down in front of me when she saw how upset I was upon returning from the meeting.

"I have a house. Fully paid for, including the land it's on, with taxes being paid by some unknown source. I have a family in Sweet Briar, Georgia, although, for some reason, I can't let them know I am part of their family. Not yet, anyway. I have a bank account opened in my name in said town with the fifty thousand sitting in it, and a debit card was in my mother's attorney's possession, ready for me to use. And I have a few pieces of ancient-looking jewelry that is supposed to be priceless."

"Georgia!" squeaked Molly, since that was one state under her hometown of Asheville, North Carolina. "But that borders *my* state!"

I held up my hand to dissuade any further comments. "Wait...it gets even better! I have a small trust that has paid me about two thousand dollars a year since my birth, which explains the wad of cash I was just handed. If I agree to not just *visit* Georgia and this mystery house, but *move* there permanently, I will be wired an additional fifty thousand dollars. I will get a thirty-three-thousand-dollar annual increase to my yearly trust, which means I could look forward to a thirty-five-thousand dollar a year income. *And* I have an intriguing list of tasks I must do—according to my mom's directives—that I can only read once I get inside said house and find it. Like somehow, somewhere along the way, she knew she would be asking this of me and left a letter of further instruction. And it's in a house I had no idea I owned! When could she possibly have done this, and how long had she been planning all of it?"

I pressed my hands to my face then slowly ran them down until they just covered my mouth and looked over at Molly, who just sat there blinking.

Mr. Pearce was apologetic but very firm in his declaration that my mother's orders were to be followed precisely as described. No word of who I am was to be given to any resident of Sweet Briar should I choose to go see the house. The key was already in my possession, as it was the one in the black box, and it would open any door to this mysterious home. It's ornate style and apparent oldness made me wonder at the age and condition of the place.

I had to agree to these terms plus sneak in so as not to alert anyone of my presence, then leave and go check into an inn or motel and pretend to be visiting the town. Or pretend to be a person looking to settle into a new area if I decided to stay. I was to declare that I was an artist, which I was in a way since I would scour areas looking for tossed junk to turn into art pieces. Despite what my mom said, I made some neat reclaimed art, if I said so myself. I was also instructed to avoid any Dolce, Sweet, or Croy relations and just to observe them until I understood the situation better. If I chose to keep the house, I had to search there for further instruction.

What situation, and what instruction, from whom or

what? Another note from Mom? But that answer my attorney could not or would not give.

"I'm sorry, Lily, but this is all Jessica left for me to pass on to you," was all he said.

The final stipulation had been the strangest of all and one I worried about because it made my mother sound like the nut Leo proclaimed her to be. Although it did seem as if she lost her mind when she put these decrees together—whether or not I wanted to admit this to myself. My last instruction was to keep the jewelry safe and not to show it to anyone or ever wear it, not until I fully understood what I was walking into by returning home. Mom was adamant that the lone ring among the pieces was definitely not to ever be placed on my fingers. Ever. Until I understood all.

"Curiouser and curiouser, Alice," Molly stated as she began to smile at this news.

"You think? I certainly feel as if I've fallen in the Looking Glass. I'm just waiting for a white rabbit or talking caterpillar to make this day complete."

"Looking glass? With that last proclamation, I'm afraid you will be heading off to Mordor soon carrying your own form of the One Ring." Molly snickered at her own joke. She too went the movie reference route; there was a reason we became fast friends.

"So, let me see it. You *are* wearing it, right?"

I pulled the silver box chain I strung the ring through out of my shirt and held it dangling for Molly to inspect. She whistled in appreciation at the ornate platinum ring. It had a center black opal surrounded by bright blue aquamarine stones that formed an intricate eye shape. It was a lovely if weird piece that did seem to give me a sense of bizarre hubris for having it on me.

I didn't worry about letting Molly in on such momentous news; she had earned my trust in so many instances over the last three years. But I did have something troubling me. There were countless times, especially in the previous few months, where Molly had come through with a loan, dinners brought to the hospice where I sat vigil, a water bill or electric bill paid. I felt not only remorse over that I had to gratefully accept such offerings, but now with this small windfall, I wanted to pay Molly back for such generosity—charity, really.

"Oh no, you don't." Molly surprised me with a finger stabbing at my nose. "I can read your face like an open book, Lily Sweet. I am not taking one penny of your inheritance, nor am I going to hold a bit of it over your head for any kind of repayment. What kind of friend does that? I mean, really!"

I started protesting immediately. "Because it's the right thing to do—"

"The right thing to do. Pfft. Listen to me, missy. I gave you that money because I *wanted* to help you, wanted you to have it. I never once expected you to be able to return it to me, so why would I want it back now? Do you have any idea how fast that fifty thousand can disappear? Even if you decide to run off and stay in Georgia, leaving me behind—and don't get me started on that, because I just may begin crying right here and now. Do you seriously think that the second fifty thousand is going to find the first pile and start making babies? It's not, like, a massive lottery win. Thirty-five thousand a year is a bit of a security blanket, but you need that to live on. And that jewelry, for all you know, might be worth nothing but sentimental nonsense."

I started blinking rapidly and gave Molly a dewy-eyed look.

"You'd really cry if I moved away? You'd miss me?"

She already guessed that that was precisely where my decision had me leaning, a clean break, a new adventure, a fantastic journey, I hoped, to discover the region where I had come from. Basically, going back to a place I never knew *was* home. I weighed all my options and surmised I could not leave this mystery alone. I had to learn about my relations and where I came from and maybe get the answers as to why my mother left all those years ago. It was too good a mystery to pass on, and I knew I'd need time, time that a week or two of snooping could not give me, to find those answers. So, with a lump in my throat and tears in my eyes, I looked at my dear friend as she continued berating me.

"This is what you come away with, woman? What you focused on? That I'd be upset should you choose to run off to Georgia and leave me behind? Well, focus on the fact that you have a life-changing decision to make, and not only that, you have to decide if this list of demands from your mother is a worthy pursuit or just the rantings of a lunatic. Because, bless her soul and may she rest in peace, your momma was a nut."

CHAPTER 4

hat have I done?

I had already worried most of my nails down to nothing. Now I was gnawing at the skin around my thumb and staring at a man staring back at me who could give Uncle Jesse from *Dukes of Hazard* a run for his money. I am not into stereotypes, but someone forgot to give this guy the memo.

My truck had decided to give me issues once I crossed over from Otto, North Carolina, into the small tourist town of Dillard, Georgia. I was driving along just fine—Depeche Mode cassette cranked high—straining what life was left in my speakers. Yes, cassette. My truck was so old it didn't have a CD slot or Bluetooth anything. The cassette head unit was the newest installment that truck had and was probably done in the early eighties. I had just crossed the state line and looked down at the space under my passenger seat and whispered, "You're home, Mom." That's when my truck had a fit. *Not* a good omen. I looked up at the sky. *Gee, thanks.*

It made a bang sound then started making a repetitive clunking noise from somewhere under it. I pulled into the gas station with a service shop attached to it and tried to explain to the lone mechanic what I thought might be the problem since I had never heard that noise before, especially coming from my vehicle. He stood there, scratching his head for a long moment, squinting and blinking at me like I had several multi-colored heads and was speaking in tongues.

I was apprehensive, because while the gas station seemed to be thriving, the mechanic shop looked like it was being cleaned out and closed down.

"You ain't from these parts none, are ya?"

Oh, lovely, the stereotype was indeed alive and well.

"Um, no, I am from New York." I waited for the commercial for hot sauce to come to life with folks popping up all around me yelling, "New York City?" But nothing else happened other than a wad of tobacco flying out of the man's mouth and narrowly missing my left boot.

"You know, my great-great-great-grand-daddy fought in The War. Mebbe he met up with some of your kin."

Lovely. I was about to tell Bubba here that I was born in these parts when I remembered at the last minute to curb my revelation in light of me supposing to stay incognito for the time being. I smiled wanly at him instead and said, "About my truck? Do you think that noise means something critical?" I glanced over at his name tag. "Stan? Do you think you could figure out what's wrong and if I need to stay here, or can I go on to Sweet Briar like this?"

"Name's not Stan. That was my daddy. I'm Stu."

Have you ever gotten so frustrated you felt the next thing to set you off would result in you finding yourself in a jail cell once you woke up from having blacked out? The reason you blacked out had everything to do with the fact you were probably bludgeoned from behind by the police because they found you pummeling an idiot repetitively all the while screaming obscenities. No? Huh, must just be me, then.

I had an excuse. I hadn't eaten today…heck, I didn't even have any coffee because I couldn't find a coffee shop open since leaving the Asheville, North Carolina, area in the wee hours of the morning, hoping to get to my location by nine. I needed my coffee. I remembered heading out thinking surely someplace would be open twenty-four hours and have decent coffee…nope.

"Okay, Stu, do you think this is serious, the noise…from my truck?"

"Might could be." A long pause. "Might not."

I turned away and began rummaging through my purse on the front seat and pulled out a Chapstick, which I uncapped and began liberally applying to my lips. Stu did not see that this was a tactical maneuver to keep me from wrapping my hands around his neck. I didn't think he appreciated just how close he came to death at that moment.

"Well, what is it? Can I keep driving this thing, or should I leave it here and come back for it when you've fixed it?"

The sheer exhaustion of my trip finally hit me, and I was about to walk away from my truck, Stu, and the State of Georgia and find a one-way ticket to New York State. However, that's when a man in a pair of jeans and a plaid shirt that fit him like a second skin, showing off a lithe but muscular frame, came around the building. He had sandy medium blond hair and matching five o'clock shadow. What? I can look. Stu suddenly became animated and rapid-fire explained to the mystery man just what he thought might be wrong with my truck.

Huh.

Stu almost seemed to know what he's talking about.

Mr. Lithe turned and gave me a friendly once over. No, I was not offended. I mean, I'd just done the same thing to him. I'm not a hypocrite. He must have liked what he saw because he walked right past Stu, heading in my direction.

He gave me a flash of a smile, which showed off perfect straight white teeth and a tiny dimple on his cheek, and introduced himself.

"Name's Jake. I don't know much about fixing trucks, though. I'm from Sweet Briar, a few towns over. Stu tells me you are new to our area?" He said this as he peered over the top of his sunglasses, giving me a peek at his light baby blues.

Welp! There was a God if this was what the men of Sweet Briar, Georgia, were made of.

"Um, yes. Lily. Lily Hogan." I had decided to use Molly's last name for the time being to remain anonymous since I didn't know who a relation might be. "I'm down from New York State looking for a change of scenery and thought this part of the country would have what I need for my art. I'm an artist."

I knew I sounded like a dork, but I couldn't help myself since I suddenly morphed into a teenage girl swooning over the cute jock. Shoot me now, please.

"An artist? Nice. What media do you work in?"

Good looking and had some depth. Most people would just ask what kind of art I did...but media? That's got intelligence written all over it. Of course, now it made me feel self-conscious because even the most enlightened people gave me strange looks when I told them I scoured garbage bins and flea markets. Not to mention that I went through people's garages and even drove around picking up random stuff on the side of the road to turn into sculptures and whatnots. It wasn't that I was embarrassed about what I did; I just had a hard time with people's perceptions and prejudices. Some warmed to my work right away and saw the beauty and hard work I put into it, while others wrinkled their noses and asked, "You make actual money with that stuff?"

Yeah, those are the folks that had given me a bit of a complex.

"I sculpt. I actually do modern pieces out of found things."

"Well, that sounds like a fun profession."

Jake smiled, and I felt a bit dismissed until I realized he was distracted by a U-Haul pulling in. Then he said, "Now, here is someone who can help you with your truck issues. That's Lorcan Reid. He owns a mechanic shop in Sweet Briar. If he can't figure it out, it's time to call in the wrecking crew."

Another handsome man with rich brown hair and abundant laugh lines started walking toward us. I felt a fissure and chalked it off to the sight of another hunk in my presence. He, too, filled in what he was wearing nicely, a pair of jeans and a simple black t-shirt. Yeah, there was a God. However, I could immediately feel a bit of tension in the air between the two men, and Stu actually looked a bit nervous. Interesting.

"What lies have you been telling this lady about me, Carter? Whatever he said, it isn't true."

He directed that last bit down at my five-foot three-inch frame with a smile and extended his hand, which I was surprised to see was smooth and clean. Bad me for immediately assuming all mechanics would have greasy, stained hands like my buddy Stu. We shook, and I looked into his warm brown eyes. He really did seem like a lovely person, but I couldn't deny that charge in the air between the men.

"No lies. Just told Miss Hogan here, who is visiting from New York State, that you were the best mechanic in all of Sweet Briar, if not the state of Georgia."

Even with that glowing accolade, both men stared a long minute at each other. I supposed there was definitely some unpleasant history between them. Lorcan smirked and looked away first, back at me. Stu looked between the two men and nervously mentioned hub bearings and tie rods and differentials, which was all Chinese to me. Lorcan held out his hand, and for a minute, I thought he wanted to hold mine. *Down, girl.* Then I realized he probably wanted my truck keys. I knew I was blushing and ducked my head while I dug through my bag again but was unable to find them. I heard a throat clearing.

"You might want to try the ignition. It's where yeh left 'em."

Stu chose that moment to contribute and just added to my embarrassment, for I was most definitely flustered by all this testosterone floating around. Jake and Lorcan's, anyway. Stu could keep his testosterone to himself.

I moved out of the way of the driver door and sheepishly smiled up at Lorcan while motioning that he should get in. As he climbed into my truck and turned over the engine, he paused and looked at me as if to say, "Coming?" I scrambled around to the other side, embarrassed when I realized I left my giant bag of black jellybeans open and had managed to spill a plethora of the little buggers everywhere as I drove and munched. Lorcan didn't seem to notice, though. I put on my seat belt and made a little wave toward Jake and Stu preparing myself for the clunking racket that freaked me out.

"I'll load Stu's things into the U-Haul then drive him back to town in my Mercedes. You got this?" Jake called out as we began rolling. Lorcan nodded yes and waved out the window. "I'll leave the U-Haul key with the attendant!" Jake smiled at me, and I thought, *He drives a Mercedes, nice.*

As we eased out of the parking lot and onto the roadway, Lorcan reached out and patted the dash.

"This is a sweet ride you have here. Sixty-seven?"

"Sixty-eight. I got a great deal on him two years ago and have been keeping him going with religious oil changes and prayer." I smiled and fondly patted the dash myself. "He's a good truck, but I don't think he was quite prepared for an eight hundred and eighty-odd mile journey south."

"He?" Lorcan smiled to let me know he wasn't belittling me.

"His name is George. It's a good solid name for a Ford truck, I think."

"George it is, then. Is your family into the hardware business or some such? I noticed the logo on your truck."

I chuckled and informed him that not only was I probably the second or even third owner of the truck, I didn't think Scramble Hardware even existed any more in New York. But I liked the old-timey look of it painted on the doors.

"What part of Upstate New York are you from?"

Lorcan was a stranger who seemed nice enough, but I didn't feel I should give him too much information, especially since I didn't know who in these parts might know my mother and where she ran off to, so I thought it best to fudge a little.

"Um, the Catskill Mountain area, a small town no one has ever heard of. What about you? Have you lived in…what was it called? Sweet Briar? Have you lived there your entire life?"

Lorcan nodded yes and went on to tell me that he inherited his mechanic shop from his father Henry, who inherited it from *his* father Malcolm. Henry was retired, driving his mom, Eileen, nuts and spending most of his days fishing. His dad was good enough in his hobby to have some for his mom to clean every night if she wanted—she didn't. I laughed along with Lorcan's description of both of his parents and the trials and tribulations of retired life. It sounded idyllic to me, who had only known what it was like being with an undemonstrative parent and no close relations.

"And your name, Lorcan, that is a different one I've not heard before. Gosh, and I am sorry if that was a rude thing to say!" There I went embarrassing myself again. Maybe it was a family name or had special meaning, and here I was making what could be construed as a negative comment about it, however unintentionally. But Lorcan just laughed and didn't seem all that upset about my asking.

"It's Irish. It means 'Little Fierce One,' or so my mother insists. She is Irish, and I think she named me that just to vex my Scottish dad. They've had this hilarious rivalry going on for as long as I can remember. Besides, he wanted to name me Angus."

"Oh, that just would *not* do. You definitely do *not* look like an Angus! Lorcan suits you!"

"Does that mean I look fierce?" His eyes crinkling in the corners made me see this was just friendly banter and that he was teasing.

Wait, was he *flirting* with me? I was so out of practice with men and flirting. Even just talking to people had been limited. I'd been sequestered away in a hospice, and I didn't have many deep conversations with my coffee customers. They were all in such a hurry to get to their jobs in the morning and get their java fix.

"You look—nice." Oh, mental palm slap to the forehead. Good one there, Lily.

Such. A. Dork.

My truck saved me from more embarrassment by making its loud, nerve-wracking noises and distracting Lorcan into what I assumed was diagnosis mode. He pulled over to the side of the road, got out, and dropped to the ground, rolling under the back end and staying there for quite some time. I waited for a few minutes then undid my seatbelt and hopped out of the passenger side, wandering over to where his legs were poking out from under my truck. He made some mechanic "hmmm" and "huh" noises then crawled out from under it. When he came back up, he had a bit of grease on his forehead as if he swiped the lock of hair that kept being unruly back in place. Hey, I noticed these details!

"What engine do you have in this baby? Do you know?"

41

"Um, I think it still has the original Ford 300ci six-cylinder engine in there, but that's as much as I can tell you. I only know that because my friend back home is dating a guy who is a car and truck nut, and he kept saying how impressed he was that it had the original Ford engine in there...and that it is knocking on two hundred ninety-eight thousand miles."

At first, Lorcan seemed impressed with my knowledge, then his eyes dulled a little as I went on and on with my explanation. I got it, a chick who knew nothing about cars, sue me.

"At least it's not a Caterpillar engine. I've spent the last two weeks fighting with one before it finally gave up the ghost." Lorcan laughed a little, shaking his head at the memory, so I guessed it was some battle he wrought against it.

"There ain't nothing like a Caterpillar engine." Where did that come from? I really needed to stop my mouth from inanely running like it was.

"Jack Crews, aka Patrick Swayze, *Black Dog*, 1998."

Whoa. That was the fastest anyone ever came back with an answer after I made one of my lame movie quotes, and Lorcan was one hundred percent correct.

"I'm impressed, sir. That was an obscure quote from an even more obscure movie that wasn't a hit or anything."

Lorcan smiled with a flash of white teeth. "Yeah, but they filmed part of it down the road a bit in Cleveland, Georgia, and my cousin Fred got to be an extra in it and everything. Did you know that?"

I smiled right back at this man who was truly easy on the eyes and stated, "Heck, I didn't even know there *was* a Cleveland, Georgia, let alone that a movie was filmed there. And I don't know your cousin Fred!"

That got a full-on laugh out of him, and we both stood

there a minute smiling at each other. Okay then, I deduced I wasn't too bad at this communicating with another human being stuff. At least he found me somewhat amusing; it could be worse.

"Here, let's get back in your truck. These mosquitos are eating me alive!"

I agreed and turned to hop back in when I saw my Pisces charm had fallen out of my pocket and was lying on the ground. I made a small "Eep!" sound and bent over to retrieve it then continued to my seat, slightly embarrassed, although I didn't think Lorcan noticed. It was a little girls' charm, and I felt a bit foolish carrying it around, but…well, it was a link to the past I had forgotten.

Lorcan joined me in the truck cabin, put his seatbelt on, and turned my truck on.

"Well, I have good news and bad news, and I won't beat around the bush about it and keep you in suspense. The bad news is you seem to have an issue with your driveshaft—looks to be a u-joint has worn out. That's what's causing the noise, and before you ask me, yes, it can be fixed. The good news is I can take it to my mechanic shop and would be happy to take care of it for you if you tell me where you are heading. I can at least try to get you settled in…unless you want it towed somewhere else?"

I blinked up at my hero and told him my plans.

"Well, you are heading my way, in fact. I am heading to Sweet Briar to scout some areas for a possible art studio since I've been considering a permanent move there if I like what I find."

I wasn't sure what I said wrong, but Lorcan's eyes clouded over, and he began looking at me with suspicion. What had I said to break the convivial mood we were sharing? I opened my mouth to say more, but Lorcan stopped me with a dire statement.

"What are you up to, miss? When we just spoke a minute ago, you pretended not to know the name Sweet Briar. Now you tell me that was your destination all along. Moreover, no one heads to Sweet Briar to move permanent like. Not without being invited first."

CHAPTER 5

I spent the better part of the last hour walking
furtively around the outside of my new home,
going from bush to tree to stump to shrub again, staying out
of sight from any neighbors' prying eyes or anyone driving
by. This was easily accomplished. The overgrown vegetation
blocked the view of the house from anyone going by on the
street.

Mosquitos were buzzing around my head, and it was all
kinds of humid, even though it was September—I was
woefully overdressed. Back north, we were getting danger-
ously close to having the first frost, but down here, it felt like
a summer day, and it *looked* like a summer day, not a colored
leaf anywhere, which helped me since the trees in the front
of the house shielded me from discovery.

I felt the sweat running down my cleavage and was glad
of my impulsive move to take the necklace with the ring off
and just put it on my right middle finger. Otherwise the
silver necklace would have turned black from my sweat by
now, making my neck the same. I felt guilty blatantly
ignoring my mom's instructions to not ever wear the thing,

but come on! It was a ring. They were meant to be worn! Plus, it looked good on my hand.

Back to my surveying the area, I noticed many of the dwellings on this street had sidewalks set lower than the homes, which were raised up on berms. It took about six to eight steps to the path below. Various porches or porticos with driveways seeming to all lead to detached garages were set behind the houses. The styles ranged from cottages to capes to stately brick—even a Tudor and craftsman-style were thrown in the mix.

This was what I found myself drooling over when I finally reached the front edifice. It was definitely overgrown and in a state of disrepair, but underneath the mess, the great bones of an actual mission-style craftsman home looked back at me. This part of Georgia didn't usually have such a glut of variances in housing, so I was rather pleased when I arrived in town yesterday, a passenger in Lorcan's U-haul. My items were added to the back with Stu's stuff, and I kept Mom's urn on my lap, thankfully concealed inside a box.

After some quick thinking on my part, I managed to smooth-talk my way out of the sticky situation of Lorcan being suspicious of my intentions. I told him I planned on moving south, hadn't heard of Sweet Briar per se, but when he mentioned it, it sounded so lovely I had to check it out, adding I was slightly embarrassed to admit to him that I didn't have set plans, so I made it sound like I did.

Then I told him I already researched the area and knew artist towns were dotting the north Georgia and southern North Carolina and Tennessee mountains, with a prominent folk college up the road near Murphy. If I moved somewhere close to all three states, I'd surely reap the benefits of being in a place where others made their living making art. He bought my excuse, I think. Maybe.

He certainly got me situated by helping me find a small

rental car and a motel just inside the town limits that he said was safe and clean, even if it was probably built in the 1950s. The proprietors were an older couple, the Murphy's; I assumed the town in North Carolina had no correlation on the shared name, but you never knew. It didn't look like the Bates Motel, and there was no scary house up the hill—or a crazy man with a taxidermy fetish. The Murphy's—Doreen and her husband Donald—didn't seem to be hiding anything.

I had just finished settling in when Doreen tentatively knocked on my door, bringing me an unexpected but much-appreciated bowl of her homemade chicken soup and even some crackers to go with it. She carried the tray in and placed it on the side table and started pouring iced tea in a glass from a small pitcher. "It cures all ailments and takes the stress of the day away. Be sure you eat up, hon. You look wore out!"

She patted my arm with a grandmotherly smile, and as she opened the door to leave, in walked Donald, carrying the last of my suitcases. He didn't say much but gave me a shy smile and tipped his cap then handed me a key in case I wanted to lock up, "even though we never get much crime in these parts." I felt cared for and safe, well-fed, and my thirst quenched with the sweetest tea I had ever tasted, and I decided the motel seemed like an excellent spot to stay until I figured out my next move.

Right now, that move was to get in the house and away from the possibility of detection. I took tentative steps up onto the wraparound porch and, looking over my shoulder several times, made my way to the front door. It was a thing of beauty even if it was decades old and a dusty mess. I pulled the ornate key out of my pocket and wondered if it would open the door to this house as my mom promised.

I put it into the keyhole and turned it over until I heard the loud *click*, and the knob twisted in my hand, letting me in. The hinges protested a bit but swung open, revealing a sheet-draped wonderland of a house that time forgot. Chairs, tables, mirrors, sofas, anything and everything covered in a white material that I suspected would shed a few pounds of dust if I dared move them.

I waited for any déjà vu moments to hit me but—nothing. I didn't know if I had ever lived in this home, but even shrouded, I could tell it was and could once again *be* a place of comfort and beauty. Holy cow, this dwelling was a stunner. Even in the dim light and the pathetic excuse of a flashlight emanating a soft glow from my phone, I could see this was once a showplace. The woodwork looked original, and the craftsmanship was top notch.

I moved from the vestibule into the main foyer, noticing the gorgeous slate floors under my feet and detail work all around me. There were built-in pieces everywhere I looked. An entry bench and places to hang coats along with two smallish windows on either side of it ended at the stairs going up to the second floor. Straight ahead was a wall that had two closed doors, which I discovered led to a closet and a half bath.

When I looked to the right, I found I was looking into the living room, which then led to the formal dining room separated by thick pillars with shelving under them. *Oh my!* A rounded stone fireplace with glass bookshelves built into both sides and a large mantle dominated the living area, and I could picture myself cozied up next to it in a club chair on a cold night...if it ever got cold enough down here. Well, it certainly didn't take me long to start falling in love with the place, and I hadn't even stepped into the kitchen.

Heading there next, I slowly went from room to room, taking in every feature this home was revealing to me. Once I reached said kitchen and spied the incredible room beyond, I knew I found a magical place I could call home. The room off the kitchen could be a family room, but it would have been described as a keeping room turned into a library or den. Bookshelves everywhere, again built-ins, and there was yet another fireplace. Windows lining both the walls in there and in the kitchen looked out to a back enclosed porch and had transoms above them, and the woodwork was everywhere, even the ceilings.

The kitchen was dreamy, no question about it. The cabinets were topped with detail molding that I suspected made a shelf that lined the entire room, and the transoms continued above each of them. Speaking of cabinets, they could only be described as well-crafted works of art. Wood upper and lower ones, with a center island painted in a greenish-blue, all topped with what I thought was black soapstone or some other dark stone. All the appliances were gone, but their spaces remained, telling me whoever did the cooking had massive ones back when this house was lived in.

Oh, was that? It couldn't be, but it *was*! A walk-in pantry to *die* for with a place for everything to make a chef, even a wannabe one, drool. Off the kitchen and den was another room, which looked to be an office, with more terrific windows and a short hall that led to a relatively large mudroom with an area for storage and a laundry spot. It even had a space for a workstation as if someone used it for crafts or sewing. In the same area was the back door, and looking out to the yard, I could see the ubiquitous detached garage prevalent in this town. A stone patio and an overgrown garden area, two garden areas really, a smallish one near the house and a bigger one nearer the garage, beckoned. There looked to be a glass greenhouse attached to it, all tempting me for closer inspection, but I decided to head upstairs first.

Once on the second level, I found three bedrooms waiting for my inspection. Two smaller ones that shared a

Jack and Jill bathroom and a larger one that had its own bath shared the space with the landing that looked to be another sitting area, more bookshelves and built-ins, and a linen closet rounded it out. The walls downstairs were painted a modest beige that most mission-style homes sported in their prime. Upstairs, however, whoever decorated went with bold, gorgeous, and highly intricate-patterned wallpaper that was still in surprisingly pristine condition. Marvelous deep greens and blues and burgundy designs on rich cream backgrounds, mostly fanciful floral patterns, gave my eyes a delight and made me want to research who the artists were that painted them—for they *were* hand-painted panels.

I peered out the window down into the yard and was only mildly disappointed that it didn't have room enough for an artist studio and workshop for me to start up. I would have to make time to search the town if I decided to stay. Oh, who was I kidding? I was staying! This house alone made up for any shortcomings I found. I did a double-take when I thought I saw a tiny black shape whisk by, but after another moment thought perhaps my eyes were playing tricks on me.

The last door I found had stairs that went up to the attic, but no way was I going to explore that dark, foreboding place on my own. Visions of spiders and things that went bump in the night had me shutting it firmly and heading back down to the foyer in a hurry. I could tackle that another day, with big, brawny men to scare away any beasties that might be lurking, waiting to pounce.

Back down in the safety of the first floor, I began to smile and make more plans. It wasn't a massive abode, but it was comfortable and seemed to have everything I could ever want in a home. Me. I'd lived in dinky apartments and rental places barely over nine hundred square feet, and I suddenly found myself in a real house complete with a front porch and multiple fireplaces. One that was absolutely charming and, well, okay, dusty, musty, and waiting for a cleaning crew to bring it to life again. But I knew I would never sell this place and would claim it as my own. Once I figured out what the deal with my family situation was. I wondered, yet again, why my mother never told me about this or why we would ever leave such an incredible sanctuary.

For it was precisely that, the epitome of everything home sweet home could ever mean to me and more!

There I was, standing in the foyer, smiling to myself, wondering where the letter my mom promised would answer more of my questions could possibly be. I was literally planning my future when a shadow suddenly loomed behind me. Dissolving my heady daydreams and startling me into a banshee shriek, a stern voice asked me what I thought I was doing breaking and entering. I whipped around—heart in my throat—and felt relieved and a bit angry when I saw Lorcan standing there.

"What on Earth is wrong with you, sneaking up on me like that? Are you following me? Why would you try and scare the bejeezus out of me?"

"I just counted three questions, but you haven't answered my one. I think you are stalling."

Smartass.

"I'm not stalling. You are." *Oh, great comeback there, genius.*

Rolling his eyes, Lorcan came into the house and looked around curiously as I took a step back and pouted. What? I could pout. He was being an unreasonable bully, and he must have been following me. Otherwise, how did he know where I was and what I was doing?

"Why are you here, really—and how did you get in?"

He looked more perplexed than aggrieved, and he was my hero of sorts from yesterday. Maybe I owed him a slight explanation.

"Would you believe me if I told you I had a key?"

Lorcan looked down at me, scoffing with disbelief, then his eyes widened when I held up the very article, leaving him a bit bug-eyed. *Ha! Take that!* Of course, in the back of my mind, I knew I had just blown part of my cover, not to mention I went against rule number one: let no one know I was there. Sigh. Bad, me. But really, what could I do? I wasn't a good liar, never had been. My mother used to tell me to get good grades and keep to the path of the virtuous, because a criminal I'd never make—not with my face that gave away any and all guilt in an instant of being asked, "What did you do?" Suddenly, I had an inspiration and decided in a split second to go with it, no matter the outcome and despite my better judgment.

"Okay, here's the thing. I am working for a realtor whose attorney in New York sent me down here because we recently found out the owner of this property passed, and we may have a buyer interested in purchasing it. That's all... nothing nefarious or anything. I have a perfectly legitimate reason to be here, and I'm in my rights to do so," I stated, chin in the air, with a look of insulted, self-righteous anger.

Next thing I knew, I found myself whirled around and pressed up against the wall, the beautiful molding pressing into my back. Lorcan's arms were on either side of my head, palms flat against the wall, his nose inches from mine, and his eyes boring into my startled ones with accusation. He smelled like oranges and spice. Wait—what?

"You might want to try a different story, sugar. This here home belongs to the Sweet family, and it is most definitely *not* for sale. Now, who are you and what are you doing poking around this town and this house? And where did you get that key?"

Oh well, crap on toast.

Okay, here's the thing. I couldn't stop looking at Lorcan's mouth. I know! Now? Hormones? But he was so close, and his eyes were that dark brown almost black that I found intriguing, his damn lock of hair fell forward again, and he definitely smelled like cedar and spices with a hint of orange bergamot. I knew he saw me look at his mouth, and then I went and bit my lower lip and peeked up at him through my long, dark lashes. My heart was slamming in my chest, and I swore I could hear his pounding away doing the same. To top it off, I hadn't had a relationship in ages, and friction always brought out the beast in me. No? Sigh...*fine.*

I pushed him away and took a deep, head-clearing breath. And that's when Jake walked in.

"Well, what have we here? In town one night and already having a lovers' spat? I got your call, Reid. What's up?"

Jake smiled and looked from me to Lorcan and back, quizzically, taking in the heat of the moment and our body language. Me breathing slowly in and out with a blush on my cheeks—damn blush—and gave him the wrong idea. Just like a man. I chose to ignore his rather insulting insinuation and tried to explain.

"No, it's nothing like that. Lorcan found me here and got all accusatory and mean and bossy and...and..."

And I started crying like a girl. No, I did *not*. Yes...yes, I did.

What was it about girls and tears and some men, making them instantly go from threatening bullies to concerned and very contrite but helpless idiots? They started patting me and holding out handkerchiefs. Who still carried around those things in this day and age? They were acting like overgrown puppies with a slobbered-on toy that they just broke in half. *Ugh, stop it already!*

"Well, what the hell did you go and scare her for?" Jake glared at Lorcan, and the tension I had felt yesterday between the two men suddenly intensified tenfold. Oh no! I did *not* want this to turn ugly.

"Scare her? She broke into this house and is pretending she belongs here, giving me some lie about an attorney wanting to buy it. She told me the owners were dead and a buyer was interested. You and I both know that's a load of bull, and you can't argue I have the right to question her intentions, damn it."

The two men shared a long look that spoke volumes, then they turned and looked at me. *Eek!* They seemed to know the history of the house, both knowing it belonged to the Sweet family. Gulp...*my* family! But why the tension and scrutiny? What if someone really did want to buy it?

"You may have that right, but there is no need to scare her, for Pete's sake!"

Jake, today's hero—maybe.

Lorcan shook his head and glanced back my way, holding his hand out yet again, and asked me to give him the key. I ruefully plopped it in his hand and went out on the front porch, arms crossed—lips pressed together in a firm line. If my eyebrows could get any lower, I'd be Bert glaring at Ernie and about to explode with a temper-tantrum to beat all temper-tantrums. My tears were forgotten, and indignation was back front and center.

I was more embarrassed at this point than scared and just wanted to get away from both of these men more than I wanted to see what they planned on doing next. Lorcan just ignored my countenance and followed me, Jake on his heels, then he turned around, pulled the door shut, and placed the key in the lock. When it turned, once again securing the house, both men were startled, and they spun around, giving me an incredulous look. My frown went to a smug, told-ya-so grin.

I plucked the key out of Lorcan's hand, stuffed it into my pocket, and took in a deep breath, then let out a massive sigh in a big whoosh that blew my bangs up off my forehead. I faced my two accusers and held my head up high, shoulders back, and tried to sound like I was right, and they were the ones who had no reason being anywhere near me or the house. Holding my hands up in a placating manner, I began to talk.

"Listen, my business is my own, and I really don't have to explain anything to either of you. I don't know how you," looking at Lorcan, "found me, or why you," looking at Jake, "would follow behind him. And how either of you knew where I'd be or what I am doing. But this is *my* concern. You are just going to have to take my word on it, even if I am a stranger in these parts and just newly arrived. You both need to leave me be."

Turning quickly, I stomped my way across the porch, around the side, heading toward the back of the property and garage area, since that's where I left my rental. It was on the small side street in a spot I thought would leave me unnoticed—fat chance, with these two shadowing me! I worried they'd give chase and cart me off to the local authorities, or worse, throttle me until I spilled my guts, so I wasn't watching where I was going. That was my downfall, literally.

I was halfway across the side porch when my foot crashed through the floorboards, and I went waist-deep into a hole of my making. When I went to pull myself up and out, embarrassed at my gaff—even though falling through the rotting porch wood wasn't my fault—I happened to glance down. That's when I saw the skull.

I heard someone screaming in the distance and felt myself falling into what one could only describe as an abyss, then everything went black.

CHAPTER 6

*I*t's never a good thing to find yourself lying on your back on a driveway, blinking up at the sky, with two cops and a paramedic looking down at you—their service lights flashing nearby. It took a minute for my brain to process everything and replay the series of events that got me on my back in the first place. House, walkthrough, lovely home, Lorcan scaring me, argument, Jake, misunderstandings and such. I remembered everything up until the cave-in and oh!

The skull!

I sat up, or tried to, but sort of pitched and rolled, feeling an incredible amount of pain coming from the top of my head. What the heck?

Other than pain and the uncomfortable sensation of lying on the ground, I could hear birds chirping in the nearby trees and felt a slight wind blowing. The sky had become overcast like it might rain later on in the day, especially since the humidity was now so thick, I was sure I could cut it with a pair of scissors. I heard a buzzing sound in the distance, which sounded like someone had a chainsaw out and was clearing trees or brush. The occasional car going by behind the hedges and a dog barking like it wanted to be let back inside made the weirdness of being dazed and in a fetal position in front of strangers even more curious. The first responders seemed concerned but perplexed, and I opened my mouth to say something when one of them spoke before I could utter a word. "You dropped her on her head, Reid? Really?"

"Hey, she was a dead weight, and it isn't easy carrying about a hundred forty pounds of dead weight out of any hole and off a porch. I did what I could!"

Lorcan looked sheepish but defensive simultaneously when I was able to swing my head in his direction to look at him.

Wait a minute...

"One hundred and forty pounds?!? I'm barely one hundred and eighteen pounds fully clothed, thank you very much!"

No one took notice of my protest, and all the men moved away to discuss my condition further, leaving room for the paramedic, a woman, to keep checking me over.

"Let it go, hon. They're all the same. Men! If they don't grump about something or the other, they open their mouths to insert their big feet up into them—and they gossip like hens and usually get everything wrong. Whiny bastards, all of them."

Her name tag said Shirley Jones—like the actress who played Mrs. Partridge in that old TV show. She had a mop of curly blond hair and a kind smile, even if she was wearing way too much makeup for the daytime, let alone for any professional paramedics to be wearing. She looked like someone from the 1960s ready for a night out at the clubs complete with bright blue eyeshadow, and mascara that would make a giraffe jealous. Those could *not* be real lashes. I figured she was about my mother's age, and she was trying to get me to pay attention to her directives.

"Three...two...five...look, I can see how many fingers you are holding up. No, my vision isn't blurry. Can I just get some help up, please, Miss Jones? I don't need any medical help or a ride to any hospital, maybe just an aspirin and a glass of water, really. I'm fine."

"It's Shirley. Now darlin,' that there hunk of a man heaved you out of a deep hole, flung you over his shoulder—which makes me kinda wish I was the one a-hurtin'—then managed to drop you plumb on your head. *Plop!* Right on the drive. You're darn lucky he didn't crack your skull clean open. I don't know what he was thinking."

Shirley put her mini penlight away and helped me to my feet. I wobbled for a second but righted myself, then turned to where Lorcan, Jake, and the cops were having a pow-wow. Both Jake and Lorcan glanced my way for a second then glanced at each other, and the look that passed between them had my alarm bells going off. It was as if they were two naughty boys keeping a secret, and it was evident from what I could hear they were not telling the police the entire truth. Well, that was interesting. Especially when the officer in charge asked them once again how I came to be on my head; their uneasiness was palpable.

"I must have tripped, Glen. She was on me one minute and on the ground the next."

He made that sound slightly risqué.

The officer he addressed turned out to be the sheriff, who just kept scratching his head, while the other officer, obviously a deputy, wrote stuff down in his notebook, the tip of his tongue sticking out of his mouth. He kept giving me furtive looks and smirking like I was an imbecile. I glowered at him.

"Tripped? How come that sounds like you just made it up, Lor?"

That voice came from behind me, along with the crunch of gravel. As I turned, the first thing to hit me was the fact that, yet again, I was being confronted with what any red-blooded woman in America and beyond would consider one fine specimen of male yumminess. Yes, I believed that was the proper term for what my eyes beheld. And oh, were they looking upon a sight to make them sparkle. Tall, dark, handsome, and formidable—serious male supermodel-worthy yumminess. Black hair, piercing blue eyes, and a no-nonsense physique. What was it with this town and handsome men? There didn't seem to be an end in sight. Lorcan and Jake were great looking, but this guy was breathtaking. Even Shirley began to simper and bat her eyelashes—which threatened to fly off her face with abandon—while she put in her two cents.

"That's what I was a-sayin,' Detective. How did this wee little gal get plunked on her head when these two boys are stronger than gorillas in a sumo match?"

Sumo match notwithstanding, she had a point.

The second thing I noticed was how the newcomer stopped short when he looked my way, his face clouding with momentary confusion. He was about to say something, but he was distracted by the shouting coming from the people prying up the floorboards of the porch, which sent him heading their way. Then it registered with me what Shirley had uttered. Detective? Why was there a detective here? Not that my libido was complaining or anything. A detective for a possible break-in and head thumping? Then it hit me. The skull, again. I assumed it was attached to a skeleton, and that meant there was an unexplained death on the premises of my house—not that they knew it was my house. This was not looking good.

BETTINA M JOHNSON

* * *

"WELL, that was an interesting morning. Are the two of you going to explain just what happened back there?"

I looked from Lorcan to Jake, waiting for them to say something that would convince me I wasn't hallucinating from the bump to my noggin. We were sitting in Jake's office in the break room after learning he was the county defense attorney. I found myself handing him a dollar since he told me to retain his services so he could represent me. Okay, then.

After I did, he pulled Detective Chase—and what an appropriate name that was—and the two other officers aside, and he and Lorcan had a few words with them. Next thing I knew, everyone was shaking hands, and the police were patting me on the head, wishing me well and warning me not to fall though any more rotting floorboards. What the what? Shirley Jones proclaimed me fit enough to be released into the care of the gorillas with a wink my way and that she'd check in with them tomorrow to see how I was getting on. They left my rental at the house for now, and Jake drove me over to his office, which wasn't too far away. Even in my distressed state, I took the time to admire his Mercedes, noting how nice it felt to be sitting on leather so soft it felt like butter.

"Don't you think you've got this backward?" Jake, giving me a stern look, passed a glass of iced tea my way since I was obviously still rattled, and he insisted nothing settled the nerves better than a tall glass of the stuff.

I took a sip and instantly felt my blood sugar enter the danger zone for developing onset diabetes. What *was* it with these southern folks and their heavily sweetened iced tea? Holy cripes! That could take the enamel off my teeth and would keep me in a state of zippy delirium for the next hour or two! Don't get me wrong, it was incredible...nothing up north tasted anywhere near as good as what I just sipped, but I knew I'd regret drinking it when the sugar high was over, and I slipped into a coma. And I thought Doreen's tea was sweet! Egad.

"What are you talking about? I saw what you did back there, or, well, I know you did *something*. Somehow you convinced a police detective to forget why he was called to a scene where a body was found, that I was what you assumed to be breaking and entering, and that you," I looked Lorcan's way "had dropped me! I want to know how, and I want to know why and—just what is going on?"

There was that glance again. Both men seemed uneasy and took a few moments to sit there, blinking with furtive looks going back and forth, but finally, resigned, it was Lorcan who spoke up.

"Obviously, you know the answer to that question as well as we do. And we didn't convince anyone of anything. I just made sure the sheriff and his deputy understood you weren't a threat, just a damn fool who wasn't looking where she was going, and suggested you liked old houses and was taking a look around town. Yesterday when we met though, why didn't you tell me you were one of my kind? Why keep it a secret? Just who are you, anyway?"

It was my turn to blink but in confusion.

"One of your kind? Who are you, Michael Hutchence? Why throw 80's lyrics at me?!"

Great, now "Need You Tonight" by INXS started playing in my head, making this bizarre conversation go into a surreal mode.

Lorcan smiled at me. "I'll take that as a compliment of sorts, but that's not what I meant, and you know it."

Jake just looked confused, so I assumed Lorcan was a fan of the Australian rock band—he even favored their lead singer around the eyes—while Jake was clueless. A pity since they were one of my favorite bands.

"I'm sorry, guys, but I don't know what you are talking about."

I said this as I sat back and pushed the glass away from me, crossing my arms over my chest in a defensive posture and frowning at both of them.

Lorcan cleared his throat and, looking pensive, leaned forward, forcing me to return his stare.

"You hit me with your power, Lily. That's why I dropped you. I was taken aback when you zapped me, not to mention it hurt like a bit...uh...it hurt a lot."

I gave him my squinty stink-eye at his almost faux pas, but then it turned to befuddlement as his words sunk in.

"My power. Zapped you," I stated, dully.

"You're obviously a witch, Lily. A dark one to boot, if I had to guess. Why didn't you let us know? I would have taken you to see the Council yesterday to introduce you. Instead, you pretend you are some Yankee coming down here on an invasion mission to take property away from one of our people."

Wow. I must have a concussion. Maybe I was delusional, and my hearing was whacked. Did Lorcan just call me a witch, like a *witch*, witch? Hold on, he said...a *dark* witch? I shot up like a cannonball and backed away from the table. I didn't want to turn my back on the two of them in case I wasn't in some kind of concussed state and they were about to do something nefarious to me. A witch? Wait—power? I *zapped* Lorcan?

"What's wrong, Lily?" Jake stood as well but stayed on his side of the table. "You don't have to fear us. We are in a different Council, you from up north and all, but we take care of our own, especially if you are visiting the area. Common decency should have had you making yourself known to us before arriving in town, though. Especially by someone of your persuasion. But we would have welcomed you. Unless, of course, you *are* here under false pretenses. Did you mean to do us harm?"

I wet my lips and felt my breathing coming out in quick bursts of air. Thinking I might be having a panic attack or something. However, I managed to squeak out an answer.

"You're crazy. Both of you. You are both totally insane. I'm not a witch. I have no idea what you are talking about, zapping and Councils and dark anything. I am a girl from Upstate New York, who should have *never* come down here to this nutty town just to get manhandled by thugs who drop me on my head and then tell me I am a…a…there are no such things as witches!"

I screeched out this last part and look toward the door to plan my escape route. Lorcan, seeing that my distress was real, lifted his hands and, in a calm voice, told me it was okay and that they meant me no harm—and to please sit. He said that last part like there was no room for argument, however.

I paused, acknowledging the quiet intensity coming from him, and slowly, but reluctantly, shuffled to my chair and took a seat. That's when he lowered his hands and gave me back my glass of iced tea. Or, should I say, he moved the glass without touching it, so it slid across the table to come to rest directly in front of me again. That's when I almost passed out a second time. I was gobsmacked! Did I just see that?

I raised my eyes to them both and found truth there but still questioned my sanity. Because, well—I couldn't be a witch. Right? Wouldn't my own mother have told me something so monumentally important? Wouldn't I have known myself by some happenstance that what they were saying was true? Especially since this wasn't some Harry Potter moment with Dumbledore about to show up to take me off to Hogwarts. I mean, really! Even more so, the dark witch comment indicated I'd be sorted into Slytherin—yeah, no, thank you! I'd pass.

"But I've already told you, I'm not a witch at all! Witches are old and ugly."

Both men laughed at this comment, appreciating the *Wizard of Oz* reference at the same time, and it broke the tension. A bit.

"No, seriously, guys. I can see you believe what you are telling me. And I just witnessed that glass move of its own accord. I'm not sure what I did to you, Lorcan, to have you drop me like a sack of potatoes, but I can assure you. I'm not a witch. Don't you both think I would know something like that? I don't even know what this means, because I assume you are telling me you are, what? Warlocks? Isn't that a male witch? Wizards? Do you realize how outrageous it is that we are even having this conversation?"

Jake walked over to my chair and squatted down in from of me.

"First of all, never say warlock, because that is kind of insulting in the Witch World. Wizard isn't the correct term, either. We all fall under the same word, witch. Second, you were highly upset at finding that skeleton under the porch today, Lily. When Lorcan began pulling you out of your predicament, you went into a fight or flight mode of sorts, and, well, you fought. You hit him right in the back with a burst of power that I am sure is going to leave scorch marks, if not some black and blues, that will take weeks to disappear. Unless we have a healer tend to him."

I heard what he was saying, but this just couldn't be true. He registered my continued doubt because the next thing I knew, Jake reached out and grabbed my arm, jerking me to my feet, and it looked like he meant to strike me.

Despite Lorcan's cry of alarm and my utter lack of knowing what I to do, I reached up as if I was going to defend myself from a perceived blow. All of a sudden, blue light shot out of my fingertips, and Jake went flying back toward the counter knocking into the mini-fridge and coffee maker, which shattered, spilling hot coffee everywhere.

"Jake! Oh my gosh! What did I just do? Are you okay?"

Lorcan jumped up and ran around to the other side of the table, helping Jake to his feet, then grabbed a paper towel began wiping up. Both men looked at me ruefully and took their seats once more. Lorcan pulled his phone from his pocket and began texting someone while Jake stated the obvious.

"Well, if you didn't know you were a dark witch before, you certainly know you are one now!"

CHAPTER 7

*T*he three of us sat there staring at each other for what seemed like hours, but in reality, it was just a few moments. Well, how did you like that? I was insane. Clearly, I was suffering hallucinations brought on by my head having an untimely meeting with the ground. No, I refused to believe what they were saying. Even with the evidence—snaking blue sparks pooling out of my fingertips without my knowing how or why. My poor brain was exhausted from the long trip, the stress of the repairs needed on my truck, and the excitement of the day and could not cope, obviously making up things that, I was sure with proper rest, could easily be explained. So, insanity it was.

"You are not insane, Lily."

Lorcan smiled, a look of sympathy in his eyes. Despite that, I chose to be mad at him. He got me into this, after all—chasing me out of the house and being all threatening and mean. The big meanie.

"You obviously had no idea. And from the look on your face, I can tell you aren't lying to us. You are going to need some help sorting all this out," Jake stated.

I liked him slightly better since he was the one who told Lorcan to stop yelling at me and, well, I was feeling sorry for myself and wanted to lean on someone who showed me the most support. I felt needy right now; sue me. However, upon reflection, both of these men bullied me, so I felt my lower lip going into a monumental pout. Again.

I was saved from giving them both a piece of my mind, which would have been heavy on the snark and short on the, "poor me," when there was a knock on the office door, and in walked Detective Chase. Oh boy. He's come to arrest me. Or at least question me about why I was at the house finding skeletons. I sat up straight and began to tremble like an arrow about to be sent flying from a bow.

"Exciting day, huh?"

Okay, I didn't expect that coming from the police detective, but both Jake and Lorcan stayed in their relaxed positions and didn't seem upset nor surprised to see him arrive. I figured they were about to throw me to the wolves, since they didn't owe me anything and I was technically, to them anyway, breaking and entering. Now how to hide the fact that I'd gone insane. Yes, I was still going with that over being a witch. Work with me, people.

I must have looked like someone who saw a ghost. That's when the detective turned his chair backward and straddled it, sitting across from me, his cologne, which reminded me of a dark forest after it rained, distracting me almost as much as his intense eyes. He looked me over—not in an insulting way—but I could tell he liked what he saw. I think we were having a moment. No really, it's what I chose to believe, anyway. You can think what you want, but I was certain something was happening between us, despite my being so nervous. Those deep blue orbs were twinkling, he looked at my face, then down to the ring on my finger, then over to Jake and Lorcan, who nodded the affirmative. Then he looked back at me and said, "Relax, Lily. I'm also a witch."

Had all the men in this town, the cute ones anyway, lost their minds? Was this some kind of joke they did to all the newcomers? I mean, Stu didn't do this to me, and I was starting to feel like I perhaps misjudged the guy, falling for the cute factor and losing my acuity. I bet they gave me something to drink that made me see things. I distinctly remembered not having anything other than iced tea, it tasted normal, but one never knew.

Detective Chase spent a few moments regarding me in a disquieting way. Suddenly, I saw a kind of recognition in his eyes that didn't make sense. It was quite alarming. To add to the uncertainty, he abruptly stood, looked at both Jake and Lorcan, then ordered them to their feet.

"We need to go back to the house right now, guys, immediately."

Confused right along with me, both Jake and Lorcan had their questions forestalled by the very determined detective, who turned on a dime—but not without grabbing my arm, albeit gently. Then he guided me out the door to his vehicle. At least it wasn't a police car—and I wasn't cuffed.

* * *

"What are we looking for, Brian? Lily is spooked, and having a tech team working outside on the porch with those remains isn't helping the mood here. Is she in trouble?"

Oh, so *now* Jake was all concerned about my mental state.

Although he yet again was the support I needed, arm around my shoulder and tossing glowering looks around the place. Okay, he's my favorite hunk. The place in question was the living room I had just been daydreaming in that morning. It was indeed raining outside. Those clouds that moved in earlier followed through on their promise, but it didn't seem to hamper the technicians removing the skeleton from the property. It did cool the air, if slightly. Detective Chase didn't answer Jake's question right away but directed his gaze once again toward mine and shook his head a little.

"I thought I recognized her earlier, but the excitement outside distracted me from the obvious. Then you took her to your office, Jake, and it had to wait until I came by and remembered."

Wait. Recognized me? What was he talking about?

"What do you mean, recognized her? She's new to town and all, Brian."

Lorcan spoke up from his position, leaning against the entry to the room. He'd been withdrawn and sullen ever since I knocked Jake clear across the break room, and I couldn't blame him. I was rather glum myself. But now, I was downright freaked out. A body under a porch of a house I now owned notwithstanding, the detective said he recognized me. But how?

I was about to reiterate my newness to Georgia, but was stalled by the detective walking over to the mantle, reaching up to what I assumed was a painting hanging on the wall, shrouded in white linen. He carefully pulled the tarp off what was indeed an oil painting, and everyone in the room gazed upon the subject looking serenely back at us. It was my face. Whoa. It *definitely* was my face, but on a woman that was wearing clothing from the early nineteen hundreds, if I had to guess. She looked to be a slightly older version of me—or what I would look like in about ten years. So that put her in her mid to late thirties, possibly, when this painting was commissioned.

"What is going on here?"

I asked this to no one in particular, but all three men swung their faces to mine. Every single one of them had a countenance that was downright accusatory. *Uh oh.* Time to come clean, methinks.

"Don't you think you are better equipped to answer that question Miss, ah, Hogan, is it?" Detective Chase asked, looking somewhat skeptical that whatever I would reply with would be nothing short of a bald-faced lie. *Well, gentleman, time for me to come clean and wipe those looks off your pretty faces.* I walked over to a chair and didn't bother to remove the covering but sat, motioning them to do the same. Each man complied, but I noticed they all chose seats on the opposite side of the room, facing me. Fine, *be* that way.

"Hogan isn't my last name. I used a friend from New York's last name because I hoped to remain undetected for a bit before coming clean." I saw identical looks of suspicion and alarm cross all three faces and held my hands up. In a tumble of words, I stated breathlessly, "I am not trying to pull a fast one here or do anything nefarious. My real name is Lily Sweet, and I just found out this home belongs to me."

Dead silence. Okay, *cringe*. Maybe that was a poor choice of words, what with a body of sorts out on my side porch and all. But that was what my statement was met with, along with incredulous looks from the three men. Their faces were so comical. I actually caught myself before I could snicker—I didn't think that would help my cause at the moment. "Look, guys, detective, really. I have everything here in this packet from my mother's attorney. It proves what I am saying is true. I have my birth certificate, the deed to this house, driver's license, a letter from my mom, papers, everything to prove the verity of my words. I am as surprised as you are because I had no idea she was going to do this to me. I never knew I had family, well, much of a family, and she kept things from me my entire life. This is all new to me, too."

Detective Chase stood up and walked over to the portrait once again then, turning to me, he asked, "Why would your mother do this? Where is she now? I have questions I'd like to ask."

I looked down at my hands and felt a lump growing in my throat. The last thing I expected was to feel a swell of morose and overwhelming sadness, but I looked up and quietly told the three men about Jessica.

"She passed away from cancer. It was recent—so much so that I am still in shock over it even though she had been ill for over two years. I really am from Upstate New York, but I just found out I was born here in Sweet Briar. My mother was Jessica Sweet."

Never had I seen such pain cross the faces of three men so quickly then disappear just as fast. Yet my pronouncement was met with acceptance. It was as if, by having the obvious pointed out with the painting as proof, and my words backing it up, they all chose to acknowledge the verity in my statement.

"And she never once mentioned you happened to be from a powerful witch family?"

The detective looked at me with hooded eyes, but I thought I detected a spark of something in them that I couldn't put a name to quite yet. Interest? In what way?

"No. She never spoke of life before New York. She was, well, she had some mental issues."

Lorcan came up to me and squatted down so we were eye to eye.

"I know your name is Lily, but I didn't make the connection. I was just a kid myself when she took you away from here and disappeared, never to be heard from again—and now she never will."

He beamed then. However, the look was tempered with a sad countenance. But the warm twinkle in his eyes from the day we met was back again—his attitude changed once more.

"We played when we were both in diapers. My mom and

dad live next door to your Aunt Iona. I was always included in your cousins' Douglas and Nora's, playdates. Jake, too. We all grew up together or would have. If she hadn't done a runner with you."

"That makes us sort of related." This was from Jake, who kept staring intently at me, which I was finding unnerving. "My mother, June, is the sister of Judge Haywood. Owen Haywood. He happens to be married to your aunt. It makes us part of the same family but not by blood, more of extended relations. Mom runs the local general store here in town, June's Emporium, and is going to freak out when she hears all this. She was best friends with your momma."

I looked over to Detective Chase, who hadn't spoken since my revelation.

"So, Detective, does that make us related as well?" I asked rather cheekily to hide how blown away I was by all this news.

He smiled and walked back over to where he'd been seated and plopped onto the chair, sending up a poof of dust.

"No, Lily, and it's Brian. We aren't related or never played as babies. I was about five and a half or six to your three years by the time you left. You, Lorcan, Jake, and Nora are the same ages, roughly. However, I do know my father was intensely in love with one of the three Croy sisters. Your aunt, Iona, is the eldest, your mother Jessica, the middle daughter, and young Adelaide was baby of the family; she was the one he was smitten with—then Adelaide went missing. He had already been married to my hapless mother for three years, when Adelaide disappeared just before your own mother took off. When Adelaide left, he became depressed, but we didn't realize how severely until he went and hung himself after your mother ran away with you all those years ago, leaving my broken-hearted one to raise me on her own."

Oh, well, *damn*.

* * *

IF I THOUGHT my morning and afternoon were sensational, nothing could have prepared me for the evening that I was now encountering. I think the analogy was, "Prodigal Son Returns." Only in my case, I was—in fact—a girl. Much to my surprise, the menfolk suggested we head to my aunt's home, which was around the corner from mine and one house over, so that if I went to the edge of my backyard and looked diagonally over the fence, I'd be looking into hers. This meant Lorcan's parents were either directly behind mine or on the other side of my aunts. Small towns—got to love them.

Last week, I thought I was an orphan, all alone in the world, without a future or resources, no money, nothing. Now? Now I was sitting across from a woman who most definitely was my Aunt Iona because she looked so much like my own mother, it hurt. She had the same red hair fading to gray that my mother had, and her eyes were a dark cornflower blue with crinkled laugh lines etched deep on the corners. Her face was flushed, and she looked both excited to see me and sad upon learning of her sister's passing.

"That's it, then. I'm the last one. And here I am, the oldest of the three and the only one living, for surely the remains under the porch is our dear Adelaide?"

This she directed toward Detective Chase, Brian, as he asked me to call him. Weird, since his announcement left me feeling slightly awkward, all things considered. But she looked back and patted my hand as if to say everything would be all right. I had nothing to reply to this, shocked into silence. Could that poor, unfortunate soul be my missing aunt?

"One can assume, even though I hate doing so. But I can't think of anyone else it could be. I don't believe another female went missing all those years ago except Adelaide, then

Jessica, taking Lily here with her. We will have to run tests for verification. Still, the medical examiner already confirmed the skeleton is that of a young woman. I think it's only a matter of weeks before we get a positive ID. Unless I can convince them to rush the tests."

This news brought me nothing but distress thinking something horrible must have happened to my mother's little sister, the young lady who was holding me in that photograph. I pulled it out now along with the photo I had of my parents and me and passed them on to my aunt. How weird that was. I had an aunt who welcomed me with a warm hug and a gentle voice that hinted of her Scottish roots.

I suspected she must have been born in Scotland, but my mother and their younger sister were from the States because I never once remembered hearing any sort of brogue when Jessica spoke. Aunt Iona gasped then took the photos from me and regarded them with a melancholy smile. How sad it must be for her to find out she lost two sisters in one day, one several weeks ago now, but the other twenty-one years or so ago. My heart went out to her, and I placed my hand on her arm in comfort. I looked up as a striking blonde walked in with what could only be her twin brother following close behind.

"Dear Adelaide? Please, Mother, spare me your drama. She was a nasty piece of work, totally evil, and we all know it. Just ask poor Brian here what that harlot did to everyone —especially his father and mother. And now the prodigal daughter returns, I guess. Have we figured out if she is as evil as Lorcan says she is?"

Hey! Wait—Lorcan said I was evil? The woman, who could only be my cousin Nora, slithered her way across the room and wrapped herself around the man in question, who looked rather uncomfortable. I opened my mouth to protest, but Jake spoke first.

"Totally uncalled for, Nora. Beyond rude, and it really makes you look like an insecure wench."

Nora just stuck her tongue out at Jake then cooed up at Lorcan, who looked my way apologetically, but I chose to ignore him. Hmm. I wonder what that's about.

"Hi, I'm Douglas. I guess we're cousins. Nice to meet you."

Well, at least one cousin seemed pleasant. Douglas reached out to pat me on the shoulder as he passed by then sat down next to his mother.

"Of course, we will need a DNA sample first before we really welcome you into the fold."

Well, so much for that; passive-aggressive rudeness at its best, thanks *so* much, Doug.

The words and attitude stung. After all, I grew up never having family. To suddenly find that not only did I have one, but they're prolific *and* all of them are witches? Okay, that was finally settling in my brain as a possibility I was willing to entertain. To have two relations instantly take shots at me was a bit more than I could handle at the moment. I stood up in a huff and reached for my photographs when Aunt Iona did something totally unexpected. What it was, I had no idea, but suddenly both Douglas and Nora shot up, hands to the sides of their heads, and began making anguished noises of distress. It was like a Spock mind-meld, total *Star Trek* woo-woo stuff. I couldn't help but squeak in alarm, because it looked like that was precisely what Aunt Iona was doing to the twins.

Out of nowhere, I heard myself yelling.

"Stop, please. It's not worth it. I can handle a few slings and arrows. Please, Aunt Iona—stop."

And just like that, it was over. Douglas and Nora both sat down hard and shot nervous glances at their mother while giving me venomous ones—Nora, at least. Douglas was downright contrite and immediately apologized. Cousin

Nora was made of sterner stuff or had a fool's reckless heart because she just started in again as if her head wasn't just being turned to mush.

"Oh, honestly, Mother. Do you think you can fling spells around without the Council hearing from me? Attacking your own daughter to protect a renegade witch, a possibly dangerous dark one to boot, and not get in deep trouble with them? I'm only looking out for you! How can you trust this person? She claims she didn't even know she was a witch."

Jake, yet again, spoke up for me.

"Don't be an idiot, Nora. Look at her. She looks just like the portrait in the house. How many times did we sneak in there and stare at it before the Council finally closed up the place for good? As for the Council, two of the thirteen Elders are Lily's kin, one of whom is your own father! Do you really think they'd take your side in a petty complaint? Lily is a Sweet *and* a Croy. There is no doubt of that. Not only that, look at her hand. Do you see what's on it?"

I felt beyond uncomfortable as all eyes swung to me, well, my hand and the ornate ring upon it.

Everyone gasped a little, and Nora, feeling contrary I guess, had to have one last word on the matter.

"She probably stole that from the house after breaking in today. I don't care who she looks like. I don't trust her."

"If you can't control your tongue, daughter, then leave my home."

Aunt Iona looked about ready to spit bullets and opened her mouth to continue when there was a banging in the hall, and a lovely, fair-haired woman with vibrant brown eyes and a kind face came rushing in.

"Where is she? Where is Jessica's girl? Oh…oh, my!"

Turning toward me, the woman stopped short and almost fell over in shock. Jake rushed over and caught her just before she toppled, propping her up in his arms.

"Mom, it's okay. Let me introduce you to Lily. Lily Sweet, this is my mother June, June Haywood, now Carter, and as I said, she was your mother Jessica's best friend."

June held shaky arms out to me, and I went over to her tentatively as she pulled me into a great big hug. Weepy and misty-eyed, she leaned back and took a good look at my face then proclaimed, "Oh my word, but she looks just like Adriana. She is the spitting image of her great-grandmother."

Everyone was nodding yes in agreement when Lorcan finally found his voice, shocking everyone into frozen silence when he remarked, "Indeed, she does. Now, who is going to inform the Italians?"

CHAPTER 8

*F*or the last two hours, not only did my evening continue in a whirl of confusion, but the theme song from *The Godfather* kept playing randomly in my head, distracting me from what everyone was saying and decisions that were being made without my input. What the heck could be so wrong with the Italians that everyone was acting all weird about them finding out I showed up on their doorstep, so to speak?

I was now sitting in June's back kitchen in her charming store, trying not to yawn and slowly blinking with exhaustion. The fact that half of it looked like a regular old-time general goods shop, and the other half looked like a witch theme run amok, left me hoping I'd have more time to explore once I was done being resettled into my new digs and had at least another night's sleep in me, for I was about to drop.

Yes. I was moved from the loving care of Doreen and Donald Murphy and their motel, much to their disappointment, to a small apartment over June's shop—at least until my house could be aired out, dusted, and reopened. Although

I was a bit hesitant, what with the skeleton and all and my house an active crime scene. June was explaining to me that the wards were more potent in the center of town. And that, while the motel was a safe place from most attacks, nothing could beat being in the heart of Sweet Briar if and when an attack came.

Attack? What?

Pausing when she saw my look of alarm and confusion, June patted my hand and reached for the pitcher of sweet tea. I now knew it was called that in these parts, having been schooled on the matter tonight. I gratefully accepted another glass. Yet how any of these people thought I'd get any sleep with that much sugar coursing through my veins was a complete and utter mystery.

"Oh dear, Lily. You have no idea what I'm going on about, do you? No matter. In time, all this will seem old hat to you, and you'll understand everything. I promise. I just cannot believe in all these years, your momma never told you one thing about who you are or, more importantly, *what* you are!"

I ducked my head, embarrassed at my ignorance. I was obviously being pitied by everyone. Well, everyone except Nora, who, when I was having my living arrangements sorted out, sniffed in an elegant but ultra-snotty way and declared she'd had enough drama for the evening and had no intention of watching the Italians devour me. Ah! There— cue the music again. I was waiting for Fredo to come bumbling in and assault me. I kept looking around for rosary beads! Not that I believed all Italians were "connected," especially since I *was* one and certainly never benefited from the brotherhood. However, all this talk had me wondering.

"Mrs. Carter…" I started.

"June. Please call me June." She smiled back at me.

"June. About these Italians I keep hearing about. I assume they are my Dolce relatives. I mean, what is wrong here?

Why all the nervous banter about them finding out about me?"

June sighed and looked away, her hand going up to her cheek, and she seemed to be thinking of how to answer my question without making a long story out of an explanation that needed to be short. She, too, could see my droopy eyes and stifled yawns.

"Okay, hon, let me give you the short version tonight, then get you upstairs and tucked in, all right?"

When I nodded the affirmative, she smiled and settled in for what I hoped would be the promised short version, but even if it wasn't, her next words would have woken up a narcoleptic sloth.

"Well, you see, it's not *all* the Italians we are worried about. Just one. Your great-grandmother must not know of your coming home just yet until we figure all this out. She has never gotten over what happened back then—Adelaide taking off for parts unknown in the middle of the night, then Jessica disappearing with you, followed by your father. We assumed he went after you but never heard from him again or had any sign he was alive. No credit card usage, no contact, no trace of him anywhere. Well, that boy was her pride and joy, her only grandson, and he carried the family name even if it was changed to Sweet. Carlo, Charles, was the heir. Well, *you* are the heir, but he was her beloved boy, the light of everything she loved, never to be heard from again. So, you see, they, the Italian half of your family, are very upset with the Croy women, and they will do every-thing to defend Adriana—and what she might do when she discovers your return."

Whoa. Wait…no, *whoa*! The lady in the portrait, my *great-*grandmother was still *alive*? But how could that be?

"How old *is* she?" I blurted out rather indelicately, spitting tea everywhere then taking the time to pat the table—and

June—down in embarrassment, reaching for some napkins. Then it hit me.

"Wait, hold on. My father—he left? Disappeared? Meaning, what? He could still be *alive* and out there somewhere? Mom told me he died! He obviously never came for us, because I am sure I would have remembered if a man ever showed up in our lives, but one never did."

I sat back, and the stress of the last few days finally slammed into me, and tears began gathering as I blinked to keep them at bay. I placed my hands over my face, distraught, and I didn't even know if I wanted to continue this rediscovery of my past. I reached up to stroke my tiny kitten earrings, looking for some small bit of comfort. I knew I needed a bed and soon. More than likely, things wouldn't seem so dire in the morning, but right now? Right now, I needed a good, long cryfest.

"Oh, honey. I'm so sorry all of this happened to you. I should have been a better friend to Jess, her best friend. But, well, you see, we had a huge fight about a month before she left. It was over Adelaide running off and everyone so upset. I confronted her, knowing she should've had an idea where her baby sister went, and why. But she screamed at me to leave and never bother her again. I was so shocked! We were like sisters! I always felt like the fourth Croy sibling growing up, we were so close. Jess looked different, too, drawn and pale. She jumped at every little thing."

June paused to take a trembling breath. "I went to Iona and told her about the fight. After that, Jess refused my calls, saying I betrayed her. She distanced herself from everyone in the town, and your father went along with this although he seemed despondent and distracted. The self-imposed break from family and friends lasted a week, then one day, we found out Jessica ran away with you in tow and that your dad was gone as well. None of us understood. The last we heard from him, he telephoned his grandmother, stating he was going to find his wife, his family, and keep them safe. Then he disappeared into the night with no further explanation, even though Adriana demanded it of him. We never heard from any of you from that day forward. What I don't understand is how could you not remember some of this, dear? You loved your father so much."

I looked up at June with tears in my eyes, my face a mask of distress.

"June, I can't remember anything. Anyone. I thought him dead. I still can't remember even though I'm back. I hear what you are saying, but I have no recollection of Adelaide or my dad, Aunt Iona, any of you. I know other four-year-old's have better memories than what I guess I was given, but I truly don't remember this town, its people, my family, or my past."

Then I let the tears I'd been hold in flow out.

June, sensing I needed privacy to cry it out, helped me from my chair and walked me to the back door that opened to a small vestibule. It was a mudroom, really. It had a door on the left that went to the side yard. On the right, a staircase led to my apartment above. She got me upstairs and to my small but comfortably welcoming bedroom and helped me turn down the bedding. Before June left me to settle in for the night, she gently proclaimed, "I will explain more tomorrow, and let your aunt know what you've told me, so you don't have to keep going over everything. Get some rest." Then she departed.

I had acquainted myself with my little apartment earlier upon arrival. The back stairs reached a small landing that led to my door. When you entered, you walked into a tiny living room with a small fireplace then continued to a door with my bedroom and bath beyond. From the living room, there was a secondary door, which led to a kitchenette barely big enough to eat a bowl of cereal standing up, but it had everything I needed in miniscule form. A door off the kitchen opened to another staircase, which was very narrow and steep, that led down to the store and must have been used to run supplies upstairs when this was part of the storage for June's shop. June's Emporium. I thought the name fit it perfectly. The secondary door was kept locked, but the key was hanging on a hook on the wall beside it. I loved every square inch of the place.

Tonight, though, these things didn't matter to me, as exhausted, I crawled into bed. Not even bothering to change into pajamas, I kicked off my shoes and pulled off my socks, then rolled over onto my side and looked out the window. I regarded at the box that held the urn filled with my mother's ashes. I had kept her with me, not sure yet what I planned on doing with her cremains.

"Well, Mom, you sure had plenty of secrets."

Light flashed out my window as thunder sounded far in the distance. It was cracked open just a bit, but even that much, I could feel a cool breeze coming in and listened to the rain falling steadily. The sound was soothing and calmed me a bit, but I didn't think I would be able to fall asleep—not with all these thoughts going round and round in my head. Morpheus, however, had other ideas, and I was soon in a dreamless, deep, exhaustion-laced sleep.

CHAPTER 9

J was sitting on the side porch drinking coffee and watching the town come to life the next morning. I was surprisingly calm—considering all that I had going on and all that I knew was coming—when I heard June come out. Her own coffee cup cradled in her hand, she sat next to me.

"Sleep well, hon?"

I could not believe how deeply and solidly I had slept the previous night and told her so as I continued watching the local business owners go about their morning routines. From our vantage point, I could see most of the right half of the square's businesses. It was a hazy morning; the humidity was thick again after last night's rain. Once again I noted how it felt like a summer morning, not the autumn chill I had left back in New York. Bugs were buzzing by, and the only sign that it was fall came from a few crows that were calling out to each other from the rooftops of the local businesses. Some of those businesses sported the odd fall leaf-colored decorations in their windows, with a few early pumpkins dotting the doorways here and there.

The town was adorable, something I had observed on my disastrous recognizance the previous day. Main Street in Sweet Briar was everything you would expect from a small and thriving artist colony and folk village in the North Georgia/North Carolina Mountains. Businesses were on either side of the street with a central square that was park-like, and then the main thoroughfare continued on the other side. A police department, a courthouse, a barber shop, a bank, a beautician shop, a café, a bookstore, a dress shop, Lorcan's garage, a funeral home, an old-fashioned drug store that boasted a soda fountain, and a retro diner all lined one side of the square, with the more artistic shops on the opposite side.

This included a candle shop, a small folk-art studio with a potters' shop behind it, a craft store with all manner of beads and baubles and charms hanging in its windows, a metaphysical store with psychic readings advertised, an herbalist shop, and a hardware store with a small woodworkers shop on the side. Okay, the last two weren't artsy or witchy, but the little woodworker shop inside the hardware store had folk art pieces in the window that looked like old-time whirligigs. It was right next door to June's place.

Branching off of Main, on the picturesque side streets, little pubs and restaurants and a bed & breakfast shared space with the more common businesses you'd find in any town. A few churches of various denominations, the Chamber of Commerce, professional offices, as well as an inn at the far end of town up on a hill, rounded out what I already had logged. An Ingles Grocery Market and Walmart were on the outside limits of the village about ten miles away. There was even a working payphone just in the county's limit. You hardly saw those anymore!

June's Emporium was on the artsy side of the square, and hers was a catch-all general store with a few staple groceries, candy, office supplies, gifts, and cards, along with all manner of oddities not normally found in the real world. Just this morning, when I came down to greet her, I found her polishing a massive witches' cauldron! Many of the artisans had studios sprinkled in and among these businesses. The result was a town begging to be explored.

I remember passing a few flea markets and a farmer stand plus several different schools on my way into town and knew there was a library somewhere near the elementary school, which was one block off of Main. There was also an agricultural fairground a few towns over and several unidentifiable buildings that I'd have to check out when I next had the time. It reminded me of so many of the small Catskill Mountain tourist towns from back home that I felt myself relaxing and thinking this might just work out for me if I could pass my upcoming familial interrogation.

"I love it here, June. I know I've only been here a few days, with a large blemish tainting one of them, but, well, it's just a darling town!"

I knew I was gushing, but never having had a home, suddenly finding my very own place to restore, decorate, and live in was thrilling. Then I remembered the skeleton who was probably my aunt Adelaide, and my face clouded over, my smile slipping away.

"Don't let poor Adelaide ruin your homecoming, Lily."

Did everyone around here know what I was thinking all the time?

"That poor girl has been laying under that porch, and you can bet Brian Chase will get to the bottom of it. He's like a dog with a bone, and the Witches Council will lend their aid, don't you worry!"

"See? That's just it, June. Witches Council. The fact that witches are real—that I'm a witch. How can I be one if I didn't even know they existed? And how do I know who is and who isn't one? Are *you* a witch? Is it even rude for me to ask something like this? And how do the regular townsfolk handle having witches in their community?"

I knew I threw a barrage of questions at her, but my frustration was growing, and all these queries just spilled out of me. June just chuckled, shook her head, and patted my back in that motherly way she had.

"Oh, sweet child, all in time. All of these questions of yours will be answered. And no, I'm not insulted you asked, and the answer is yes, Lily, I am a witch, just like, well, not exactly like you, but..." She sighed, looking off across the square as a car slowly came around, heading toward her shop, cutting off what she was about to say.

"There is Brian now, probably coming to update you on your home and whether or not the tech team is done, and you can have it back. Not that I want you to leave any time soon. You take all the time you want to stay here and let me fuss over you. I never had a daughter of my own, and you, the daughter of my best friend! Let me have a bit more time spoiling you."

Another smaller sigh came out of June, and she excused herself, telling me not to worry, that she'd be right back. I had a feeling she was going to get a pitcher of sweet tea and some glasses for the three of us and had to steel myself for the coming onslaught of sugary sweetness.

Before the detective reached the shop, I saw him slow down and start talking to a woman who looked an awful lot like my cousin, Nora. It looked as if she was heading to the beautician shop, and didn't that just figure? A woman like her had to look her best for an inquisition, after all. And I suspected that was precisely what I was going to face once I met this Witches Council.

I suddenly squeaked in alarm when a shadow blocked the sun as I looked up to see a straggly man, with a small potbelly, and long dirty hair, scrutinizing me. I backed away as he leaned forward, his gaze going from me to the detective and back in a nervous way, his breath smelling of alcohol.

"Can I help you?" I managed to get out, hoping June would come back out and shoo this character away.

"You're Lily Sweet. You just came back. You look like your daddy. Why did you come back now?"

Okay, then. This was someone who knew my family, but I was at a disadvantage.

"I'm sorry, but should I know who you are? Are we related...or?" *Lord, please no!*

"You look like your daddy. I know his secret. Charles Sweet. He was a no-good rat. But that's not what I come to tell you."

He looked off to where Brian was now finishing up his chat with Nora and getting ready to head my way. The mystery man's eyes widened when he saw this, and he hurriedly continued his rant.

"I need to tell you secrets. Only you can know them. About your mother, Adelaide, Charles, all yer kin. Jess didn't have to run. I have some things you need to hear. Meet me. Tomorrow at eight o'clock in the mornin' at your place. I'll be waiting for you."

Then he squirreled away as fast as he appeared. I called after him, "Wait. Do you know who killed my aunt Adelaide? Do you have any information? Can't you wait for the detective?"

But the man had vanished around the back of June's shop just as the detective in question pulled in the driveway. Getting out of his vehicle, Brian headed over to me with an inquisitive look on his face.

"Was that Chad Barwick I saw running away from you? But you wouldn't know who he is or what he looks like, so why am I asking? I'm sorry. Good morning, Lily. How do you feel today?"

Shaking his head, Detective Chase, Brian—I had to get used to the change in address from the previous day—sat next to me just as June came out. This time it was more coffee and some yummy-looking biscuits with some sort of jam.

"Just in time Brian, dear. Here, have yourself something to eat, and here's a cup of coffee. I'm sure you have been running on steam, what with the remains and the Council all up in arms, not to mention our dear Lily's kin all atwitter about her return."

I turned to the, *um*, Brian and told him of my encounter. He and June both laughed and assured me old Chad was harmless. Okay, then. I stopped myself from saying what he had asked of me, and I was sitting there wondering why I wasn't forthright with what he told me, when Brian spoke again.

"Well, that's kind of what I'm here about. The Council, that is, and Lily's relatives. A meeting of sorts has been called for. All the essential Elders plus any kin that would like to come and meet Lily over at the Hall will be in attendance. I'm here to escort her."

Wow, that was fast. Escort? That sounded ominous. Was I in any danger? These were witches, after all.

"Er, is everything okay here, guys? Am I in danger? A police escort kind of sounds formal—maybe too formal?"

Brian smiled at me and tried to ease my concerns.

"Nah, this is just how the Elders like to do things. Trust me, everyone is excited to see you and such. It would probably be a party with all the works if it weren't for Adelaide being found under your porch. As it stands, they are all delighted you are back and just wanted to get to know you, introduce you to the Council, and get you inducted into it.

I'm sure they will help answer all your questions if they can. This will be a good thing, Lily. Trust me?"

He said this with such a tender smile and a twinkle in those gorgeous baby blues that I found myself smiling right along with him. Okay, I also felt electricity, and my mouth was watering a bit; the man was sitting so close to me I could smell his heavenly cologne, and loved the look of his five o'clock shadow. *How has he managed that at nine-thirty in the morning?* I wondered.

"Can I have, like, fifteen minutes to make myself a bit more presentable?" I was slightly mortified to realize I was still in yesterday's clothing and sitting there barefoot.

"Go ahead. I will just have me another of these earth-shattering biscuits and more coffee. Go knock yourself out."

Smiling, I ran upstairs and unlatched my suitcase to find them empty. *Oh my gosh! Where are my clothes?!* I started thinking all manner of dreadful things when I realized June had probably helped me unpack before I arrived last night since she and Jake went on ahead to get my possessions from Murphy's motel while the relatives fussed over me and made plans. Lorcan, dropping me off, had promised my loaner would be returned to the rental place since he was almost finished with my truck. That was quick; he must really know his stuff like Jake said.

Throwing open the closet doors, I found most of my clothing neatly hung. I grabbed a cute sundress, white with red and yellow flowers on it, and matching red sandals and one of my mother's button-up cream sweaters in case the temperature changed, or it was cold in the Council building. I ran into the bathroom and turned on the shower, brushed my teeth, used the facilities, then hopped in, the warm water soothing my nerves a bit. I knew I was getting all wound up about this upcoming meeting, but I wanted to look my best and give an excellent first impression to all the relatives I would meet. *How many could there possibly be?* I wondered.

I took what had to be the quickest shower in the history of showers, hopped out and toweled off, then started drying my long black hair. Realizing it would take all day, I added some Moroccan Oil and pulled it into an attractive bun with a few tendrils hanging down. It would dry a bit more on the way, and I knew it would look good; my hair was one of my best assets. Slipping on my underthings and then the dress over it, I donned my sandals and grabbed my makeup.

I didn't want to glam up. I wouldn't try to compete with dear Nora, the witch—oh wait, yeah. Well, I didn't want to come across as too overdone or too whatever these folks expected a New Yorker to be. I just did a simple outline of eyeliner, a light mascara, and lip gloss and called it a day. I put a small, cheap necklace with a tiny heart I'd picked up around my neck and considered switching out my rather childish kitten earrings for the only other ones I owned, tiny pearls surrounded by aquamarines that I never could recall ever wearing, but I decided against them. They'd just have to take me as I was, quirky kitten earrings and all. Grabbing my purse, I headed out the door and down to a waiting Brian.

"Well, that was a lot quicker than I expected," he said with a cute chuckle.

"Should I be insulted at your assumption all women need hours to primp?"

I smiled at him to counter my stern words, and he just laughed some more.

"Well, you certainly were faster than I thought you'd be, and let me just say, you sure do clean up pretty. Come on, Lily Sweet, let's get you to the Council and introduce you to the world of witches!"

Okay, so I would arrive in a police car not on a broom. Wait—*did* we ride brooms? *Yikes!*

CHAPTER 10

J didn't know what I was expecting, definitely something more along the lines of the Wizengamot in the Ministry of Magic from the Harry Potter books. The Council of Witches in Sweet Briar, in comparison, looked like an Ikea catalog mated with an aromatherapy shop. The result was a light, bright, soothing, pleasant-smelling office, piping New Age music. We walked into a reception area complete with a desk. Looking around, I also spied office space and elevators. These led up to second-floor conference rooms and two auditoriums, one large and one small. I really had to let go of my preconceived assumptions, because I had a feeling more surprises were coming as far as all things Witch was concerned. I was currently cooling my heels just outside the smaller auditorium, yet again gnawing on the side of my thumb.

June wasn't invited to this meeting, so I found myself sitting with my aunt Iona and Cousin Douglas. The only non-relative with me was Brian, who I hoped wasn't here as police presence in case things got out of hand, although why they would, I had no idea. At least his being there settled my nerves some, and it didn't hurt that he placed a calming hand on my shoulder when he noticed me anxiously fretting. We were waiting to be called into the "reunion," as Aunt Iona called it. I was sticking with High Inquisition until I could judge for myself how welcoming the rest of my family and the Elders would be.

Suddenly, the door to the small auditorium swung open toward us, letting a chatter of many voices reach my ears. *Gulp!* It sounded like a full house. I looked at the elevators and started calculating how fast I would need to bolt to be able to reach them, press the button, and hope for a quick escape before Brian and or my relative hoard jumped me. My uncle Owen, *Judge* Owen, came into the hallway before I could make haste, and the butterflies that were flitting around in my stomach suddenly lodged in my throat.

"They're ready and waiting for you, Lily."

I looked him up and down when I noted he was adorned in a luxurious, dark purple hooded robe that went all the way down to the floor. Ah! This was more like it. He definitely screamed witch rather than judge, and it dawned on me he was one of the Elders, which made sense, I guessed, since Jake mentioned it last night. I gave a wavering smile to no one in particular and rose to my feet, following my small group into the chamber.

Dead silence and intense stares.

Then quiet murmuring started, heads leaning close in and whispering behind hands from some of the people in the room. Others keeping their ardent scrutiny fixed squarely at yours truly, but quite a few faces were open and friendly and wore attentive smiles. *Okay, focus on them, kiddo.*

"Can everyone please be quiet and let me present and welcome our dear, long lost Lily back to the fold?"

Uncle Owen's voice was soft but commanding, and everyone complied, making me get a clear picture of what he must be like on the bench—if the witches had a courtroom set up like the regular folks, that was. Who knew, maybe he did double duty with witches and, er, humans alike. I had to ask if there was a term for everyday people, or I was going to start hearing "Muggle" at every turn. The thought made me giggle, and I heard a voice to my left ask, "Do you find us amusing?"

I turned toward the voice and found a very striking woman with long, golden-brown hair and intense green eyes regarding me with a combination of curiosity and caution. She was also in a purple robe, so I had no idea if she was a relative as well as another Elder, because sitting in her area were more people similarly garbed—a total of twelve—with four in more ornate robes than their brethren. Hers was like Uncle Owen's, so I gathered she was indeed an Elder.

"Um, no. I just, I'm a bit nervous."

"Oh, Gloria, leave her alone. She's probably overwhelmed with all of this pomp and ceremony."

The woman who made that statement came up to me and placed a hand on my arm. She was one of the most stunning individuals I had ever seen. She had vibrant golden skin and gorgeous brunette hair that cascaded in glorious curls over her shoulders, her eyes were similar to mine, and she reminded me of someone. Wait! Me! She looked a bit like me! Her eyes, anyway. I certainly did not see myself as having the grace and beauty of the woman in front of me. We stared at each other for a full minute in silence, and then she nodded her head and turned to face the group.

"With certainty, this is Carlo's daughter. Face notwithstanding, her aura aligns with his. But we should still determine if she commands the power of her ancestors through that ring she is wearing."

All eyes went to the object in question, and I heard quite a few gasps. Clearly, the ring my mother intimated I keep off my hand caused a stir among those gathered. I raised my eyes back to the woman, and she smiled at me then blew my mind with her next words.

"Welcome, Lily. I am your aunt Chiara, your father's sister."

Well, just—wow. My mouth was hanging open, and I fought the urge to reach up and close it like I'd seen Daffy Duck do in cartoons more times than I could count. Indeed, an inane, "Hi, how ya doin'?" would not suffice for this moment, and I was convinced everyone concerned was starting to suspect I might be a tad slow, so I mustered all the poise and confidence I could gather, which wasn't much. I plastered what I hoped was a sincere-looking smile on my face and put my shoulders back.

"Aunt Chiara, such a pleasure to meet you."

I saw her eyes soften, and she reached for my elbow and led me to the front of the room.

"I, Chiara Dolce-Becker, claim this woman, Lily Sweet, as heir and Dark Witch in the House Dolce." My aunt turned to me and quietly instructed me to bow my head. Before I knew what was going to happen next, she placed a rather intricate white gold filigree circlet studded with precious gemstones on my head. There were diamonds, emeralds, amethysts, rubies, and sapphires, surrounded by smaller peridots, alexandrite, opals, and pearls. The center stone was an Aquamarine—my birthstone. She then placed a leather necklace around my neck that sported a rather simple pentagram on it with a tiny black cat, a moon, and another aquamarine on it.

"These would have been yours by now, my dear, had your mother…"

"Had her mother not been the coward she was and

destroyed the life of my Carlo, putting this entire town in peril."

This came from a voice in the back of the room, her identity hidden by shadows. It was a female voice, and at first, I wanted to blame Cousin Nora, but I knew it couldn't be. This voice was older, much older. Like antediluvian old. Methuselah's mother. Yeah, *that* old. It sounded like a voice you'd expect to hear coming from an open crypt on Halloween, calling out to wayward travelers that she was going to steal their souls. What? I had a very vivid imagination, and I knew this person was not going to give me the warm fuzzies.

As the tension in the room mounted, I could hear soft footfalls making their way down the center aisle. As the woman got closer to the front, and the light, I couldn't believe what I was seeing. A tiny old lady dressed all in black, imposing, just as I suspected, but instead of a bent old hag, she was ramrod straight, had a queenly countenance, and her eyes were alert and focused. But the most surprising thing about her, was how youthful she appeared. Obviously, this was my great-grandmother, for who else could it be? If I had to take a guess, I would put her in her late sixties, not the late nineties or, gulp, more she must be. The most incredible thing about her was the fact that I now knew exactly what I would look like when I reached her lofty age. Well, I deduced someone got word about me to the old woman!

"Grandmother, please, not now, not here. Please, let's not start again. You cannot call Jessica a coward when we still have no idea what caused her to run away. Moreover, Lily is not to blame," Aunt Chiara said on my behalf.

"No, she is not!" said a voice from the front row. "Great-grandma, please, she looks just like you! And Lily is Uncle Carlo's daughter. How can you be mean to her?"

The person speaking was a pretty brunette with chestnut

locks that were curly and bouncing around her head as if they had a life of their own. Her gray eyes flashed with anger, and she came up to stand next to me, giving me a brief, tight hug.

"Mama, please make Granny stop this. She isn't the leader of the Council anymore. By right, it should be Lily, here. But you are in that position...so...so just make her stop!" She turned to me and hit me with a huge grin. "I'm your cousin, Andrea. Chiara is my mother. My dad, Stephen, would be here, but he is at our bakery in town. I hope we become best friends, Lily Sweet!" This she emphasized with another enthusiastic hug.

"Lily Sweet," spat the old woman. "Liliana Dolce. That should be her name. But no. My son had to marry that lunatic hippie-woman from Northern Italy, change the family name, run off to a commune, and leave the fold. Comes back a few years later with the only two good things to come from that ill-fated marriage, my grandson Carlo and my granddaughter Chiara. Then they both were killed in a car crash somewhere in one of those Asian countries on the other side of the world. Bah!" She stamped her foot down on the floor, walked up to me, and I swore she grew in size to match her ire.

"Are you or are you not a Dark Witch?"

Okay, Wizard of Oz flashback notwithstanding, I wasn't about to go all Dorothy on the old lady. Therefore, I reined in my usual snark and tried to answer her with a modicum of respect.

"I'm not quite sure exactly what that means. This is all new to me. I have only recently been told I am one by Jake Carter and Lorcan Reid—and Detective Chase, Brian. They all seem to think I am. I actually zapped Lorcan and sent Jake flying across a room, but I'm not sure how I did it!"

Interest sparked in her eyes.

"Zapped? You performed magic? Let me see. Now!" she commanded.

"Grandmother! Stop!" Again, I was saved by Aunt Chiara, who rested her hand on the old lady's shoulder. "All in good time, and now is *not* that time, if you know what I mean."

Her words registered with my great-grandmother, whose face suddenly got crafty as her eyes shifted to all those sitting in the auditorium.

"Fine. But the girl comes to me soon. I must know what she has in her."

And with that, she slowly but regally swept out of the hall and into the corridor beyond. You could feel the tension rush out of the room with her.

Andrea grabbed me and started making the rounds, introducing me to everyone in the gallery. Most of the people there were related to me in some way or another. My head began to spin with the realization that I had quite a massive family and suddenly wasn't so alone in the world anymore. I just wasn't sure yet if this was a good thing or not. Oh, Lily, be careful what you wish for—a little too late for that.

I spent the next two hours in a meet and greet of sorts. A whirlwind of faces and names, none of which I would remember clearly without dedicated practice—and more time with each individual would help. There were quite a few I felt sure I would rue the day we ever met and would try to avoid at all costs. Thankfully, most of my relatives were marvelous and entertaining. They welcomed me with open arms. The Scot-Irish side were gregarious and welcoming, and the Italians were gracious and warm—other than my great-grandmother. Therefore, I didn't know why anyone had made such a big deal about them the previous evening.

As I said goodbye to the last of my newfound family, Andrea sat down next to me and wiped her brow. "Whew!

That was a lot of work. So, what do you think of the relatives, and can I buy you a cup of coffee and a cupcake or something? You must be running on empty about now!" She asked me this with a wide grin on her face. I was going to like this cousin. Anyone who offered me coffee and cupcakes had to be someone I could put on my exclusive favorite person list.

"You're on!" I proclaimed, my gaze landing on the last of the stragglers leaving the room. I removed the circlet and leather necklace and placed them carefully in my handbag.

"Well, most of the relatives seem great. Last night, Aunt Iona and a few others seemed worried about the Italian half not welcoming me, or, well, I am not sure what the fuss was over since everyone seems to like me, with a few exceptions. Who the heck is that bunch leaving just now?"

I surreptitiously nodded toward two heavy-set women with over-processed hair wearing sour expressions, who spent most of the morning giving me dirty looks. They all but insulted me when I greeted them. Throwing, snide, silly remarks my way that were meant to upset me—it just left me feeling sorry for their obvious insecurity. I assumed they were part of the Italian brigade, and they were followed by a tall, skinny, pale man who reminded me of Jafar from Disney's *Aladdin*.

Andrea looked in the direction I pointed and sighed. "Oh, that's Teresa. Not Teresa like you, and I would say it. Te-ray-zah, she demands to be addressed, and her mother, Ursula. The lanky dude is her husband, Teresa's I mean, not Ursula's. He's from some far off country that I can't keep straight. No one can remember his name, so we all call him Guy." She giggled after saying this, and I couldn't help but laugh along with her.

"They are harmless but think they are more important than they'll ever be. Don't pay them any mind—no one around here does. Just avoid the beauty shop in town that Nora goes to—I've been hearing rumors on how she's been treating you! Stay away from that place since they own it and go see Gloria. She's the witch that called you out a bit earlier —one of the Elders. She didn't mean anything by it, that's just her way. She gives a mean haircut and does it from the ground floor of the B&B she runs—the big one just off Main Street here in town."

I made a mental note to stay clear of that bunch and go check Gloria's place out when I needed her services. Then my eyes met another group of people leaving, and I felt the same derision coming from them.

"Ah, Todd and Lynn something-or-other. Distantly related and think they are above everyone else because they graduated from UGA. She's a docent at the elementary school and spends most of her time laughing out loud when anyone she doesn't like finishes saying something. We think it's a mental disorder. Therefore, we all started laughing along with her and nodding hoping not to set her off. I just hope it's not dementia or something, poor dear. She keeps telling everyone her family came over on the *Mayflower* and acts like it happened last week!

"Her husband is into pharmaceuticals. We don't know if that means he's a pharmacist, a scientist and works in a lab, grows them, or takes them. My money is leaning towards takes them. He certainly seems a bit crazed and goes off on political rants and conspiracy theories over contrails. He talks to himself while driving his tractor on his farm over in Hiawassee. You can see his lips flapping as you drive by. They declared to everyone last year that they were vegans and converted to Hinduism. Ex-hippies, gotta love 'em."

Andrea certainly had strong opinions about people, but I suspected she was dead on with that group.

"So, explain something to me." I turned to face Andrea

and bit my bottom lip as I decided how to approach a delicate subject. "Your mom, my aunt, she stated Dolce-Becker as her last name, but Adriana said her son changed the name. Wouldn't that make your mom a Sweet-Becker?"

Andrea laughed out loud, tears in her eyes, and I was confused since I hadn't said anything particularly funny. She was quick to correct me, however.

"Oh, Lily. Becker, in German, means a baker. Can you imagine my mother going around with the last name Sweet-Baker?" She chortled a bit more, and I had to concede her that point. No, I could not imagine my daunting aunt walking around with that moniker.

"But then, that makes me the only Sweet in town?"

"Who cares if you are the only Sweet? I like the change in surname! Lily, I know you are clueless about all this relative and witch stuff. My mom has all the answers you seek. Let me just caution you, since you are supposed to be a dark witch, something my mom will extrapolate on further when she has more time to set aside—without distractions and interruption. I hope you will see the validity in cautioning you. My mom is the head of our Witch Council, and that is more than likely the reason everyone was acting peculiar last night. Just give her time to enlighten you, because I don't think it's my place. However, when you know everything, I will certainly help you any way I can! We're cousins, after all. But first, we need to have something chocolate!"

Yeah, she's on my exclusive list.

We made plans to meet a bit later in the afternoon at her dad's bakery, exchanged phone numbers, and with one last hug parted ways so she could run a few errands before our coffee date.

I saw Brian head out the front doors just a bit before Andrea did, and I figured he was my ride, so I needed to catch up with him. But before I could leave, Aunt Chiara came over and stopped me, smiling at her daughter's retreating back.

"You do so look like my brother, Charles. I hope this wasn't too much for you to take in, my dear. My daughter Andrea is correct. I will give reasons for all this intrigue, and very soon. Just not today. Are you overwhelmed?" She asked this with a weary smile that I suspected had more to do with how her grandmother acted and the demands she made rather than the horde of people running around checking me out and asking her endless questions. I just hoped, in the days to come, someone would expound upon everything my great-grandmother said. Especially her accusations regarding my mother, my father, everything!

"No, quite the opposite, in fact. I am tired but delighted with all the many cousins I seem to have in a hundred-mile radius. Well, most of them, anyway!" Aunt Chiara smiled at this last statement as I shook my head and continued. "And here I thought I was an orphan. But now, well, I have family all around me."

"And a place to call home. Don't forget that, Lily. This town, Sweet Briar, is your home now, despite what your great-grandmother says. She will come around, you will see. She…" Aunt Chiara looked pained when she whispered out her final words, "You see, she must."

* * *

WHEN I WALKED out of the Council Hall looking for Brian, I was pleasantly surprised to find Lorcan standing there, dangling the keys to my truck. I ran over and grabbed them, giving him a tentative hug. I wasn't used to all this touching, it still felt weird to me. But come on! That was the fastest anyone ever got good old George repaired and back to me!

Lorcan smiled but looked distracted, glancing over his shoulder.

"Thank you, thank you, thank you! I'm so relieved this wasn't a bigger issue and he's all mine again. How much do I owe you?"

"I usually charge about two hundred for the job, but since you are new in town and we both rolled around in diapers a long time ago, I felt it only fair to knock about fifty dollars off." Lorcan laughed as I poked him in the chest.

"You made that sound positively naughty, mister. Normally, I would argue, but you said I was one hundred and forty pounds the other day. Plus, you told Nora I was evil. So we're even!"

We shook hands and laughed out loud together. This was nice.

"I'm off to freshen up because Andrea, I assume you know her?" Lorcan nodded in the affirmative, and I continued, "Well, she offered to treat me to coffee and something decadent from her father's bakery, and I never say no to sweets. Must be the name!" I smiled up at him, wondering again why he looked a bit nervous.

"Good. You two should get along great. You are a lot alike, I think. She is a loyal and kind woman and has a heart of gold but can be a little firecracker when she gets mad—so never get on her bad side!" He chuckled a bit, shaking his head with some memory that I suspected Andrea played part in, and not in an endearing way. "By the way, I never told Nora you were evil. I said I suspected you were a dark witch. As for the weight, I'm a guy, and we are just dumb that way." Well, his self-effacement certainly made me want to forgive him even more now.

"You know," I said as I wrapped my mom's sweater around my shoulders, "you never did tell me how you knew

I'd be at my house the other day. Like, were you following me or something?"

I saw a blush spread across his face as he reached up to use his thumb to scratch his eyebrow. Oh, wasn't that just adorable? He shifted a bit and reached into his back pocket, pulling out an item and holding it out to me.

"Open your hand," he said and dropped my Pisces charm into my open palm. "You dropped it again when you got out of your truck last. I saw how dear it must be from the way you reacted when it fell to the ground the other day. I found it when I was doing the repairs. There it was, just lying on the floor mat. It must have slipped out of your pocket, so I picked it up and kept it safe for you."

I immediately closed my fist around the tiny charm, overcome with relief and upset with myself for not even noticing I'd misplaced it. I reached my other hand up to check on my earrings and sighed in relief to find them both firmly in place. Looking at Lorcan, I was embarrassed, blinking back tears. If he noticed, he didn't let on.

"Later that morning, I happened to notice you drive by my shop, but you didn't see me wave, so I followed you, wanting to see if you needed anything and to take the opportunity to return your charm. You know the rest. In the commotion of the day, I forgot I had it, and then we were at your aunt's and everything. It slipped my mind. I put it in my toolbox for safekeeping. I'm sorry I didn't have the time to get it to you sooner."

I went against my usual reticence and gave Lorcan another hug, longer this time, and followed it up with a kiss on his cheek. Daring of me, I knew, but I was so grateful. I couldn't figure out why this little charm meant so much to me—other than my mother left it for me. A trinket she had taken from me a long time ago, and one, she had returned upon her death, Yeah, it meant a lot. Like a *lot*, lot. I was so very touched by his compassion.

"Here a few days and already stealing men? How like a dark bitch—oops, sorry! I meant witch."

Ah, Cousin Nora. I wondered that she hadn't made an appearance today. It looked like she showed up after all. Better late than never—not.

"Nora, cut it out." Lorcan looked abashed, and I suspected she was the source of his disquiet. I wondered again at their relationship. "She was only thanking me for fixing her truck and finding something she misplaced in it."

Nora peered at the charm in my hand before I could ball it up into a fist.

"Hmm. I bet that isn't the only thing Lily dear has ever lost in that truck."

Why that—how dare she insinuate anything about my character? Laughing, Nora walked into the Council, her hand in the air, waving at me dismissively. I sent dagger looks at the back of her head and lurched forward to go after her and give her a piece of my mind, but Lorcan reached out and stopped me.

"Let her go, Lily. Save it for another day. Go have coffee with your cousin Andrea and let Nora be Nora. There is a story there, but let's save it for another day, okay?"

I pulled away from Lorcan, wondering at his words but too hurt that he hadn't said more to shut down that mean cousin of mine. With a half-smile and no further dialogue, not trusting what I might say, I turned and went to get in my truck. That's when I stopped short, discovering for the first time that my back window was no longer stuck open. Lorcan had noticed and fixed it. I turned and ran back to him, giving another brief hug and whispering, "thank you," before climbing into my truck.

Ah, George. I gave his dash a fond pat and turned his

engine over. As I pulled out of the parking lot, I swallowed the lump in my throat. I could handle bullies like Nora. I didn't have to like it, but I refused to let her ruin the rest of my day and turned my thoughts to Andrea. I headed to my apartment to get freshened up for my coffee date with my new cousin—and, better yet, maybe a much-needed ally.

CHAPTER 11

J woke the next morning with a sense of urgency but no recollection of why it needed to be so. Yesterday afternoon was lovely. I had a great time meeting my uncle Stephen, a big ruddy-complexioned ginger of a man with a quick smile and a twinkle in his light-blue eyes. He was a dedicated baker of all things German, on his side of the family, and Italian delights that he picked up by his marriage to my aunt. He even tossed in a few French treats.

His establishment was everything anyone could ever want in a bakery and rivaled those I had visited in New York City. I wondered if the townsfolk knew just how lucky they were to have such a talented baker in their midst. His pastries and cakes were to die for, but what did me in was his strudel. Never had I ever eaten something so utterly and lovingly created. The taste was out of this world, a burst of butter and apple-laden goodness, and I already worried I'd have to take up some kind of excruciating physical activity to live in the same town with his café. Still, it would be worth it for that strudel alone.

I sat up in bed and went over the last few days, trying to

figure out why I was feeling this out of sorts, when suddenly I remembered the weird man from yesterday morning. He pleaded with me that I meet him at my new home. Dare I even show up? What if he was some deranged lunatic and would try to hurt me? But no, Brian knew who he was and didn't seem alarmed yesterday when he saw him shuffling away at his approach. He certainly didn't go any further in questioning me as to what Chad Barwick, as he called him, had to say, so I didn't think I needed to be concerned. What would it hurt, meeting him this morning? I doubted he had anything important to tell me, just rantings of a strange old man. Maybe I shouldn't be quick to dismiss him, however. You never knew what some people kept secret. I just wondered how he recognized me and knew that I had returned to town. I wondered if gossip was the norm around these parts.

Noting the time was just after seven in the morning, I calculated I had just enough time to grab a shower and head over to the bakery for some coffee and another piece of that strudel before I was to meet Chad at my new place. Well, that was enough incentive to get me up and going for the day. Did I say I loved that strudel? Yeah, it's all that and more.

I stretched before getting out of bed, my eyes landing on a baseball bat that I hadn't noticed hanging over my door. It had writing on it, and I swung my legs over the side of the bed and got up to inspect it. Oh, it was inscribed with little leaguer's names, and I saw Jake's on there. This must be from when he was a little boy, and I smiled as I imagined what he must have been like, uniform and ball cap, all cute and determined he'd be the next great baseball star.

Smiling, I headed into the bathroom and started my morning ablutions, thoughts of the last few days going around my head, when it suddenly occurred to me I never did get to the bottom of what the animosity was between

Jake and Lorcan, mild though it seemed. It was ever-present, just under the surface, and I was itching to know what it was all about. I wondered if June would know and, likewise, tell me.

As I headed down into the shop, I walked in on June, pulling a tray of muffins out of the oven. Big, delightfully fresh blueberries bursting in large, gorgeously formed muffins with that coarse sugar on top. Well, I knew my visions of strudel for breakfast just faded, because these looked too good to walk away from—not to mention the fact that the woman could make a stellar cup of coffee.

"Lily! You are up early." Coming around the counter, June gave me a great big hug. I tried not to stiffen. Yet again, more hugs. I had a lot to make up for since my mom was not the demonstrative type. "I made muffins, and coffee is on." She read my mind.

My thoughts went to my friend Molly back in New York. If she could only see me now, the introvert giving and receiving hugs, she wouldn't believe how fast I came out of my shell. Sweet Briar seemed to have that effect on me. I discerned a phone call was in my future because I needed to give her an update.

"Where are you off to so early, dear?"

"Oh, I thought I'd swing by my house today and start taking inventory and figure out what needs doing. Aunt Chiara mentioned that there is nothing stopping me from setting up residence. She's having all the utilities turned on and plans on dropping off an information packet on what utility companies I need to call to set up my accounts and other things. But I am having such a lovely time with you here. I'm in no rush to move out—if you'll let me stay a bit longer, that is."

A happy sob came out of June as she wrapped me up yet again. "Oh, sweetheart, you take all the time you need. I still can't believe I have Jessica's little girl here under my roof after all these years." And with that, she handed me a muffin, and one for the road, then went about finding me a travel mug so I could take some of her delicious coffee with me.

I was about to query her on the situation between her son, Jake, and Lorcan, but then the office phone rang, and she went off to answer it, waving me off and wishing me a good day. No worries, I had all the time in the world to get to the bottom of that puzzle. Sniffing my delicious breakfast, I grabbed my purse and headed out to my truck. This was going to be a great day; I could just feel it.

* * *

I MANAGED to drive with one hand while devouring the first muffin and had just started in on the second when I arrived at my house. I knew I had lost an opportunity to speak to June about the tension between Jake and Lorcan. Not to mention a follow-up talk about how she promised to enlighten me regarding all things witch. Pondering this, I succeeded in not spilling any coffee as I pulled into the driveway. I deliberated how to bring up the subject again, then sighed. For now, I had to deal with Chad Barwick and his flair for the dramatic. As my tires crunched over the gravel and I parked, I realized I needn't worry about staying hidden.

I was just stuffing the last of the muffin into my mouth. What? Don't judge. No one was around; don't tell me you eat all dainty-like when you're alone. Swallowing the last of the muffin, I turned toward the residence. That's when my jovial mood was dampened by the figure of Chad propped up on my porch. His back was up against the side of the building, his feet sprawled out in front of him. What appeared to be a bottle of scotch was precariously held in his left hand and looked to be almost drained completely dry.

How do you like that? He asked me in earnest to meet him here for some critical news only I could know about then passed out drunk before he could tell me. I wondered if he spent the night here. Maybe he was the town drunk? Homeless? I felt a pang of remorse. I shouldn't be so careless with my thoughts because perhaps he needed help. I decided I'd get him some food and a cup of coffee to sober him up and fill his belly before I sent him on his way. I wasn't heartless. I was convinced this would be a bit of folly on my part, just meeting this guy. I sighed, knowing there was only one thing to do. And that was wake Chad up and get this little tête-à-tête over with as fast as I could.

I hopped out of my truck and slammed the door in the hopes of waking the sleeping man. Nothing. I began my approach to the side porch. Why, oh, why, was he there? Didn't he know that the skeletal remains of my aunt Adelaide were found just a mere foot away from where he was sitting? I knew I had to get over that fact, but with the visible gaping hole, I knew it wouldn't be until I got it patched up properly that I'd stop getting the willies every time I looked in that spot. Let alone walk on it.

"Hello? Mr. Barwick. Good morning! Time to get up. It's Lily Sweet. I'm here to listen to what you have to say!" This last bit came out as a shout because the man was not waking up. I was sure the alcohol had something to do with that. Ugh, I did not want to have to shake him. I barely wanted to touch him or be anywhere within a few yards of him. The reek of his alcohol-imbued body reached me before I put my foot on the first step.

Whew! That was quite the odor he had going on.

I assumed the returned humidity had something to do with the intensity of his stench. Wrinkling my face in disgust, I finally found the nerve to walk up to him and shake his shoulder. Nothing. I went to rattle him a bit harder, not to hurt, but definitely trying to get a rise out of him and get him off my porch. I was going to have to hose the boards because it looked as if old Chad had an accident in his sleep. Yuck.

I gave him a good shove, calling out his name again when his body pitched forward. The first thing I noticed was the knife sticking out of his back. Of course, my hand reached out and grabbed it; don't ask me why I did this. I watched detective shows. I knew the drill. But that's precisely what I did, reached out and grabbed it. The second thing I noticed was Brian Chase stepping onto the opposite side of my porch just as I released the bloody knife. Reeling back, I inadvertently sent poor Chad careening into the hole in the floor, head-first and feet in the air. The third thing I noticed was the sound of a train approaching, and I thought to myself, *How odd. Why is there a train coming here?* And then I blacked out.

CHAPTER 12

"*W*hat on earth were you thinking?"

I didn't want to open my eyes, because unlike the last time this happened, I fully remembered where I was and why I passed out. Maybe if I left my eyes shut, they'd all go away and let me have time to figure out how to explain what just transpired. Oh, I knew I did a monumentally stupid thing. I touched a murder weapon. Yes—murder. Because no way did old Chad get that horrible blade into his own back and fall down dead on my side porch. Nope. He had help. A murderous heap of help. And I knew I must look like prime suspect number one. Especially since I had a grip on the darned knife seconds before it looked like I pushed the poor devil into the same hole my aunt Adelaide was just pulled *out* of.

My day couldn't get any worse.

"Oh my God. She murdered poor old Chad Barwick!"

Nora. Well, I guess my day *could* get worse. Go figure? This was just great.

"Lily, I know you're awake. Your breathing changed. Open your eyes and sit up, please." This was from Brian.

Sighing, I opened my eyes and sat up as instructed and involuntarily looked over to where Chad was still stuffed into the hole, legs askew, and almost passed out again.

"Whoa, steady there, girl." I turned to see Lorcan crouching next to me, a perturbed Nora tapping her toe impatiently on the ground behind him.

"Why are you letting her just sit there, Brian? Arrest her. She's a murderess. Poor man, what did he ever do to you to deserve that?"

"How about you shut your stupid mouth before I come over there and murder you, you...you..." Okay, maybe not the best thing to say in these circumstances, but I was tired of this woman always saying snide stuff to me, and after this morning's little adventure, I was feeling a bit irritated. She could bite me. Everyone could just bite me. I turned toward Nora, glaring at her, and was about to get in her face. I wanted to let her know just what I thought of her when a small bolt of blue something shot out of my fingertips.

"Ack!" Nora's eyes widened as she squealed and dove behind Lorcan's back in mock terror. Oh, it was all for show; I could see the look of triumph in her eyes. I bet she was counting on Brian to cuff me and stuff me in the nearest jail cell. Imagine how upset she was when instead, he reached down and helped me to my feet then gave me a hug. There was that cologne again; I felt like I was being hugged by a thunderstorm and maybe held on a bit longer than I should have.

Okay, I was starting to really like these things, especially when they came from the hunk brigade.

"What?" Nora screeched. "You aren't going to arrest her? She murdered Chad Barwick in cold blood! She just tried to kill me!" *Laying it on a little thick there, hey, Nora?* We all turned toward her as she continued with her histrionics.

Finally, Brian, making sure I was steady on my feet before

releasing me, turned to address her. "Knock it off Nora, and go sit in the car if you can't behave properly. I already told you I saw what happened. I was pulling in when I saw Lily approach the stairs and go shake Chad. When he didn't respond, she shook him again, and he fell forward. Unfortunately, she reached out for the knife, which is what ninety-nine percent of civvies do in this type of situation. No one could expect that the next thing to happen was he'd pitch into that hole and get stuck. Now stop being so dramatic and let me hear what Lily has to say."

Ugh. Chad was stuck. In my floorboards? Why did this have to happen to me?

* * *

"WHY DOES this keep happening to you, Lily?"

This was from Jake, whose office we were now sequestered in, yet again, trying to come up with a game plan. We sat around his conference table, the same one I zapped him away from—was it only two days ago? It felt like weeks. Joining us was Aunt Chiara, Aunt Iona, Uncle Owen, Andrea, June, Brian, and Lorcan. Thankfully, Nora wasn't invited to this party. I heard she tried to bully her way in, with Douglas in tow, but she and her brother were turned away, much to their surprise and disappointment.

We left my property in the hands of Sheriff Glen Buford and Deputy Buford, his nephew, who would accompany the medical examiner and poor Chad's body down to the morgue in Atlanta. I, yet again, had a crew of police crime scene technicians crawling all over my porch. They gave me funny looks as Brian led me away from my property, and who could blame them? Oh Lord, was I going to be known as the town nutcase down here as well?

I was about to open my mouth to reply when a man I had

yet to meet walked in. He looked familiar, and I wondered if we were relations. That was disabused when Jake looked up, smiled when he saw who it was, and said, "Hi, Dad."

Ah, Dennis Carter, Jake's father, which explained my acuity upon seeing him enter. He greeted everyone warmly then headed over to an empty chair, but not before pausing to hold out his hand for me to shake.

"It seems you are the cause of quite a bit a drama around these parts, aren't you, young lady?" Dennis said this with a kind smile to take the sting out of the truth behind his words.

He frowned a little when I wouldn't place my hand in his but shook my head instead and looked down, mumbling, "I don't trust myself not to hurt you, sir. Blue sparks keep flying out of my fingertips, and I don't know why, or how to control it."

When I looked up, I was met with a wall of sympathetic faces, all registering understanding of how I must feel. Dennis, instead, rested his hand on my head in a fatherly gesture.

"You have to understand, a few weeks ago, I didn't know witches existed except in stories or movies. I had no idea I was one. Never in my entire life have I ever had sparks pop out of me, so why now? It can't be that just because someone tells me I'm a witch, I suddenly manifest this phenomenon!" I turned as Aunt Iona came around the table and took the chair near mine, patting my hand in the process.

"Lily, dear...it's the ring. The ring your mother left you after her death. The powers of generations of witches reside in that piece of jewelry. You obviously are the dark witch we have been saying you are, because no one else in this room could harness the potency in that ring without years of practice. You just put it on and, poof! Power." I stared at her like she had two heads. No, really, I did. Then I tried to twist the damned bauble off my finger.

Placing her hands firmly over mine, she gently chided me.

"That's not the answer, Lily. You *are* a witch. Get used to it. Embrace it. You were born into a family of powerful and great ones. Be proud of that and let any preconceived notions you have fall by the wayside until you can learn our ways and join us."

I jutted my chin out stubbornly, crossed my arms, and glared at everyone. I knew they were trying to help, but I didn't feel like cooperating right now, and okay, I was feeling a tad sorry for myself. I think I earned some time to engage in a monumental pity party here; I was good at them. Enjoyed them, even.

"Wait a minute. Hold on. June said she was a witch, but not like me. What does that mean?" I turned to June to implore her for some backup. "That means she must be, what? A white witch? I'm a dark witch. Am I...am I evil?" I gulped, and my bottom lip started to quiver. Yeah, big meanie here. I couldn't even handle being a dark superpower without falling apart. If they were counting on me to be some Maleficent or the like they were going to be horribly disappointed.

"I'm not a bad person. I cannot be this dark witch you want me to be!"

"Need."

This was from Andrea, who said it with a kindhearted look.

"Let me expound on that statement." This was from Aunt Iona again. "But yes. We *need* you to be a dark witch, our dark witch, Lily. You see, after your father disappeared, died, we just don't know? Anyway, after he left, your great-grand-mother, Adriana, endured as one of the few left that could wield dark power. But the few remaining do not have enough to protect us from what is coming."

"And what is it that's coming?" I asked, albeit reluctantly, because I had a feeling I was not going to like what I'd hear.

"Utter chaos."

I looked around the room and saw nothing but agreement in the eyes of all these people who I had only known such a short time.

"But..." I shook my head. Reason was fighting with the reality of my situation, and I was stubbornly fighting this with all I had in me. "But I can't be evil. I don't like hurting things! I don't know how to be cruel. I don't *want* to be. I don't go out and purposefully seek out the dark in anything! I just want to fix up my house and look for a place to work on my art projects, an old warehouse or barn somewhere. I want to start a new life and be happy for once. Not have this dark witch drama hanging over my head. And chaos? What does *that* mean? Am I supposed to fight something for you?"

Aunt Chiara spoke up. "First of all being a dark witch doesn't mean being evil. As for the chaos, we just do not know the extent of it yet. We have been hearing rumors from other Councils that there is a rogue coven out there. Some say it comes from somewhere out west; others are convinced they have been hiding in Florida of all places. One source has put them on the Canadian border near Niagara Falls. We don't know who they are or what they want, but if whispers are to be believed, they want to take out the old families. The dynasty covens like ours. That means the Dolce clan, and the Croy to some extent—and you are in great danger. We all are."

"When? Next week? Because I can tell you right now, I have a better chance of learning how to fly on a broom than I do of harnessing these blue sparkly things coming out my fingertips!" I couldn't believe this talk of coming danger. My plate was already full, thank you.

Aunt Chiara shook her head. "Not so soon as that. We probably have months, maybe even years. They are small and weak but growing in numbers, and we suspect they are gathering all the renegade witches without a coven, most of them criminals, to train and then attack. Our Council is doing everything it can to find these people and stop them. Maybe this will be something we need never worry about. We just don't know."

I sat there a moment, and the weight of what she was saying hit me hard. I did not want to be as evil as whatever was coming my way and said so, yet again.

"But I am not dark and I won't do dark things! I won't go out there and seek out darkness, ever!"

Brian spoke up as I took a breath to continue. "But it seems darkness came and found you, Lily. Why else would Chad be murdered on your side porch? Whether or not it has anything to do with finding Adelaide's remains, you can't argue the fact that someone did this to leave you some kind of message. We just have to find out who it is and why they targeted you. As for fighting for us and this coming chaos, as your aunt said, we have time. Being a dark witch is not what you are thinking. Your family and to some extent, the Council, will help you understand this better." This he directed toward Uncle Owen and Aunt Chiara, who nodded in agreement. "They will explain."

Dennis shook his head a little then stated, "Well, you are right, Brian. It seems they targeted Chad Barwick. Leaving him as a message of sorts for Lily." He stood up and ran his hand through his hair, then leaned on the counter near the coffeemaker and finished his thoughts. "Chad, after all, *was* engaged at one time to Adelaide. This can't be a coincidence."

What?! That poor, bedraggled man was once engaged to

Adelaide? My long-dead aunt? I pictured the beautiful young lady in the photo holding me, then I thought of the pitiful creature that was one Chad Barwick. No way.

"We were all young once, Lily." Seeing my shocked expression, Aunt Iona made a rueful little chuckle. "Even me."

"Aunt Iona, how can you even compare yourself to that man? He looks, looked..." I gulped when I switched to the past tense. "He looked older than anyone in this room!"

"Yet he was what? Only forty-eight or so, isn't that right, Owen?" Aunt Chiara spoke up for the first time. "He used to work for you, no? Alcohol aged him so."

Uncle Owen frowned and looked down at his hands clasped and resting on his belly. He sighed as he lifted his head to address the room.

"Chad Barwick was a good kid. Got decent grades, went into the military right out of high school, then became a deputy here when he finished his four years in service."

This elicited a gasp from me, and I blushed when everyone looked my way. Mumbling, "Sorry," I motioned for Uncle Owen to continue.

"He worked under your daddy, Brian. A better sheriff this town has never had since, even though he was a young one, something that can be rectified if you would just accept the position." Obviously, this was a sore spot between the detective and the judge, as Brian pushed back from the table and began to speak.

"Yes, yes...I know what you are hoping for, Owen, but I am happy to be a detective with the state, and my position allows me to keep an eye on any outside goings-on that may affect our town. You know all this, so why rehash it again?" Frustration poured off Brian, and he shook his head, looking anywhere but at my uncle.

"Okay, son. You can't blame me for trying—again. Chad

and your daddy became friends, even though he was the boss and Chad his deputy. That is, until Adelaide came between them. No one knows exactly what happened all those years ago, but one day Adelaide, Jessica, and Charles took off on a road trip to get away from the feuding duo, and when they showed up again, Jessica was a new mom with Charles, the proud father. They had run clear across the country and stayed out west, eloped in Las Vegas to make it all legal, and returned home a nice little family with Adelaide talking about going back to be a showgirl at one of the big casinos."

Uncle Owen paused, shaking his head at the memory.

"Since she was nineteen, we couldn't stop her, but we managed to convince her to stay and train, as she was a promising dark witch herself. Halfway through her twenty-second year, that itch came back, and we knew it would only be a matter of time before she left. One day she packed her things in secret, and took off, never to be seen or heard from again. It wasn't until we put Council witches on her trail, and they found no trace of her past the bus station over in Commerce that we started suspecting she met with foul play. Now we know it was a ruse of some kind because all along she was right here under the porch of your house, young lady."

Dennis spoke up then, startling me a bit because I hadn't seen he was standing directly behind my chair now.

"Wasn't Sherriff Glen Buford a deputy back then as well, and sweet on Adelaide, too?"

Uncle Owen smiled when he replied, "Everyone had a crush on Adelaide. Chad, your father, Dillon." This he addressed to Brian. "Heck, we all had a bit of a crush on her, young or old. She just had that something about her. She left a trail of broken hearts in her wake. Even Reverend Brewster, over at that Evangelical church on Piccadilly Street just outside of town, tried to court her. Imagine that, a reverend and a witch!"

Everyone in the room chuckled but me. I just looked confused as usual.

"Not Glen, though, that I know of. He had just convinced his future wife, Cora, to agree to marry him after a long and lengthy courtship. So I doubt he'd have been keen on Adelaide. I'm sure he noticed her, though. All the men did." Uncle Owen smiled to himself, recalling this.

I was mentally taking notes because I knew I had to get to the bottom of all this drama before another body showed up at my place!

"The other day, Nora mentioned that my aunt Adelaide was pure evil. What did she mean by that?" I asked no one in particular. "And Chad, he mentioned my father was bad too."

Aunt Iona sighed. "Evil? No. Flighty, impulsive? Yes. My sister did tend to cause a commotion every place she went. The men flocked to her. After a time, we worried it would get to her head, all this attention from the opposite sex. I tried to warn her not to trifle with the affections of so many suitors. She made one mistake that followed her around, but then, for a while there, we thought Chad had won her heart. When she ran off with Jessica and Charles, we thought it another one of their games." She turned to me and explained further. "You see, my two sisters were closer in age than me, and Charles was the same age as Jess. They all palled around for years and would always get up to some mischief or another."

She looked sad and picked at the tablecloth then smoothed it out before continuing.

"When they left to head out west, we all expected them to be back in a few weeks. Your great-grandmother even agreed it was a good idea to get Adelaide away from the young men. She felt Adelaide, at seventeen, was too young to settle down. My sister had just started apprenticing with Adriana, you see. However, they didn't return until almost twenty months had passed, with you in tow. It was quite a scandal, and had they not gone and eloped, I think your great-grandmother would have murdered Jessica. That Addy only stayed around for three years and broke not only Chad's heart, but almost ruined a few marriages...well, plenty of women in this town sighed in relief when she left."

June looked at me then everyone in the room and took up the story. "I was shocked. Jess never mentioned any of this to me and we were like sisters. I knew she was close to Charlie, but I didn't think they were dating or talking marriage yet. She always told me she wanted to study abroad and see the world, so I was as amazed as everyone else when they came home an old married couple." She shook her head and continued, "but they seemed so happy, so I am not sure what happened next. Nor why Addy decided to finally run off a few years later."

Aunt Chiara took up the story from here, a dark look crossing her face.

"It broke my grandmother's heart when Adelaide left. She never went to say goodbye to her, you see. They had grown very close. Then several weeks later, Jess ran off with you, but not after becoming a virtual recluse. Charles was alone in the house with her, and the only other person she welcomed in her home was June, for a time, anyway. Your father assured us everything was well, and they just needed time to get over Adelaide breaking away from the family. But then, when Jess left and Charles left, we knew something must have caused the rift and had them all disappearing as they did. I thought Adriana was heading for a break down when Jess ran taking you with her, After Charles took off, well, it was not good."

Aunt Iona slammed her fist down on the table, startling everyone in the room.

"But evil? Addy? Charles? No. None of them. For a time, the entire town thought they must have done something bad and run off before retribution caught up to them. But we never heard, never found out what caused the three of them to run. Now we know poor Addy never left. I know Jessica became paranoid for a while, but I chalked it off to mood swings or something going on, because Charles assured all of us everything was fine, and we believed him!

We all were fooled because they seemed so happy, and you were a joyful and adorable little girl by that time. Everyone was fooled, everyone except his grandmother, that is. She was fit to be tied when all of this went down. She'd been complaining for weeks that something was wrong. Now we all have to face the fact that something bad must have happened and those three chose not to let us in to help."

This was met with somber silence as the reality of what Iona said just sunk in.

"You don't think? I mean. Adriana is a powerful dark witch, no? You don't think my great-grandmother had anything to do with any of this, do you?"

Everyone in the room relaxed, and a few people chuckled at my worry.

"Oh no, dear." This was from June. "Your great-granny has a mean streak a mile wide and twenty feet deep, but as a dark witch, she wouldn't resort to common murder. No, she would have turned everyone concerned into weeds right there in her front yard then poured vegetation killer on them and slowly watched while they withered from her porch!"

That was a pleasant thought.

"Well then," this was from Lorcan, who leaned back in his chair, causing it to squeak and slide back a bit, "the question remains. Who killed Chad Barwick, and why target Lily?"

CHAPTER 13

I was sitting in June's kitchen again. I had trouble sleeping last night as the heavens decided to open up at about four o'clock in the morning, followed by lightning and thunder. I usually enjoy a good storm, but in light of recent events, I was jolted awake and stayed that way.

Now the sun was peeking through the clouds, and the weather forecast called for clearing skies and much cooler temperatures. I had donned some old jeans and an Aerosmith t-shirt, another of my favorite bands. Humming, "Sweet Emotion," I was looking forward to my day. I planned on tackling some of the rooms in my house since Brian said the interior wasn't affected by this latest incident. I was treating this as a case of falling off a horse syndrome. I intended to get right back up and not let anything deter me from setting my house in order. This was my first place, blast it all, and nothing and no one would stop me from enjoying every bit of it. Well, maybe not the porch, not just yet.

My thoughts went to Chad and I took a moment to ponder why someone would hurt that poor man. And why at my place? I felt guilty for still being excited about heading over there to open it up and air it out, but I also knew I was being irrational if I thought staying home and forgetting about it would make a difference to him. It wouldn't. Only finding out who did this and why would bring some sense of justice. And that would be up to the police to find out. Although I felt the urge to investigate, which was silly, right?

I enjoyed the fact that I could walk to my place from June's if I so chose. I was just off South Main. All I had to do was cut through her back alley onto the street behind her business, turn right and continue to South Main, and turn left. Then walk one block before making another left on the next street. My home was four houses in on the opposite side of Wildflower Lane, number twenty-eight. If I stood on my front porch, I could just make out the back of her shop through the trees that belonged to the home across the street from mine. Today, though, I thought I'd take my truck because I needed to haul some cleaning supplies, and I wasn't confident I could lug everything on foot.

I stopped by my place after the meeting at Jake's yesterday to retrieve my truck, totally avoiding the porch and the crime technicians as I did. As I was getting ready to climb in, a middle-aged couple approached me from my back yard. Another sense of déjà vu hit me, especially when I looked the man over, but this time I knew exactly whose parents these were. Lorcan looked so much like his dad, I could tell he'd be the spitting image of the man in front of me when he reached his middle years. Considering how great his father looked, I thought it portended well for Lorcan's future.

It was remarkable how so many folks in their forties and beyond still looked youthful around here—if you excluded Chad. Even Adriana looked decades younger than whatever her true age was.

Lorcan's parents were no exception. They did indeed have the property directly behind mine and wanted to come over to welcome me. Unfortunately, the circumstances weren't more pleasurable, but I thought we made the best out of it, all things considered.

"Oh my, you have had a bit of hard luck since you've arrived, haven't you?" That was an understatement if I ever heard one. This was from Lorcan's mother, Eileen, a pleasant woman with a warm smile and laugh lines like her spouse and son. She had dark hair, almost as black as mine, with the most amazing hazel eyes I'd ever seen, and rosy cheeks that complimented her fair Irish skin. Henry, her husband, definitely looked like a typical Scotsman. I was somewhat disappointed he wasn't wearing a kilt since it would suit him.

"Now, Eileen, look at how your words upset the lass! It's not her fault that two bodies were found at her place!"

Skeleton and a body, thank you, but who's keeping track?

I didn't correct Henry, and Eileen went on to welcome me and invited me over for tea some time. I assumed she meant the sweet variety and thanked them both for coming to greet me. Before they left, Henry held up a small bottle of oil he told me he used on the back gate, so it didn't squeak if I wanted to go through the yards to get to their house. They were such a nice couple and left me feeling at ease and looking forward to paying them a visit. When we parted, I asked Henry if I could borrow the oil to do the hinges on my front door, and he told me to keep it as he had several more in his workshop. Before I left, I ran back to my house and took care of that task—one thing off my list!

June set a fresh cup of coffee down in front of me, startling me out of my reverie, and I sliced us both a piece of her breakfast casserole. It had onions and asparagus, bell peppers, and ham all mixed together with egg and cheese and baked until golden, and it was delicious. After devouring my first piece, I reached for seconds, glad I intended to work hard all day to combat the calories I was ingesting.

"June, can I ask you something?" Licking my fingers off, not caring whether it was impolite, I reached for my coffee and took a healthy swig. I figured now was the perfect time to bring up Jake and Lorcan, my curiosity winning out over my reticence on getting too personal. I had mentioned meeting Lorcan's parents yesterday and used it as an opening of sorts. "It's about Jake and Lorcan. They seem friendly, but I sensed an undercurrent of tension the first time we all met on Monday, and every day since I've been with them, there always seems to be unspoken words hanging over them."

The sound of the clock ticking counted the seconds and was the only thing making a sound for quite some time as I watched June struggle with how to reply to my query. I didn't like being the cause of her discomfort, so I opened my mouth to tell her to forget I asked when she started speaking.

"I guess you might as well know the details. You are part of the family, and it is common knowledge." She sighed and looked up at me, sadness etched on her face. "I will tell you most of what happened, but the rest should come from Jake and Lorcan and only if they choose to share the details with you." Seeing the look of alarm cross my face, she tempered her next words with a smile. "No, it's not something too dire, dear. It's what goes on in an endless cycle from generation to generation. Their issue was over a girl. Your cousin Nora, in fact. Lorcan was dating her, but somehow, Jake wound up causing a rift, someone suggested he told Nora that Lorcan was cheating on her. They came to blows over it, as teenagers are wont to do, and it left some bad blood between them. They never got too specific on what exactly happened, and they aren't dating now, but there you have it. That must be what you are sensing, dear."

She got up and went over to the sink, staring out the window at her small garden beyond. "It's a pity, really, because they were all such great friends growing up, and you would have been in with them as well. Even though your aunt Iona is a good bit older than her younger siblings, she and Owen waited a bit to have children, so you are all around the same age, give or take a year or two. Who knows? Maybe your return can help heal some of those old wounds."

Maybe, but not as far as Nora was concerned, not if it involved yours truly.

* * *

As I was walking out the back door, getting ready to start my morning, I heard the sounds of a vehicle approaching and looked up to see Lorcan pulling up the drive in a fully restored, old Chevy truck. I smiled, and he gave me a wave, as he parked behind me, blocking me in.

"Hey there, stranger," I said as a way of greeting then whistled as I took in the quality of the rebuild. His truck looked to be from the mid-nineteen fifties and had impeccable green paint and a tan leather interior—also in remarkable shape. The side-rails were a rich polished wood, as was the truck bed. The words "Reid's Garage" were painted on the side in white with a cute mechanics logo of crossed wrenches. And the best thing about it was the white-walled tires that completed the package. I was sure everywhere he went that truck made heads turn. Poor old George looked like a junkyard heap in comparison.

"That's one great truck you have there."

Lorcan ran his hand down the length of the bed and gave the tailgate a fond pat.

"Yeah, she's my baby. She belonged to my granddad

Malcolm, and he left her to me. I've been keeping her going since high school. I need to introduce you to him someday. He's a great storyteller."

He met me on the steps to the side porch and sat down.

"He in his late eighties. A virtual youngster compared to your great-grandmother. So, what are you up to today?"

I held up the bucket that had some cleaning supplies in it and nodded over to the bed of my truck, which held a mop, broom, industrial-strength garbage bags, and other things I'd need to get my home in order. Lifting the bucket in along with the rest of my equipment, I turned, plopped down next to Lorcan just as the sun finally broke through the last of the clouds.

"I think I need to clean the place after yesterday, the inside anyway. I am going to have to hire someone to take care of the porch. Why are you here? Oh! I met your parents yesterday. They seem even nicer than you described. Your mom even invited me over for tea."

"They called and told me. My mom thinks you are lovely, and my dad said you are quite the looker. Watch out for him. He's a bit of a rascal. I came because I have something to show you if you have the time, which looks like you might not." Lorcan rubbed the back of his neck with the palm of his hand, something I saw his father do yesterday, and it made me giggle a little, causing him to give me a questioning look.

"I…" I never finished what I was about to say, because at that moment, the roar of a motorcycle drowned out any ability to talk, and Brian Chase pulled up, looking like every parents' worst nightmare. Seriously. I know he's a detective, but this must be his day off because he was all gussied up in leather. Pants, jacket, boots, with a white t-shirt and red bandana covering his black hair—hair that was way too long and wild to be regulation length. It made me wonder about the liberties he enjoyed at the police department. He flashed me a smile and nodded to Lorcan.

The motorcycle, a Harley, fit his personality and gave him an aura of mystery and danger. And I couldn't help noticing how good he looked getting off of it. Not to mention how sexy he appeared as he sauntered up the walkway. I felt my heart give a little hitch and had the uncanny urge to start purring. No, that's silly; I'd never purr. Drool a little, yes. But purr? Nah.

"Hi, Brian," I purred. Okay, so I lied! "That Harley is just breathtaking. I'm guessing all the girls ask you for a ride." Whoa! Did I just say that? Oh my gosh, I couldn't believe that just came out of my mouth. What the heck was wrong with me? I chalked it up to too little experience with the opposite sex, despite some fumbled attempts in college that I'd rather forget. No, really. One guy I dated back then confessed he discovered he was gay after dating me for three weeks. And I lost my virginity to that boy! Stellar track record I did *not* have.

"Well, that's why I stopped by. I have some things to go over with you regarding your house, and I thought you'd like to go for a spin."

I squealed and jumped in place, clapping my hands.

"Do I ever?!" I looked happily back and forth between both men then looked down at what I was wearing, wondering if my Keds were standard Harley gear. "Is this fine for a ride? I've never been on a bike before!"

Brian nodded in the affirmative, and I raced over to the bike then back toward him and paused to give him a hug. Yeah, definitely taking liberties here. What? I needed the practice. "Let me just tell June where I'm off to. Oh, where am I off to?"

Brian looked down at me and whispered, "Maybe it's a surprise. Do you feel up for a bit of a mysterious adventure?"

I clapped my hands like an idiot again and ran into the kitchen to tell June that I was off on an adventure with Brian then raced back out the door and paused just long enough to tell Lorcan I'd see him later then met Brian by his bike. He was already seated on his motorcycle and instructed me to climb aboard and hang on.

As we were pulling out of the drive, Lorcan shouted something about a helmet for me, but Brian waved him off and sped down the street with me squealing in glee. I leaned forward and shouted in his ear, "Maybe I should have a helmet on, no?"

Brian laughed and said, "What's the use of having a badge if I can't break the law every once in a while? I was born on the back of one of these babies. Trust me?" I nodded yes even though he couldn't see me and gripped him tighter, and off we went.

It wasn't until about fifteen minutes later that I recalled Lorcan stopped by because he said he had something to show me. Feeling slightly guilty, but not enough to have Brian turn around and go back, I made a note in my mind to apologize later and hoped he wasn't too upset with me. But come on! A motorcycle ride with the hunkiest guy in town, who had a badge, a gun, and all that gorgeous hair? I couldn't say no, and who could blame me?

* * *

BRIAN PULLED into one of Sweet Briar's three parks. This one bordered the Coleman River and had a few ball fields, a walking trail, a kiddie splash park with a playground, and picnic areas. He parked and we dismounted. I was a little wobbly, and I laughed as I got my legs back under control.

"That was awesome!" I was beaming from ear to ear and decided right then and there that no matter what I had going on, if Brian showed up at my place and offered me another ride on his motorcycle, the answer would be a resounding, "Yes!" I was still catching my breath when he approached me and lifted my chin up toward his, then reached up to brush a lock of hair off my face.

"Oh my gosh! My hair! I can only imagine what a mess it must be. I should have listened to Lorcan and insisted on a helmet." Brian laughed at my concern, and he spent some time running his fingers through my locks to untangle them, his hands pausing on my shoulders. None of what he was doing was helping my heart rate get back to normal. In fact, if I had to guess, not only was my heart slamming so loudly in my chest that he could hear it, but my face was probably all shades of red. I hoped he chalked it off to the excitement of being on his Harley, and not because I was straddling him for the last quarter of an hour.

"You look lovely. Better than lovely, in truth. You look good enough to nibble on."

Our eyes met, and I was shocked and thrilled to see a spark of passion in his. Where was this coming from? Not that I was complaining; he was grade-A perfection, and how this man was still single was beyond me.

"Am I?" Oh, smooth. I opened my mouth to say more, and that's when he pulled me to him and kissed me. It was a slow and sensual kiss that started building to something way more than I was prepared for. Just when I thought we reached a point where I was going to swoon, and yes, you would be thinking swoon in this instance as well, he broke away from me and stepped back.

"I've wanted to do that for some time now, and it was better than I thought it would be."

He had? Me? I really wanted to say something flip and worldly. I saw myself smiling knowingly and replying with some witty comment, flipping my hair over my shoulder, and looking seductive and amused.

"That was—wow."

Yeah. I think I drooled a bit as I said it.

I couldn't blame Brian when he threw his head back and laughed out loud. I was feeling like the world's biggest moron, but then he pulled me toward him again and pet my hair gently and whispered in my ear.

"You are as sweet as your name. Do you know that? You taste like licorice and smell like vanilla and make me want to do more than what is considered gentlemanly. That's the effect you have on me, Lily Sweet."

Oh, my word.

And you'd think I'd learned not to open my mouth again, but no. Not me.

"Are you sure you have the right person?"

That elicited another series of guffaws out of the man, and he told me if he got a dollar every time a perp said that to him while on a bust, he'd be a millionaire. That broke the tension a bit as he led me over to a park bench. We sat and I looked around, for the first time noticing a few kids playing on the swings gawking at us and making kissy sounds. Ugh. I hate kids. No, really, the, "aw, I just love children," gene must have skipped me when they were passing them around, and this was precisely the reason why. I was tempted to try out my new witchy abilities and zap them, but Brian's next words stopped me.

"I actually have an ulterior motive for showing up and taking you away from where others could hear me. I wanted to tell you first before everyone else finds out." Oh, no. He was going to arrest me. They thought I did it, and he going to give me the bad news then have his way with me, over and over and over until he was forced to cuff me and…

wait. What were we talking about? Oh! I was in trouble. I just knew it.

"I'm in trouble, aren't I? Are you here to arrest me?"

Brian looked confused a minute, then I saw humor flicker across his eyes then sadness. I felt nervous energy in the pit of my stomach and a sense of disquiet. I had a feeling I wasn't going to like what he had to say.

"What is it, Brian? Please tell me."

"It's about Adelaide." Okay, I didn't expect him to say that, exactly, but I nodded for him to continue. "She's gone."

Gone? Like...gone? How does a skeleton just get gone?

"Let me explain. The lab called to inform me the bones are missing. They had pushed their schedule up so they could get me a positive ID sooner rather than later, as a favor, but when they opened the drawer where the bones were stored, they, *she* was gone. They searched everywhere, but there is no trace of that skeleton anywhere. To top it off, all the paperwork we had on her, all the notes and photographs, everything, was stolen. All the security cameras inside the morgue were down. Someone went to a lot of trouble to stop us from identifying those remains."

He shook his head, and I could see he was angry and disturbed.

"The crime lab was short-staffed this week due to some training. To compound matters, they have a new employee at reception who has been making eyes at one of the security guards, and we suspect they may have been canoodling, allowing whoever broke in to get away clean. So far there are two people, besides the morgue technicians, that know of this: me—and now you. I guarantee heads are going to roll when the chief medical examiner gets word of this. My question to you is did Chad Barwick have anything else he said that tied his death to Adelaide's and would give us some kind of lead? It's almost like whoever did this didn't want Chad speaking to you, which makes me wonder if we are missing something. It gets worse, though. Chad's body is missing, too. And if that isn't bad enough, this was taped to the drawer in the morgue where his body was on ice."

I looked at what Brian was showing me and saw it was a photo taken of me crossing the street near the diner. It had a big X in red across it. What?! What was going on around here? How could this even be possible? How does a body go missing in less than twenty-four hours, along with a skeleton. Who photographed me without my knowledge? Did this mean I was next? I was freaked out, and I told him so.

"They went to all this trouble, and I might know why," I said, shivering more from the news than any weather-related causes. "This just convinces me the same person who killed Adelaide is the same one that murdered Chad. But, without any evidence, well, without a body, there is no crime, right? And this photo—maybe they think Chad had time to tell me enough for me to be considered a threat."

"Not so fast. It isn't as simple as all that. We know there was a skeleton, and you discovered Chad's body. We know there was evidence, so the crimes still stand, but this just made it difficult, impossible really, if we can't recover them both." Brian looked at me with concern. "What I need to know from you, though, is why Chad approached you. What did he have to say? Because you may just be correct in that whoever has done this thinks you know more than you are letting on. Are you positive you don't know some huge secret and are keeping it to yourself?"

Time to let my police detective know all the details of what Chad told me and what I held back. It wasn't much, but it was along the lines of what he suspected, that Chad Barwick had information on my parents, Adelaide, and happenings of the past that involved us all. But I assured him Chad never got around to telling me anything.

Now I wished more than ever poor old Chad told me what he knew the morning he waylaid me instead of insisting we meet the following day. Because one thing was obvious: someone was keeping tabs on my comings and goings and saw that man approach me, wasting no time in removing the threat of what Chad had planned on revealing to me.

It dawned on me how very likely my own life was in peril.

I looked at Brian, and he read my thoughts in an instant.

"You need to remain calm and have faith that I will find this person or persons before they make a move on you. I don't know why you are a target, other than they might suspect Chad already told you something. Even if you don't understand what he meant, it doesn't mean with time you won't figure it out. Heck I don't know for a fact that this person will come after you, but we need to practice caution. I'm having one of my officers' guard June's place, and I don't want you going off alone. Especially your house."

I started to protest because I was not someone who would cower in my room, gnashing my teeth. I wanted to find out who this person was and deal with them before they could hurt someone else. I had the blood of Chad on my hands, whether this was my fault or not. It certainly felt that way, because had I not arrived in Sweet Briar and discovered those bones under my porch, more than likely, Chad Barwick would still be alive. I couldn't live with myself if I didn't try to find out who the culprit was.

"Brian, I have to help. I can't sit sequestered away and just let the police handle this. You have to understand how guilty I am feeling right about now. That poor man…"

"That poor man is dead, and none of it is your fault, Lily. How can you even think I'd let you get involved?"

Let me? I didn't remember asking him for permission.

Police detective or not, no one was going to dictate to me what I could or could not do!

"I care for you. I have feelings that came out of nowhere that I can't ignore. I was smitten from the moment I saw you lying there on the ground looking like a crushed daisy. I want to be the man who puts your petals back in order and makes you whole again. Can you blame me?"

What was I upset about? Petals? Flowers? Yeah, whatever he wants, I was okay.

CHAPTER 14

"*I* am so not okay with this."

I was pacing back and forth in June's store, smacking my fist in my palm.

"How dare he think a few sweet nothings can discourage me from investigating this mess I'm in."

Andrea was sitting on the counter swinging her legs back and forth with a wide grin on her face.

"Did he really kiss you? Do you have any idea how many girls in this town have been vying for that man's attention, and you are here less than a week and he's already making out with you in the park? I'm jealous but also happy for you, cuz!"

"Were you listening to anything I just said? How can you go there when I have been locked away from society, practically on house arrest, all because some lunatic is out there killing people and trying to possibly get at me?"

Andrea sighed dreamily. This was not going as I hoped it would. I called her at the crack of dawn, and true friend that she was turning out to be, she ran over here as fast as she could, even skipping her breakfast. Three years my junior, the minute I told her everything that transpired yesterday, she wouldn't stop going on about our, as she put it, "make-out" session with her youthful exuberance. Okay, if I stopped to think about it long enough, I too would get a foolish look on my face, but right now? Right now, I was mighty pissed off at the man in question.

The minute Brian realized his pleas were not being heeded, he went rogue and told everyone in my family I was in danger, causing the entire clan to join forces and lock me away at June's, with guards. *Guards*, mind you! Posted at every exit! Even Douglas was perched on a tree limb, assigned to Jake's old treehouse out behind the shop, making sure I wouldn't sneak out my bedroom window and go off in search of clues at my house.

I mean, really! How could they think I'd stoop so low?

Did they really know me that well in only six days? Huh. I had intelligent relations, at least.

"How was it? Does he kiss as good as I imagined?"

I had to stop and shake my head to remove the image that suddenly invaded my thoughts and went on to chastise Andrea. She finally realized she wouldn't get more salacious details and focused on what was disturbing me, after I promised to give her a play by play of the spicy details at a later date. Who was I kidding? I couldn't wait to relive all that again, once I was over being mad at Brian.

"You have to help sneak me out of here. I need to get to my house and search for something. With all that has happened since I arrived, I totally forgot what my mother wrote in her letter to me. Somewhere in my home might be information on everything that happened back before I was born and leading up to why we left. Andrea, I need to find it before someone else thinks to search the place. I have to go there and soon! Please help?"

Andrea scratched her elbow and shot me a worried look

as she bit her bottom lip, and I could see her struggling with going against Brian and my family versus alienating me. We hadn't known each other that long, and I knew I was asking a lot of her. Imagine my surprise when she squared her shoulders and said, "Let's do this, then. I've got your back, cousin. You can always count on me!"

I knew I liked this girl.

* * *

HOW WE MANAGED to sneak out of the house and slip by all of Brian's defenses was more to Andrea's doing than anything I could have come up with. She failed to inform me the extent of her witchy abilities. Apparently, my dear cousin Andrea could make you disappear. Not in the literal sense; we still had corporeal bodies, after all, but not unlike the Invisibility Cloak from Harry Potter, Andrea could make us seem invisible to the naked eye. She'd cast a spell that shrouded us in an alternate space, still here in the present, but not quite. As long as someone wasn't looking too carefully at us, we wouldn't be seen by them. I was so excited assuming we could walk through walls like a ghost and couldn't stop myself trying before she vetoed that idea. I wound up smacking my face into a closed door. Andrea fell over laughing hysterically.

I was *not* amused.

Mumbling and rubbing my sore nose, I now found myself out on the side lawn in between the Emporium and Ye Olde Country Hardware, which was Jake's dad's place. It was nice that June and Dennis had their shops next door to each other, not to mention convenient, since they lived above his store and rented out the Emporium's apartment that I was living in for the time being.

I didn't want to go to the right then circle back around a

few blocks as Andrea suggested, because we'd have to cross the street where the diner was located. I did not want to go near the place, since so many people were dining, and I was afraid we'd be spotted despite being cloaked. We couldn't go through the backyard because Doug was there in the tree, so we chose to go to the left. That took us past the herbalist shop and the metaphysical shop before we turned left again and cut down the south side of Main Street...heading to my house. I brought a huge tote bag with me, that I normally kept my books, magazines, or other reading material in.

We slowly made progress toward our destination, with Andrea concentrating; the tip of her tongue poking out of her mouth, when I noticed a lot of police activity going on behind us. A couple of state police made the rounds from shop to shop. I figured Brian had them out asking questions and gathering information on the case this morning, although I wasn't absolutely certain. I did remember him saying most the state police weren't "our kind," except for his division, and he could keep an eye and ear out as one of them rather than taking the sheriff position everyone else seemed to want him to take.

We finally reached Wildflower Lane and turned left one more time, making our way stealthily to my place. Looking around, we didn't see anyone that would hamper our plans, and before someone did show up to stop us, we crept up the front path. Those wonderful overgrown shrubs and hedges, once again, blocked anything we would do next from view from the street. What I did do next was pull out the ornate key and unlock the door. Holding our collective breath, we sighed in relief when it swung open without making a sound, and we closed it behind us, now safely inside.

"Jeepers, I haven't been in here since I was about six, and all us kids would sneak in to stare at Adriana's portrait. None of us believed that crotchety old woman could be this beauty painted here. But now that I see you, and both of you are virtually identical, I can see how she must have once looked."

I didn't know whether or not to be insulted on my great-grandmother's behalf or because Andrea described her in a way that I was sure if I, too, reached that lofty age would assuredly mirror.

"Where do we start?" Andrea spun around slowly, taking everything in, much as I did, when I remembered the little room off the den and kitchen.

"Let's go check out a place I found last time I was here, just off the kitchen; if I'm not mistaken, it's an office."

Leading the way, I weaved through the house into the kitchen then entered the room in question. I could make out what appeared to be plush chairs, a settee, a coffee table, end tables, lamps, and a desk. The entire place had bookshelves taped off with plastic, I assumed to keep dust and dirt from getting to the tomes behind. I risked opening the wooden shutters to let light in and had Andrea help me begin to uncover everything in sight. What we revealed was indeed an office, and I felt my pulse jump in anticipation. We'd have to work with the light coming in from the shutters since I knew Aunt Chiara was still in the process of having the accounts switched to my name.

It was a masculine space but was also dotted with feminine influences. The desk and shelves were a rich mahogany, and the furniture was fronted by deep, rich, jeweled-toned fabric, emerald green with gold threading. The backs of the furniture were upholstered in a floral-patterned material that complimented the front, and the balance was one that made me think both my parents spent time here, together. Before everything fell apart. I paused, letting the emotion wash over me, then moved past it, knowing I had nothing to do with what happened back then. At least I hoped not.

"Jackpot!" That was from Andrea, who managed to open

the drawers that I anticipated be locked, when she held up a small key. "Found it on that bookshelf over there!" Could it be that easy? I certainly hoped it would be the case. She then held out what looked like a day minder—more diary than ledger. It had my mother's handwriting in it. I took it from Andrea with a thanks and slipped it in my big bag.

We spent some time going through each drawer, and while there were indeed papers I knew I would need to go through when I had the time—and permission, *thanks,* Brian, we found nothing that jumped up and said, "Private, for Lily's eyes only!"

Just as I was about to give up on the top of the desk, I leaned to the left, my hand gripping the side. I heard a click and a small panel opened in front of me. Oh my gosh! A hidden compartment. Moreover, sitting in the small, closed-off space was an intricate wooden chest about the size of a child's jewelry box about fourteen inches long by six inches tall and six inches wide. The wood was carved in patterns of leaves and flowers and birds and looked to be hand-crafted. I was about to reach for it when I heard someone clear their throat.

"Can you ladies tell me why you are in here when I was told you were safely locked away at June's?"

I looked up to see Deputy Beau "Bubba" Buford frowning down at us from the doorway, all the while working what I hoped was gum and not tobacco in his rather copious mouth, with lips to match. He looked like a catfish chewing on a school of tadpoles. I turned my head toward Andrea, giving her an inquisitive look because I believed we were still hidden from sight.

"Sorry, I let the glamor go. It was too difficult to concentrate on a search *and* hold it in place." Andrea looked mortified and gave me a look that was riddled with guilt and a tiny bit of fear, as if she thought this one transgression would make me decide she wasn't a worthy.

"Deputy Buford! Well, imagine meeting you here." I was going for innocent ignorance or something along those lines, but I saw the look of apprehension cross his face as I stood up and reached out to shake his hand. What did he think I would do? Zap him? Well, that was something to consider, if I knew how the darned power I had worked, that was.

"Now you can just stay right there while I call the sheriff to come get you and bring you home. No sudden moves like, you hear?" Like I was a criminal and in my own house, too! Well, honestly!

"Wait, Beau, isn't it? What a lovely name you have." He squinted at this as if trying to decide whether or not I was poking fun at his name. I was. He didn't have to *know* that, though. "I remember you from the other day, and I was so relieved to see you and Sheriff Buford on the job looking out for little old me." Okay, maybe that was laying it on a bit thick, but I saw the big brute start to not only thaw, but preen from all the flattery I was throwing at him. "It's so nice to have big, strong men around to protect us women from any nasty business. I am *so* grateful for all you did that day."

Chest puffed up now and a smile on his vacant face, I knew I scored a good one when he re-holstered his walkie-talkie and started droning at me like a bee in heat. Just ew, but I knew I had to take one for the team, well, duo anyway, to get us out of this mess.

"Well, now, I was just doing what any good officer would do to protect a fair maiden such as yerself, such a pretty little thing and all alone in the world. I kinda know what it feels like, what with my very own daddy spending most of his life in a jail cell before he passed on and the entire town talking behind my back for years. That is until my uncle saw fit to give

BETTINA M JOHNSON

me a chance to prove what an asset I'd be to the community."
He finished this with a rather gross smile, seeing as how it was
indeed tobacco in his mouth, which he proceeded to spit onto
my dusty floors with complete and utter lack of manners.

Suddenly, he was in my personal space and making me
regret the damsel in distress act. He took in the entire length
of my person, slowly from top to bottom and back up again,
although his eyes stopped suddenly and disturbingly at my
chest, making me regret choosing the skimpy t-shirt that was
one size too small for my figure in my rush to leave earlier.
Licking his lips, he continued, "Mebbe you and I could get to
know each other a bit better over some drinks." Oh,
heavens *no*.

"Oh, well, I don't know how things are done right and
proper down here." I purred this out, looking into his beady
eyes. I was gagging on the inside. I was trying for Scarlett,
but suspected I was coming off more like Carol Burnett
doing her comedy sketch. "I might have to take you up on
that idea. I just *love* a man in uniform." Drool was dribbling
down one side of his face, I kid you not, and my revulsion
was going to give me away if I couldn't figure out how to get
out of this mess in a hurry. Thankfully, Andrea made to
move out of the room, and the big oaf lunged to stop her.
While they were otherwise occupied, I grabbed the small
chest and slipped it into my tote.

"Now, Andrea dear, let this big man do his job and stop
distracting him." My words were like a magic elixir, making
Bubba pause his manhandling my cousin and turn back to
me. "Why don't you let her run along and get Sheriff Buford
so we can have a little time to continue our chat?" The anticipation in his eyes made me want to vomit buckets, but he
waved Andrea off. She gave me a look of incredulity, but I
nodded slightly, giving her a wink and tilting my head
toward the exit, hoping she knew I was trying to buy time

while she found help. The dawn of understanding crossed her face, and I looked back toward Bubba as she slipped out of the room to hopefully would find someone to deal with this Lothario before I regretted making myself the sacrificial lamb.

"Now, honey lips, why don't you come over here so we can get to know each other better? I always wanted me a raven-haired witch." Bubba pulled me down onto the settee.

Was this joker for real? Like, ugh, I was truly going to win an Academy Award for acting if something didn't happen quick to stop this little drama from playing out. He made a move to kiss me, and I put my hands on his chest to shove him off of me when I heard yet another cough coming from behind us.

"I'm sorry to interrupt this little, um, whatever I am interrupting, but I believe that is my quarry, Deputy Buford."

Brian.

Oh, just great. The look he was giving me could freeze an entire lake in five seconds flat. I jumped up.

"It's not what you're thinking, Brian, I..."

Standing up, the ridiculous deputy had the nerve to put his arm around me and pull me into his chest.

"Aw, shucks, detective. I was just getting to know this here doll a bit better since she was making sounds like she wanted a taste of old Bubba here."

I did not, well, maybe in the course of my acting too well, one could see how he'd come to that conclusion.

"Well, I am sure you will both have time for that at a later date. Right now, she is coming with me, and you need to leave this house immediately and report to the sheriff. Do I make myself clear, deputy?"

Bubba saluted, which I was sure wasn't protocol in this situation, then to my amazement and disgust he planted a big, sloppy, wet one on my mouth and said, "Catch you later, babe." Then he sauntered out of the room and went clomping though the house and out the front door into the yard, peering around like he was about to nab more criminals trespassing on the property.

"Brian, it's not what it seems." I about gagged as I wiped Bubba's drool off my lips.

Brian held up his hand to stop any further discussion. He grabbed my elbow and all but dragged me out of the room, but not before looking around first. When I went to hide my tote bag from his view, I realized it was no longer there, and my head whipped from side to side, wondering at its disappearance.

"Looking for something?"

"I…no, I just wondered what you were looking for. Brian, listen, this wasn't what you are thinking. I was trying to stall for time while Andrea found someone to get here and stop Deputy Buford from arresting us, or worse. I, he…"

"Do you think I care what you were or weren't doing? Darling, I don't care one way or another who you choose to be with. But right now, I am taking you back to June's so you can answer some questions and I can make some sense as to what it was you were hoping to find here."

He didn't care? I felt like a small, insignificant bug for all of five seconds, then I got mad. What did he mean, he didn't care? Didn't he hear what I was trying to explain about this situation? I would show him someone who didn't care! The nerve! Holding my head high, I marched out of the room and out of my house. I almost made it all the way out, too, if Brian hadn't yanked me backward by my shirt. Holding his hand out and tapping his foot, I realized he needed my key to lock the front door. Pulling it out of my pocket and slapping it in his hand, I scowled as he turned the lock and pocketed it instead of returning it to me. *Oh yeah, buddy? We will see about that!*

I think we both realized at the same instant that I wasn't wearing a bra, not stopping to properly dress when Andrea stopped by earlier and we decided spur of the moment to sneak out. I could see him struggling with this and decided to torture him in his moment of weakness. I stepped in closer and looked up at him through my lashes. I could see his nose flare and his eyes widen, then I reached up and slapped his face, hard.

"That's for insinuating I'm a slut, mister."

I turned and stomped off my porch, but not before retrieving my key out of his shirt pocket in a quick move. Still wondering where my tote had gotten to, I was fuming all the way to Brian's police car when I thought of Andrea. Had *she* managed to grab it and run since Bubba was too occupied with yours truly? I certainly hoped so and that she had the wherewithal to get it into the general store, up the stairs, and into my apartment without detection. But of course, she could manage that with her talent. Now all I had to do was clear the air between me and Brian, although right about now I was itching for a fight, and I suspected my brooding detective was, too.

* * *

BACK AT JUNE'S EMPORIUM, I was annoyed to find a delegation of sorts awaiting my return. I knew this would not bode well for my freedom and went into major sulk mode. My relatives, which constituted of my aunts Iona and Chiara, my uncle Owen, and cousin Andrea were joined by Dennis, June, and Jake Carter, and Eileen, Henry, and Lorcan Reid. They were acting ridiculous, and Andrea looked as if she'd been crying. That distracted me enough take the time to raise my eyebrows in an unspoken question, and she gave me a small nod with a sly little smile, then her face crumbled back into a look of woe. Douglas, who was found asleep in the tree-house, was sent home.

"I don't want to sound like I'm scolding you, Lily. You are a grown woman and all, but we were just trying to keep you safe." This was from Aunt Chiara, who looked more upset than the rest of those assembled.

"I don't think she needs a babysitter at all, not if she is as powerful as you all say."

This came from behind me, and when I turned, I knew the source of Aunt Chiara's disquiet. There, wrapped up in an old shawl and perched daintily on a chair in the corner of the kitchen, was my great-grandmother, Adriana. She gave me an appraising look and sniffed, "Not that I can see much of anything special in this one so far."

I looked around the room and noticed everyone staring back at me except Lorcan, who looked bent. Then I remembered yesterday and felt guilty for running out on him like that. This lasted all of five seconds when I grew exasperated with all these new men in my life and how they were acting. I had my own mind. I didn't need their attitude!

"You look exhausted. When you're done scolding, *detective*, maybe everyone should realize she's has a rough couple of days and is still new to this town and all of us and deserves a break." This from Jake. Oh, that's it, he's staying my favorite. The rest could just go out and jump in the nearest lake. I smiled gratefully at him and turned to address everyone else.

"Look. I know you are trying to keep me safe here, but you have no idea if I am the target. We don't know why this person killed Chad Barwick, and it could be totally unrelated to the bones that were found under my porch!"

When everyone, including Jake, gave me incredulous looks, I realized Brian must have told them all that the skeleton went missing along with all the files, photos, and notes—not to mention Chad. And then informed them of the photo of me with the red mark through it. Well, how do you like that?

"Enough of this. Liliana and Andrea, come with me. I am going to see what you can do to defend yourself." Adriana turned and sniffed at everyone in the room. "Keeping her locked away is a stupid idea. The rest of you stay here and continue arguing. I have more important matters to attend to." Granny stood up and took me by the elbow, nodding for Andrea to follow. No one dared stop her from taking the two of us away—they certainly seemed relieved when she led us to the stairway to my apartment. I supposed they figured I'd be safe upstairs with my great-grandmother watching over me.

Once we made the ascent to my rooms, Adriana settled herself into a comfortable armchair with a sigh then turned to me and said, "Okay, enough dawdling around. Show me what you can do."

CHAPTER 15

*D*o you know what it's like trying to make magic happen when you have no idea how you did it in the first place? No? Well, join my party, because I was clueless. I spent the next three hours up in my room, missing lunch, with a dour old lady with bad manners and a sharp tongue, trying to convince her I wasn't some kind of imbecile witch reject. Despite Andrea trying to help me focus, all I managed to do in those three hours was break into a sweat and stop myself from crying like a baby. Yeah, dark witch extraordinaire, *not*.

"Maybe we should just give up. Obviously, what I did was some fluke, and I'm not really a witch like the rest of you." Adriana reared back and all but spat at me, making me shrink away in alarm.

"Not a witch! Not a witch? Carlo's daughter? I think not. As much as I rue having to admit it, those Croy women are fairly powerful witches in their own right, so yes, Liliana, you are indeed a witch. What I wasn't prepared for was this apathetic quitter you seem to be!" She emphasized this by banging her hand down twice on the armrest then sitting back in consternation.

"Quitter? I am *not* a quitter!" I stomped across the room and leaned down, my nose all but touching hers, and did my own hissing back at her. "Never once in my life have I ever quit at anything, old woman. I am just trying to get it through to you that I never knew I had magic, so how can I know what I am supposed to do? How do I bring it out of me, anyway?"

I didn't see Adriana reach her hand up and point her finger at me. I did, however, feel myself flying backward through the air and flinched, waiting for my body to slam up against the far wall. When that didn't happen, I opened my eyes and found myself hovering in place, effortlessly held there by my tiny granny, the wicked and deranged old bat. She even had a smile on her demented face.

"Put me down."

"Make me."

"Put. Me. Down."

"Make me."

"You're not being fair!"

"Bah!"

This was going nowhere fast. I struggled and was sure I looked like some kind of mental patient having fits in mid-air—like that girl in *The Exorcist*.

"Listen you, old hag, you put me down right now or I'll...oomph!"

Well, she put me down all right. I was unceremoniously dumped onto the floor and sat there, smarting, while Adriana wheezed out a hacking chuckle or two.

"That wasn't very nice."

"Neither is this." *Whap!* She smacked me on the head from across the room with a flick of her wrist. Andrea just made a small "eep" sound, mouth hanging open.

"Ow, hey! Stop that!"

Smack! She did it again, then again, and ouch! *Again!* Terrific. My great-grandmother was a sadist. How nice. Hell, she was old enough to have probably known the Marquis.

"Stop it now. You are hurting me, you freak. How would you like it if I waved my hand and knocked you out of your chair?" I pointed at Adriana for emphasis, and the next thing I knew, the miniscule woman was toppled onto the floor as a puff of blue smoke snaked out of my fingertips. Andrea screamed. I joined her.

"Oh my gosh. Oh no. I've killed her! Andrea, help me! I killed my great-grandmother!"

That's when we heard the horrifying sound of maniacal laughter coming from her prone figure.

Before I knew what to do to shield myself, I was once again flung into the air and, this time, slammed into the doorframe. In one fluid moment, Adriana was on her feet and positioning both hands in front of herself, made a crushing motion with them. I felt my throat constrict and could not believe my own kin would torture me like this. I was convinced she intended to kill me. In a burst of anger, I felt something click in the pit of my stomach and experienced the sensation of it coiling up my body until I was sure some unholy malevolent horror was sparking out of my eyes. I welcomed it and looked directly at my great grandmother.

Much to the amazement of everyone present, I slammed my hands together then drew Adriana toward me until we were both hovering in the air, face to face. Then I smiled at her and whispered, "Enough?"

Her eyes, locked to mine, gleamed with wicked merriment, and she nodded yes. We both took in a deep breath then let it out slowly and floated down to the floor together.

* * *

IT ONLY TOOK another two hours of instruction for me to comprehend the basics of what I could do but not how to control it quite yet. Oh, I would need more time and practice to get up to speed with what Adriana said she felt was my true potential, but for now, I was thrilled I could do what was necessary. I just had to convince her I had no intention of being a dark witch after we solved this mystery. That I *was* a witch I was coming to terms with; it was hard to ignore when you could lift your granny in the air and such, but dark? Nuh-uh, not me, no way.

We were all exhausted and hungry when Adriana suggested we hit the diner on the square for dinner. Now that I was able to summon up the magic inside me, Granny didn't seem so intimidating. Assuring June, who was the only person still downstairs by this time, that she could handle any trouble coming at us, Adriana waved off my offer to drive us the hundred or so feet to the diner with an imperious sniff.

"I walk everywhere. Why do you think I'm so limber?"

And off she went, not even looking as she crossed the street, but then again, who around here would run her over? One of the things I learned while Andrea and Adriana were instructing me was the workings of this town. Every single person that lived and worked in Sweet Briar either had ties to witches or *were* witches. Those that weren't, and yes, they were just called humans, were affected by a glamor put on the town by the Council.

This was how Sweet Briar could be a huge arts and crafts destination for tourists, yet they wouldn't see the magic and couldn't hear us talking about it. It would just sound like we were talking about an entirely different subject. None who visited or neighboring townsfolk, seemed to find the overabundance of witchy stuff disturbing. In fact, it was a huge draw, especially during the renaissance festival seasons of spring and autumn. The town hosted several fairs throughout the year and was a few weeks away from the fall season kicking into high gear.

Another good thing about my day of lessons with Granny, she told June to call off the posse, that I would no longer be locked away and need everyone guarding me. My great-grandmother assured her I was more than capable of zapping a foe with enough energy to make them cry—maybe not destroy them utterly, not yet, but definitely make them think twice before coming back for more. That kind of felt nice considering she was writing me off as a reject this morning.

We entered Joe's Diner circa 1962, and I wondered if the namesake of the place was still around. My question was answered when one of the waitresses shouted out an order, "Joe, two specials, and don't skimp on the gravy this time. Hi, ladies, what can I get y'all to drink?" I was struck speechless by the visage in front of me. She was giving Flo from the old television show *Alice* a run for her money. Beehive hair and seventies makeup, complete with bubblegum that she was gleefully popping and snapping as she took our orders.

"Cheeseburger, fries, chocolate shake, kids will have the same." Adriana ordered for us. Not only was I taken aback by her choices, but that she thought we'd eat what she ordered without argument.

"I don't want cheese on mine," I piped up, earning a derisive glare from Granny. Okay, so I was going to get a burger and fries, but she didn't know everything about my preferences.

"Don't you think that's kind of an unhealthy choice for someone your, um..." Too late to notice Andrea's eyes go wide, I'd already put my foot in it. The waitress snickered and went off to place our orders, leaving us three glasses of iced water and a stack of napkins in her wake.

"Age? Are you calling me old, missy?"

Okay, I did *not* want to touch that with a ten-foot pole. Adriana had to be pushing if not already far past the hundred-year mark. I never did get around to finding out from anyone, and now I was stuck having to backtrack from my faux pas. "Um…"

"Well, so what if I am? You're only as old as you think! Plus, witches have great metabolisms and are long-lived. I come in here once a week and order the same damn thing and have since they opened their doors. Isn't that right, Joe?"

The man himself came out from the kitchen carrying three plates, heaping with fries and juicy-looking burgers, the waitress following with our shakes.

"That's right, Annie. Ever since my dad, Joe Senior, opened the place. Don't let these young'uns pick on you." Joe winked at us collectively and set our orders on the table then hurried back to the kitchen as more orders came in. Annie? Really? And look at her, she simpered at him. Gross.

"Now, what are you going to do about this murder business, young lady? Do you have any suspects?" Adriana asked this as if it was perfectly normal for me to be investigating the crime while I sat there staring at her like an imbecile. Forget that I was distracted enough by the most incredibly delicious burger I had ever eaten in my life. I was just trying my shake, which was as amazing as the rest of my meal, when she hit me with that query.

I choked a bit and took some time coughing while Granny sat there munching away on her fries, never blinking, patiently waiting for my response. She kept at it in a freaky disturbing way, fry…dipped in catsup…into her mouth…munch, munch, munch, repeat. All the while her eyes were boring into mine as she kept a blasé look on her face. Andrea finally found her voice, having not said much for most of the day.

157

"Grandmother, how can you expect Lily to look into a murder? She isn't a detective. She wouldn't even know where to start!" Thanks for the vote of confidence, cuz. Even though she was absolutely correct in her assumptions. Andrea shook her head, looking at me like my great-grandmother had lost her marbles—she was right about that one, too. She proceeded to give me an *oh, well, just go with it* shrug and took a huge bite out of her burger.

"Nonsense. Liliana is a dark witch. She will figure this out before any detective. Especially one she has been canoodling with."

I all but spit my shake onto everyone and everything then gulped, causing yet another round of choking. How could she possibly know what Brian and I were up to the previous day? There was no way she *could* know. Andrea certainly didn't have the time to broadcast our little make-out session to anyone.

"How did you? What do you mean…?" I sputtered, but Adriana just waved me off.

"Oh, spare me, kiddo. I know everything you are up to, good and bad. Who do you think taught Santa Claus? Now answer my question. Do you have any suspects yet?" The waitress, her name tag said Sheila, was just coming toward us when she heard what Adriana said, and she dropped the glass she was carrying. Water and ice went everywhere, and she rushed off to get stuff to clean up the mess.

"Hmm…might want to ask Sheila if she knows anything. She sure reacted odd to what I said just now, and I find that a bit suspicious, no?"

"First of all, I am not, I repeat, *not* a dark witch. Second, there is no way I am looking into this murder. And finally, how did you know what Brian and I were up to? Not that I am confessing anything here, so you can wipe that smirk off your face."

"Wouldn't you like to know, missy? Don't you think I figured out you two decided to play Sherlock and Watson just by the fact Andrea here cloaked you so you could sneak off to your house? Now stop all this nonsense and get to work. Here." With that statement, she handed over a small notebook and a pen. "Write down who you suspect may know something and we will start interviewing them."

What was wrong with this diminutive, psychotic imp? Was she mental? Maybe insanity ran in my family, galloped even. That had to be it. I could see it finally register with my great-grandmother that I had no intention of admitting what we were up to as I slid the items back toward her. She sighed as she pushed her plate away. A plate that was literally licked clean of food, mind you.

"Fine, if you won't, then get out of my way. I will figure it out on my own."

"Wait, what are you talking about? There is no way you can discover who did this. And then what? What can you do about it?"

Adriana looked at me like I was speaking in tongues.

"*Do* about it? Why, I will set a trap. Then nab the sucker. Buona Sera."

With that, she got up, brushed off her clothes, and waltzed out the diner, a small wave toward Joe as she passed. She left us the bill to pay.

CHAPTER 16

"What do you make of that?" Andrea shook her head as we watched our spry little great-grandmother skulking across the street, again not watching for traffic, causing two cars to have to swerve so as not to hit her. "I've never seen her act like this in all my years!"

"You're asking me?" I raised my eyebrows at my cousin and leaned back on the plush vinyl cushion of the booth we were sitting in, pushing my almost-empty plate away from me. "You've known her all your life. I just met her, and I am sure she was dead serious about investigating these murders. Adelaide and Chad have got to be connected in some way. I don't like coincidences, and that would be one wild coincidence, no?"

Andrea paused, a fry halfway to her mouth. "It sounds like you are already committed to continuing with this investigating stuff. Are you? I mean, I'm happy to resume being the Louise to your Thelma!" She nodded eagerly when I looked sharply in her direction.

"More like Ethel to my Lucy, but…yeah, I guess so."

Truth was I didn't like that someone chose to target me

just because I stumbled upon those bones and Chad decided to seek me out. I was minding my own business, not trying to cause any trouble; now suddenly a man was murdered because of me, and I felt I owed it to him to find out who did it and why. The idea that Adelaide's remains, and Chad's body were out there somewhere, snatched from the morgue, left me beyond disturbed. I wanted this person to pay for these crimes, and I wanted to be the one to make them do it. That made me a snoop, not a dark witch. I wanted the law to deal with them as well. I had to intention of taking out the bad guys myself. Right?

* * *

THE NEXT MORNING WAS SUNDAY, and I intended to sleep in and then soak in the tub for an hour. I was sore from my witchy lessons and previous days' events. I also spent a good part of last night writing things down in the notebook Adriana had left for me. There wasn't much to it, but I did make a note to go back and speak to Sheila about her reaction yesterday. I was a little nervous about doing this. I wasn't a detective, and I was sure a clue could slap me in the face, and I wouldn't even notice it, but I had to try. Anything was better than sitting around waiting for the police to figure it out.

Andrea said she'd meet me after Sunday service, and we'd get started on our investigations. I was a bit surprised at the church thing, figuring church and witches wouldn't mix, but she had laughed at me and said all the candles and incense were a perfect fit, and she didn't think God would mind us being there, since He—or She—had created us. The tiny Roman Catholic Church was entirely made out of stone and sat on a hill on the north side of town. It was next to the inn and was surrounded by an old graveyard. Many of my ancestors were interred there, or so I heard. I thought I might check it out, but not this morning. I was enjoying lounging around and stretching my tired bones.

The other prominent churches in town belonged to the Methodists, Presbyterians, and one Evangelical stand-alone, just outside the town, called the *Holy Redeemer of the Most Everlasting Lord* or some such, and I assumed the good Reverend Brewster resided there. I put him on my list just for the fact that he was someone who was interested in my aunt Adelaide back in the day. I also knew that Dillon Chase, Brian's father, might have messed around with her, but he was deceased, so he would be of no help, not unless witches could speak to ghosts and he happened to be hanging around town.

My problem was being new to the area and not knowing the dynamics of all parties involved. Hopefully, Andrea would shed more light on some of the possible players. I just hoped I wouldn't be putting her in any danger by allowing her to investigate with me. Especially since I found out she was more a cloak and dagger kind of witch and not a zapping people's brains out one. She did indeed grab my bag with the wooden box and journal in it and left it in my room, out of sight of prying eyes. I still hadn't had the time to take a closer look at the box, but I was disappointed that the only thing the journal told me was my mom was organized and paid her bills on time, at least back then.

One other thing I wanted to tackle today if I found the time was to scope out a place to set up my artist studio. I was not hoping for much, but still, someone had to have a warehouse with good light or an old barn, something not too expensive and near town, that I could do my art projects in and maybe even start selling some pieces for once. Andrea said she knew of a few places and would speak to some people, but it wouldn't hurt to keep my eyes open today as we wandered around.

I was going to head to the bath for my relaxing soak when my phone dinged, and I saw I had a message from Lorcan. *I'm downstairs, out front. If you are awake, get out here, quick!* Groaning in misery, I knew I wasn't going to get that bath in, so instead I texted back I was in the shower and he'd just have to wait. My thoughts turned to Brian, and I sighed. Yeah, well, we may never find out where we were headed now, since we seemed to be on the outs already.

Taking another hurried shower, leaving my hair out of the wash to be done at a later date, I pulled on clean clothes and put my unruly mane up in a high ponytail. Slipping on sneakers, I grabbed my bag then rushed down the stairs and out the side door. I skipped checking in with June when I realized she would more than likely be at church herself with the store closed for the day. Locking the door behind me, I spun around to find Lorcan pacing up and down the gravel drive.

"Hey, what's up?" I felt a bit awkward, considering the last time we were out here I ditched him for Brian. He gave me a warm smile, so maybe he wasn't as upset as he seemed yesterday. I didn't like the way I treated him and made a promise to myself I would be considerably more tactful if a situation like that arose again.

"I was just checking in on you. Andrea told me you were up late and had a breakthrough with Adriana. She also said you had some things to do today, and I thought, since you were heading out with her after church, the two of us could grab breakfast then I could show you that thing I mentioned yesterday."

I was thinking, since he didn't flip out or scold me, he had no clue just what me and my cousin were planning to do. This was a good thing, because I didn't think I had it in me to fight anyone today. Mentally, I was still asleep. Actually, breakfast and, more importantly, coffee sounded good about now, so I readily agreed. As we walked across to the diner, I tried to get out of him what it was he wanted to show me, to no avail.

"Nope, I want to show it to you. Not tell you about it." He said this with a secretive smile, and it just made me more intrigued. As we walked into the diner, I saw Joe in the back, flipping pancakes, and wondered if he ever took a day off. He saw me and gave me a smile and a wave with the spatula. I noticed Sheila in the back taking an order, and she looked our way, but before she could head toward us, another waitress, her name tag said Donna, came over with two menus and seated us. She looked similar to Sheila with a bit less of a beehive, but definitely a retro hairstyle, and her makeup was yet again seventies' chic.

"Coffee? You must be Lily Sweet. I can see the family resemblance. Heard you have had a run of bad luck since you came to town." When she saw the questioning surprise on my face, Donna continued to explain. "My boy told me all about it. He's the deputy in these parts; Beau Buford. Took quite a fancy to you, missy."

She looked over at Lorcan and squinted a bit, as if he was moving in on territory that had already been claimed by her precious son. "Heard you were planning on looking into these murders. You might want to be careful to not get in the way of the professionals. Even though my Beau likes you, told me you were making eyes at him he did, he won't tolerate no amateur getting in his way of solving this crime."

My face registered shock.

"Oh, your great-grandmother was already in here telling us your plans. You might want to get a handle on her flapping her gums." She snickered, then she went off to get us our coffee.

Lorcan was frowning and shaking his head back and forth in disbelief.

"What are you thinking, Lily? You can't possibly be considering getting involved in this. You could be in danger. And what did she mean by all that stuff about you and Beau?"

"Oh no, you don't. Not you now, too. I am tired of being told what I can or cannot do. And what business is it of yours who I like or not? You aren't my keeper!" I saw the hurt flash in Lorcan's eyes before he looked away. Didn't I just tell myself I'd treated him poorly and needed to make amends? Here I was being a butt again. I reached my hand out, placing it on his arm.

"Look. I'm sorry. I didn't mean to shout and be so antagonistic. I've had a time of it here, Lorcan. Ever since I arrived, it has been one thing after another. As for Bubba—Beau, not that I owe anyone an explanation, but I needed to distract him so Andrea could get away, and well, I may have gone a bit overboard in the flirt department. I think I am going to pay for it, though, since he seems to have decided I'm his little woman."

Lorcan sat there staring at me a minute then started to laugh. He shook his head and was about to reply when Donna arrived with the coffee and went on to take our orders, but not before shooting Lorcan another dark look. He ordered the breakfast special, which consisted of two eggs, two sausage links, bacon, home fries, a short stack of pancakes, and an orange juice. I ordered my own short stack of pancakes and a side of bacon. When Donna left to get our ticket over to Joe, Lorcan leaned in and continued what he was saying in a whisper.

"You may think it was harmless flirting, but be wary of Donna's wrath. She thinks the sun rises and sets on that boy of hers...and she won't take kindly to you teasing him.

Unless, of course, you really are smitten with our fine deputy Buford, that is."

This he said with a serious expression but then laughed out loud when he saw my look of horror. We were halfway through our meal when I noticed Sheila peering at me furtively then quickly look the other way when we made eye contact. That was strange. This behavior today and her unfortunate glass-dropping incident made me think my great-grandmother might be right, and I should see if Sheila knew anything.

Donna came back over to us to refill our coffees and drop off the check, which Lorcan picked up. I stuffed the last of my pancake into my mouth, then, seeing he had just enough orange juice left to wash it down, I grabbed his glass and drained it all.

"Brat!" Lorcan's eyes crinkled as he looked at me in mock anger. I stuck my tongue out at him and told him to get used to it; I always stole food and drink. It came from wondering where my next meal was coming from. His eyes immediately sobered, and I mentally smacked myself for bringing our jovial mood to an abrupt end.

"You don't have to worry about that anymore, Lily. You can take anything I have, any time."

I smiled thinly, trying to hide my embarrassment. Lorcan glanced at the check, and I didn't bother arguing with him for paying my share. He offered to take me to breakfast. I'd treat him another time. Our eyes met, and he seemed to know what I was thinking.

"You can pay for me next time." I swore that man could read minds. When he excused himself to go use the restroom, Donna followed his progress to the back of the restaurant with a scowl then turned to me, popping her gum, and using her pen to scratch behind her ear, making her beehive hairdo jiggle a smidge.

"You need to go see Rita over at her psychic shop. She had reason to get rid of your Aunt Adelaide all those years ago, you better believe it. But be careful. She's crazy. You know, I haven't seen poor old Chad in months. I was surprised to hear he found you. Did he show up at your place or something? Not that it matters much. He was crazy. I would discount pretty much anything he had to say."

I was about to ask Donna to expound on her theory when I noticed Sheila standing right behind her, eyes wide, like she had something to add but was afraid. She was staring at Donna as if fascinated by what she was hearing.

"But Rita, now, that there would be my main suspect. I think your great-grandma agrees. There has always been something off about that woman, always doting on that boy of hers and making him neurotic. Oh! And you need to add the reverend's wife Laura to your list of suspects. Who else do you have on it, anyway?"

"I…um, I don't know why you think I'm looking into the murders. I can assure you I am not, despite what Adriana says."

Donna gave me a knowing look then noticed Sheila standing behind her.

"What's your problem? Don't you agree with me on this? Everyone in this town knows how hard Rita took the betrayal. You should know yourself just how upset she was, still is, if I had to guess. Wasn't your brother hoping she'd break off her engagement to Dillon and run into his arms? Maybe Lily here needs to look into him as well. He is a bit challenged mentally, after all."

Donna looked over at me then patted Sheila on the shoulder and shook her head.

Sheila was round eyed and opened and closed her mouth a few times, looking like a fish running out of air, then spun on her heel and went into the kitchen, but not before knocking my handbag off my chair, spilling the contents. Donna had a steely look about her and turned back to me again. "You go talk to her brother Stu. He'd be on my short list, if you know what I mean. Just remember what I said about Rita. When her husband went and killed himself, she went right mental."

I thanked Donna and waited for Lorcan to return. Rita Chase went on my list of suspects, as did Stu. Wait…Stu? It couldn't be, could it? I'd have to ask Lorcan if Sheila was indeed related to the befuddled mechanic I met on my first day in Georgia. Then try to find out how all these people were tied together.

Lorcan confirmed the Stu Donna mentioned, and my would-be mechanic Stu, were one and the same, and that the day I came into town, he was moving all his equipment out of his closed shop and in to Lorcan's. His plan was to only take the odd job now and then, as he was going into semi-retirement due to an aching back. Plus, Lorcan stated Stu was busy with other commitments. Just what those were I couldn't fathom.

Lorcan and I were just coming out of the diner when we saw a tow truck approaching us, a man waving his arm out the window. As he got closer, I realized it was Stu! Go figure. He leaned out the window and shouted to Lorcan.

"Hey, man. We had two separate accidents out on the highway, and they wanted to bring them both to you. I got this one, but the wrecker is at your place with Sheriff Glen. You need to get over there quick. Someone rammed his deputy but good and pushed his vehicle off the road into the ravine. He was on his way back from interviewing some folks when it happened. Maybe the killer followed him! Beau is at the hospital. Someone needs to tell Donna. He's banged up pretty bad."

I looked in alarm at Lorcan and told him to go ahead with

Stu, and I'd tell Donna. Rushing back into the diner, I wasn't paying close enough attention to where I was going and slammed into Sheila before I could stop myself. I blurted out what happened to Bubba, and to my surprise, the waitress turned as white as a sheet, then she dropped to the ground like a bag of rocks. Joe saw what happened and shouted, then Donna came running out of the kitchen. When I repeated what Stu had said, instead of reacting like a mother should, she seemed angry. She actually glared at me, then reached for her bag behind the counter and yelled to Joe that she was heading to the hospital and needed to borrow his car. Grabbing keys from under the counter that I suspected belonged to Joe, Donna ran out the door with everyone's well wishes for Bubba's health. She waved her hand in acknowledgment and was gone, leaving the customers shocked and whispering amongst themselves. I was helping Sheila up and got her settled into a booth. Her face crumbled when she saw Donna's retreating back.

"Don't mind her. She's not really mad at you," she whispered quietly. "She relies on that boy so much, when you told her what happened she needed someone to be mad at, and you were the messenger, so..." Sheila finally looked directly at me and sniffled. I handed her a few napkins and decided there was no time like the present to interview her. Thankfully, Joe walked an order out himself, nodding at me that it was all right with him to continue settling his waitress's nerves.

"May I call you Sheila?" She nodded yes and gratefully accepted the napkins wiping her eyes. "Can I ask you why you reacted the way you did yesterday when we were here and again today when I told you about the accident?" She sighed like someone about to unburden her soul. At least, I hoped she would.

"I'm sorry about that. All this excitement is too much for

169

my nerves. It's just with Adelaide being found and Chad being murdered—it opened wounds that have be shut for quite some time. I reacted the way I did because my brother Stu was sort of involved with all the drama, but inadvertently. When I heard your granny talk about looking into it, I thought of him and got worried. He had nothing to do with those murders. He was sweet on Rita, that's true, but he knew she only had eyes for Dillon. Plus, he is years older than her! He's a dear soul, and I'm afraid the police will see him as an easy target if they get pointed in his direction, despite who he is. Trust me, Stu had nothing to do with nothing."

Sheila blew her nose, loudly, then continued.

"When Donna told y'all to talk with Rita over at her metaphysical shop just now, well, it all came rushing back to me, and I acted like a silly goose. It was a mess back then, emotions all over the place, and all over hormones! All the young men around here always get stirred up around pretty young witches, and there was quite a few. But none could hold a candle to your aunt Adelaide. That girl had all the men in this town under her spell. Not that she had to ever consider using magic on them, no, Adelaide didn't need any love potions. She just had *it*. You know?"

Sheila wiped her eyes again and then blew her nose once more for good measure.

"I don't want Stu to get all riled up over this again. He never got over Rita, I think, seeing as he never did marry. Heck, I can't recall him ever dating no one. He's my baby brother, so I worry. Me and Shirley came first, and Stu was basically an oops baby! About shocked the entire Jones clan when my momma wound up pregnant at her age!"

"Shirley? Shirley Jones, the EMT? Is she your sister?"

"That's right! You met her when you got dumped on your head the other day. She's my big sister, never got married, either, but it don't bother her none. She likes having lots of boyfriends and can never seem to settle on one. Another one running around this town causing trouble, She has a good heart, though and everyone loves our Shirley. Daddy says she got a roving eye and is as bad as any man. Me? I used to be a Jones, now I'm a Polk. I got married right outta high school to my Gordy. He's the town's garbage collector, owns his own truck, and runs his own business. We will be married thirty years this May."

I congratulated her prematurely and thought about all she said.

"What do you think happened to Chad?"

Sheila turned pale, making me worried she might faint again, but instead she leaned forward and said, "It's obvious, isn't it? Someone knew about them bones found under your porch and killed Chad to keep him quiet. I'm guessing he knew who done her in—once he heard you found Adelaide. Find that person and you find the killer."

Sheila's eyes widened and she broke into a cold sweat, making me wonder if she knew more than she was letting on. "You need to find that person," she looked up suddenly and gasped, "before they get to you next."

CHAPTER 17

*A*s I left the diner for the second time today, I realized Lorcan never did get to show me whatever it was he'd been trying to show me for the last week. This time, it wasn't my fault, so I didn't feel too guilty about it. I heard someone shout my name and saw Andrea rushing toward me from the village green. I waved, then something caught my eye. There was a tall woman standing outside the metaphysical shop called The Mystic Fox. She had gorgeous dark auburn hair that cascaded down her shoulders, hair that you could never get from a bottle. She was wearing clothes that complimented the shade, a multi-hued blouse in turquoises and greens with a dark brown flowing skirt. I wondered if this was the Rita that Donna said I should speak to, Brian's mother.

"Good morning, cousin. You look like someone who's already had a busy day." Andrea gave me a quick hug and stepped back, peering intently at my face. "And someone who seems upset. What's up?"

"You're right on both counts. Wait until you hear all about it."

I filled Andrea in on Lorcan's visit, breakfast, and hearing about the accident from Stu—and how someone had tried to harm Bubba. Then I told her about interviewing Sheila. I was a bit shaken up by her ominous words and said so, shivering a bit as I did, which made Andrea frown. She scratched her elbow, and I could tell she was taking in all I said. Finally, she looked up and smiled.

"Well, we better get cracking on this case before someone does try to harm you. We also need to keep practicing your defensive magic so you can protect yourself."

"I'd have better luck with a Glock, I think."

I was still worried I wouldn't be able to harness my newfound magical ability in time to stave off any attack on my person, not trusting my inexperience, despite yesterday's progress. We started walking toward my truck when I paused and asked Andrea something that had been bothering me since I found out I was a witch.

"Can I ask you what the difference is between a dark witch and a, what…do we say light witch or good witch? I know you guys tried to explain some of this to me already. But why is it so important that I be this dark one? How cab being dark *not* mean I have to do bad, evil things?"

Andrea had the good sense to realize it was a sore subject with me, so she didn't laugh, but I could see she was amused. She motioned that we continue to my truck, taking the time to gather her thoughts before responding. Climbing into my Ford, we paused before driving off, and she turned to me to explain.

"It's not as simple as dark equals bad and light equals good. Every witch is capable to be good or bad, depending on how one defines this. Basically, we all know the difference between right and wrong, but a dark witch has unique abilities. They can harness dark magic…wait, let me explain." I opened my mouth to protest yet again, because there was no way I would ever accept doing bad things, but Andrea pushed forward before I could say anything. "Lily, a true dark witch is a rare being. You can have any witch go down the wrong path and do horrible things, but a dark witch uses their magic, but for good purposes. They are very rare because most would use dark magic and become evil and do unspeakable things for their own gain. But a true dark witch would do malevolent magic for the good of all. Does that make sense?"

I sat there letting George idle as I considered what Andrea just told me, all the while slowly shaking my head in the negative. I wasn't sure how someone could do malicious things and still be good.

"Lily, didn't you ever in your life face someone doing something so revolting that you felt the urge to stop them and with a good dose of righteous anger?"

I thought back all those years ago to the little girl I was, defending that kitten from the clutches of the mean-spirited boy. "Maybe?" I mean, I was a child. I didn't know if what I was feeling could be considered "righteous anger," though. I was protecting a small kitten from a terribly abusive boy who was taunting me with it. But, well…

"Oh my gosh, Andrea. I felt it. Back when I was almost four…I remember something coming up and out of me to stop a boy from hurting a kitten. All these years I've stuffed it and decided it must have been my imagination. But I truly felt justified in stepping in and making him stop hurting it."

Andrea smiled at me and continued. "Only a true dark witch has been given the power to harness the kind of magic needed to be a moral compass. No one but a dark witch could be an arbiter of good by smiting down those that would do evil things. You hold a lot of power in your hands, cuz, and are invaluable beyond measure. Basically? In a word, you *are* Karma."

Karma, huh? Why did this bit of news make me even more reluctant than before?

Putting the truck in gear, we made the short drive over to Rita's place of business, and I got myself ready to tackle another interrogation.

* * *

WALKING into The Mystic Fox was what I supposed entering a witchy candy store was like for some people. Crystals and wands, potions and tarot cards, anything and everything to do with witchcraft and spellcasting was in a hodge-podge of displays. Candles in every shape and form lined a section of shelving on one wall and gave off interesting and delightful scents. Figurines and animal totems shared space with how-to books and single parchment spells wrapped in ribbons. The overall effect was one that gave an air of professional witch shop meets tourist trap. I loved it instantly, even the New Age music being piped in on the sound system, I recognized the *Aquaria* album by Diane Arkenstone playing softly. A good choice!

Looking to my left as we progressed through the store, I spied a glass door that opened to a small enclosed courtyard which shared space with the herbal shop next door, Fox Den Herbals. I wondered if Rita owned both shops and had a partner. The woman herself walked through the dangling beaded screen from the back storeroom into the main shop when she heard the bell over the door.

"Good morning, ladies. How may I help you?"

Andrea smiled and introduced me. "Rita, this is Lily Sweet, my cousin." She looked over at me and continued, "Rita's mom was one of the first witches to open her shop on the square, and she passed it down to Rita when she retired.

It is a treasure trove for anything and everything you might need or want."

We greeted each other warmly, and I turned to Andrea with a question. "What do you mean, 'one of the first witches to open a shop?' Wasn't this always a witch town?"

Both women exchanged a smile, and Rita explained. "Well, we weren't always so open about practicing our craft in a commercial way, but the Council of Elders decided we might as well profit while living our lives, and they came up with a way to both practice our craft and have a lucrative tourist trade by making the town an artist and folk village. Then they put up a glamor to shield us from mundane folk, and the town was literally born overnight into something new. We were encouraged to open shops to grow tourism, and Mother was first to jump on board with my place here. The herb shop next door followed a few years later."

That certainly answered my question on whether or not she owned both shops.

"Is it difficult, running two places?" I asked her, glancing at the side door.

"Oh no, not at all. I have a lovely woman who is a master herbalist and an avid gardener working for me. Just wait until next June when Samantha gives you the biggest, juiciest tomatoes you've ever seen. Do you cook?"

"I'm trying. I've actually gotten much better since..." I paused, realizing the lump was back, and I had difficulty finishing my explanation. "Since I did all the cooking for the last two years of my mother's life. She used to do it all, and I'd watch and try to learn, but when she got too ill to continue, I took it up."

Rita looked sad, and I saw a shadow cross her face. Then she looked up and smiled at me with a look of sympathy.

"I'm very sorry to hear about your mother. I remember

her, although we weren't close. I was a few grades ahead of her in school."

"Thank you. Actually, I am sort of looking into this murder with Andrea, and somehow your name came up as someone I should speak to?" I didn't say as a suspect, but the change in her demeanor was marked.

"I know nothing about what happened with Chad. It is horrible, but I know just as much as you, I'm sure." She almost shouted.

"Rita, what about Adelaide? Brian thinks those bones under Lily's porch must be hers. It would be too weird for them *not* to be. Do you know anything that could help us?" Andrea seemed to have better luck with her query, yet we waited almost a full minute for Rita to speak as she collected herself, getting her temper under control.

"You're asking me about Dillon. No, it's okay, don't try to deny it. I loved my husband, probably much more than he loved me. I won't say he *didn't* love me, but he was infatuated with Adelaide. I believe he was obsessed with her. Many of the men in this town were. She was like a siren with the men swarming around her like worker bees adoring their queen."

Rita got quiet again then looked up in anger. "I had nothing to do with murdering that girl, although I wanted to. I really did." She looked at our shocked expressions and softened her manner. "You see...Dillon and I, well, we weren't married yet, he was much older than me by about seven years, but I loved him so much, and, well, I was already eight months pregnant with Brian. He told me he loved me, and we planned to marry, but one day I came home early and found them in bed together, Dillon and Adelaide. He jumped up all upset, apologetic and embarrassed trying to explain, like he could! He was slightly older than *me*, but Adelaide was easily twelve years his junior! What was he thinking? Well. We all knew he *wasn't* thinking, was he? At least not with his

177

brain. I turned and left but he followed me right out the front door, and in his birthday suit! I wanted to kill them both."

Rita paused then took a deep breath, letting it out slowly as she continued. "But even worse than the betrayal was her treatment of Dillon. She refused to speak to him, see him, acknowledge that he was alive. He almost threw away his fiancé and unborn child for this girl; it changed him. We worked things out between us, at least for Brian's sake. I forgave him, eventually—and even considered forgiving Adelaide. She was so young, barely seventeen! As mad as I was with Dillon, though, it couldn't compare to how much I grew to hate your aunt. You see, she treated Dillon like a conquest, once won, no longer a concern. And that day, as I waddled out the door, I could hear her. I swear she laughed wickedly at my shame, reveled in it. I heard her. At first, I thought she was crying, but no. Adelaide had absolutely no remorse for what she did."

Tears were slowly running down her face, and I felt over-whelming sadness for this poor woman and anger toward my callous aunt.

"He never got over it," she continued. "I know it. When Adelaide left, well, I am sure you know the rest of the story. My poor Dillon—and Brian, it took me years to get him out of his shell after he found his dad the way he did."

I was shaking in anger and disappointment. How could Adelaide do that to a pregnant woman? I was ashamed, although it wasn't my fault, I didn't hurt Rita, but someone in my family had. Then it hit me, Rita had lost her husband to suicide and had to deal with the fallout I was sure Brian went through—and while I couldn't *see* her as a murderer, she certainly had a good reason to remove my aunt from her life. Despite my being sympathetic, she remained on my suspect list until I could figure out a way to clear her off it. Had Rita killed Adelaide leaving everyone to believe she'd run off only to have hidden her under my porch all these years?

* * *

"WELL, THAT SUCKED BUCKETS."

I was heading to my truck with Andrea following me, feeling like the biggest meanie on the planet for making Rita relive that horrible time in her life.

"What did you expect when we took this on? Sunshine and roses? You knew it wasn't going to be easy, trying to track down a murderer and solve two crimes!" Andrea scolded me, slightly exasperated by my glum mood.

"I know, but I didn't think it would hurt like this. Confronting Brian's *mother* is not high on a list of things I ever thought I'd be doing. How could Rita marry that man, whose heart belonged to another woman, even though the woman in question toyed with it? Woman! Adelaide was a child, barely legal at that! Poor Brian, he only knew his dad for what—six years, seven? His father spent most of it still secretly obsessed with my aunt!"

Andrea eyes widened in realization, and she stopped me before I got in my truck, giving me a quick hug.

"Sorry, cuz, I can't imagine how difficult that was, hearing those things about your aunt. Rita being Brian's mom, yeah, that did suck, especially since you and Brian seem to be getting close."

We couldn't stop now. I told Andrea this, then thought we should probably question someone else today, and turned to her again.

"Who do we go see next?"

Andrea deliberated a moment, then she sighed and said, "Might as well go see the Brewster's and kill two birds with

179

one stone. I will go over his relationship with your family on our way to his place."

"The reverend? Just how woo-woo is this church he's the head of, anyway?"

Andrea started laughing and replied, "Oh no. This you have to see for yourself. Trying to explain that bunch will make me wind up on the sofa in some shrink's office!"

Well, this was going to be interesting at least.

CHAPTER 18

*O*ow. Just...wow. *The Everlasting Love of The Lord Upon High Holy Redeemer Evangelical Church* was just as fantastical as its name implied. It looked more like a dentist's office than a church...with peeling pink shutters. It was just outside the town limits heading back toward Rabun County.

No ornamentation in sight, unless you counted the plethora of pink flamingos sprinkled around the front and side yards. I didn't know flamingos were standard church protocol. It didn't have a cross, but it did have a neon sign in one window that blinked "Jesus Saves!" Well, it would, but the sign had two letters blown out, so it said, "Jesu aves!" At least there were geraniums planted in the window boxes, but as we got closer to the front door, I realized they were plastic. That was one way to keep from having to water them. Speaking of water, on either side of the walk leading to the entry were little kidney-shaped ponds, but instead of koi I only saw one large toad poking his head out of the algae, looking morose. I feel you, buddy.

I heard music coming from inside the building. It

sounded like a choir practicing for service. As we walked in, we could hear them starting up another round, and we paused to listen:

"Alas, and did my Savior bleed
And did my Sovereign die?
Would He devote that sacred head
For such a worm as I?"

I cringed, because I was positive their Savior did indeed bleed—but from the *ears,* after hearing such caterwauling coming from His faithful. Not one person seemed to be in key, yet all were enthusiastically singing at the top of their lungs. A woman was in front on a small spinet piano banging away, not caring if the choir followed along with her. A man was sitting in the front row, head in hand, and slowly rocking forward and back. He was either the choir director or the reverend himself, and I couldn't blame him for swaying in misery. I wanted to crawl into the coat closet and cry.

"Now Beulah, you let Miss Hettie be heard. You stepped right in front of her and started competing with your alto to her soft soprano, and she can't be heard."

I looked over at the woman the pianist scolded. Beulah, I presumed, who was towering over an elderly lady, sniffed in disgust. The smaller woman, standing just behind, looked as if a mild breeze could toss her a mile into Kingdom Come. This must be Miss Hettie. She proceeded to look up at Beulah and sneered, then sat down. She folded her hands primly on her lap, but not before sticking her tongue out.

I giggled, and she looked our way. In a soft voice, Hettie said, "We have visitors, it seems. Perhaps they are looking for Jesus?"

This she directed at us, and I had the urge to ask her if

they lost him again, but I held my tongue. The man jumped to his feet and did an awkward walk-trot toward us, hands outstretched in a welcoming way. His bald head shone like his wife polished it every week along with the furniture. He was tall and scrawny but had a pot belly and jowls that looked like they belonged on a much larger man. The overall effect was disconcerting.

"How nice. Please, come in." He pumped my hand, then Andrea's in welcome. "I'm Reverend Oliver Brewster. Are you ladies looking to hear the Good Word?"

"Praise Jesus!" all the choir women shouted.

I jumped and might have made a "nya!" sound as I took a step back.

"Um, actually…"

"You are good Christian women, no?"

This came from the woman who had been playing the piano. She gave us both a stern look that didn't bode well. Turning her attention to me, I got the once over, as she made note of the purple streaks in my hair, earning me a scowl.

"I'm Andrea Becker from town, um…Sweet Briar, that is. This is my cousin Lily. She is newly arrived and…"

"New? Have you come to join our little place of worship, then?" The reverend smiled at me in apparent anticipation of a new lamb for his flock then glanced noticeably down at my cleavage, making me pull farther back.

"I was just saying today to my dear wife, Laura here," he acknowledged the woman at the piano, "that the Good Lord works in mysterious and amazing ways, and wouldn't it be nice if he sent us a few new faces to help, um, enhance our choir for the better? Praise Jesus, for he sent you our way."

"Praise Jesus!"

Again, from the choir. Laura looked at us shrewdly then glanced at her husband, and her frown deepened. I was disturbed when I realized her face now resembled a pug dog.

"She doesn't look like she's here for singing praises. Are you good Christian women, or not?"

Her chin jutted out, and if smoke snorted out of her nose, I wouldn't be surprised in the least.

"I...um, yes, I mean, I'm Catholic..."

The collective gasp that resounded amongst those gathered gave me a hint of just what they thought of *that* little proclamation. I wondered what they'd do if they realized I was a witch and turned to Andrea for help, raising my eyebrows, eyes wide. I was sure, in that moment, I looked like a Christian—one that just found out Nero started playing his fiddle, sending me to the lions.

"Catholic? Roman Catholic?" This from Laura.

"A Papist? Oh my!" Hettie cried, adding her two cents and putting both palms on either side of her face.

"Idol worshipers!" This came from behind us, and I spun to find yet another miniscule lady, this one with blue-tinged hair, wearing glasses, a wool coat and a scarf—even in this humidity. She peered up at me. "My name is Minerva. Do you enjoy worshiping the Devil, dear?"

> *"Was it for sins that I had done*
> *He groaned upon the tree?*
> *Amazing pity, grace unknown*
> *And love beyond degree."*

Beulah started bellowing from the top of her lungs, causing everyone to jump. We all looked at her like she lost her marbles as she imploded in righteous lunacy.

"God saves all, except heathens! They shall fall into the pit of Hell and be devoured by Satan and his minions! Begone from us, foul woman, and take this defiler with you!"

Beulah imperiously pointed to Andrea, then me, then to the door we had entered. I was about to turn and run when

Laura said, "Oh, stuff it, Beulah. She's Catholic. It could be worse. After all, she could have said she was a Yankee."

Oh, well, was I ever glad in that moment that I didn't have a heavy New York accent, but the upper part of the state's more country-sounding one.

"Actually, my cousin just moved here from New York and…"

More gasps, and these were downright scary. The looks I was now getting made me think they saw me as Sherman, reincarnated, back in town and ready march to Atlanta again, burning and looting all the way. Even the Reverend Brewster was looking askance at my person, as if I fouled his congregation with the stench of my unholy New York-ness. He shook his head in sad contemplation.

"Perhaps you are here for another reason, then? Nothing to do with our worship?"

At least the reverend tried. Laura and the rest of the ladies looked like they wanted to get a rope and find a nice sturdy tree. Minerva even tittered a bit. She was still behind us.

The sudden arrival of a woman from a side room, who cleared her throat before addressing the reverend, was a much needed distraction. Her voice had a silky-smooth melodic lilt, and she had a pleasant smile on her face as she spoke.

"Perhaps your visitors would like some tea in your office, Reverend? I noticed them arriving and I've set out four places for you."

Her words broke the tension a bit as the choir ladies clustered together, whispering and clucking in disapproval.

"That will do nicely, Sukey. Thank you."

The reverend dismissed the woman and held his palm forward, suggesting we follow. As I turned to leave, I felt a tug on my sleeve and looked down to see the tiny blue-haired lady peering up at me. Minerva, again.

"I will pray for your unholy soul, dear."

Smiling and nodding a bit, she teetered out the way we came in, not giving me a chance to thank her. Or kick her, as it were. I was sure she was off to her next KKK meeting. She probably brought cookies.

I turned back and went toward the side door, Laura following close behind us, cutting past her husband. Perhaps she wanted to remove my cleavage from under his righteous gaze. Yuck. She spun around and placed a hand on his chest, stopping him in his tracks.

"We will be right with you. First, I must speak with my husband. Go on ahead with Sukey. She will get you settled."

Laura held the reverend in place as she said this, making sure he couldn't follow us to his office. He looked abashed and slightly disappointed as I passed. I guessed my chest was uplifting him in wonderous and mysterious ways, and being parted from it, even momentarily, was causing him pain. I had a feeling Laura would be doling out some pain of her own.

We followed Sukey inside the chamber and settled in our seats, thanking her for the offerings before us. Sweet tea, cookies and scones, and even a small box of chocolates sat on a table on one side of the office. The reverend's desk, piled high with all manner of papers, would not have been able to accommodate such a spread.

"Thank you, Sukey, is it?"

The woman chuckled, her dark skin contrasting with her yellow dress and white apron.

"Oh, child, my name is Susanne, Susanne Washington. Miss Laura does like the old ways and calls me the old slave slang word for Susan, Sukey. It's fine, hon. I don't mind it none. They pay me well enough, and it beats not having a job. Plus, I do rightly pray for them often, and maybe someday they will stop acting like 'Fools in the Rain.'"

"Led Zeppelin?"

"Oh, you know it, honey, you know it!" Susanne smiled and shook her head at the silliness of it all. "I do love that band."

I was delighted with this convivial woman and asked, "Do you attend this church, too?"

Susanne really laughed at my question, then. She apologized when I looked confused. "No, child, I go to the AME church north of Sweet Briar, almost to the North Carolina border."

She paused, seeing that I was even more perplexed.

"That means African Methodist Episcopal Church. It's just north of town near some old rundown rental cabins by Ridgepole Creek. My daddy used to be the preacher. We have ourselves a right grand time of it there. I do believe we sing a might better than these folks! Praise Jesus!" This got us all snickering, which seemed a bit scandalous, all things considered.

"You come pay us a visit anytime you want, okay, sugar? Both of you young ladies. Can't miss us. Just head north from the square, and when you see a sign for Ridgepole Creek Cabin Rentals, look across the street, and there stands our little church, tucked in the woods."

We thanked Susanne again and said our goodbyes as she left. The Brewster's entered the office, suspicion written all over their faces. Laura even looked around as if we might have tucked some precious trinkets into our pockets or, worse, did some foul Catholic ritual in their absence.

"Now, what can we do for you ladies?" This was from Reverend Brewster, as Laura sniffed at his continued niceness.

"I recently returned to town after years being gone."

Andrea and I rehearsed what I would say before we arrived, hoping to shock the reverend into some kind of confession if he was guilty, or make him uncomfortable enough to give it away in his facial expressions.

"You see," I continued, "I am Jessica Sweet's daughter, Adelaide's niece, and I've returned to Sweet Briar to discover the place where I was born and reconnect with relatives... and *friends*."

I emphasized this, never taking my eyes from his, and immediately noticed a blush growing up his neck and spreading across his face. He drew back and sputtered a bit at my proclamation, but it was his wife, Laura, who gave away far more than I expected.

"Another Croy harlot disgracing this holy establishment with her presence. I won't have it, Ollie. I mean it. Purple hair and wanton ways, pure evil, you both need to leave, now!"

She jumped up from her seat and pointed to the back door, even stomping her foot in her obvious fury. Yeah, the purple streaks instantly heralded devil worship in all its glory. I barely stopped myself from rolling my eyes.

"Now, Laura, please don't get all riled up. That wouldn't be the Godly thing to do. As Christians, we owe it to these ladies to see what they came here for and guide them unto the Light."

Considering I was supposed to be a dark witch, I thought that would be a lesson in futility and was about to say so. Andrea, however, was more mature it seems, because she coughed slightly, giving me pointed look, obviously willing to continue putting up with this nonsense. Then I thought of Chad Barwick and sighed in resignation.

"Why don't I go sit in the chapel with Mrs. Brewster here while you and Reverend Brewster have a talk?" Andrea, again quick on her feet, gave us the perfect solution to the problem of having both suspects in the same room. Laura was about to protest, when her husband, unexpectedly, found his backbone.

"Enough, woman. Go talk with this young lady, Andrea. I will remain here with Lily." The way he said it posed no argument, and his wife sullenly followed my cousin into the other room.

"Now, what can I do help ease your mind and remove your stress, young lady?"

Ugh, why did everything coming out of his mouth sound so dirty? The more time I spent with the Reverend Brewster, the more I wanted to chuck him into a chipper-shredder.

"After all, your momma's sister Addy was a *good* friend of mine back in the day, mmm hmm. She was a right sweet gal." Yep, his eyes were again fixed on my cleavage.

"I want to know if you or your wife had any bones to pick with my aunt, no pun intended, Reverend. Surely by now, you've heard her remains have been discovered. I am looking into her murder, and that of Chad Barwick's, and going up every alley I come across." I decided to go the "in your face" route, since this joker was getting on my nerves.

"Little lady, are you suggesting I might have had something to do with that evil? I am a man of the cloth! A man of God! I don't know how you could even consider such wicked things."

Old Ollie was working himself up in a righteous lather.

"I adored your aunt Adelaide, and let me tell you that girl was sweet on me. Why, had she been a more God-fearing woman, I might have taken her for my wife instead of my dear Laura, bless her heart."

"Why now, Reverend, that makes your wife go on my suspect list. After all, she must have suspected you were *good* friends with my aunt Addy. But if not, do you have any idea who could do such a thing? Not to mention do in Chad Barwick to keep him from talking?"

I'd decided to keep the pressure on, although slightly worried the good reverend might burst the vein that started pulsing on his temple. Once I mentioned his wife, his turn-around was instantaneous.

"I would look at that harlot, Rita Chase. She had some nasty business go on between her, Adelaide, and her husband Dillon, although he weren't her spouse yet, even though her shame was out there for all to see. With child and living I sin. She has that heathen shop in town and always had a hot temper. Then there is Harley Jacobs. He lives on his momma and daddy's farm on the other side of Sweet Briar from here. He was sweet on Deanna Fredricks. Her sister Donna is a waitress at that diner in town. Deanna suspected Harley had been sniffing around your aunt and about had a fit when she heard someone saw them kissing behind his barn one day. Mind you, that Deanna is, well, everyone knew she was the town slut back then. You couldn't tell Harley that, though; he wouldn't hear it. She was engaged to Harley by that time, and rumor had it the two of them ran off and eloped, but he came back to town a few weeks later and never did mention her name again. Donna said she took up with a musician or something from Chattanooga. Deanna was a wild girl, another one with a temper. If she wasn't off devil knows where, I'd make her my prime suspect. But since maybe that's what broke them up, I would put Harley on the top of my list."

He paused, removing a handkerchief from his pocket and wiping his brow, his eyes once again flirting with my décolletage.

"Some of the boys asked him once what happened, but he wouldn't speak about it to no one. Started throwing chairs around the bar and walked out. Never did hang around town after that, just stayed on the farm, working his cows, unmarried to this day."

He sighed, wiping his brow once more.

"You can ask Donna. She has always struck me as a God-fearing woman, well, after her fall from grace. After that no-good man of hers got himself tossed in jail the first time, she showed up here begging for repentance, confessing she had that brat Bubba out of wedlock and was a soiled woman. I put her to work cleaning this place until she landed the job at the diner. She could tell you who to look at. I sure did miss having her around here all the time. I heard rumors Donna caught Ross, that's her no-good man, in bed with her sister and your aunt at the same time. Woo-boy! Imagine that."

The look on my face must have made him understand I had no intention of doing such a thing. Clearing his throat, he realized belatedly he let me see the type of man he was. I wanted to assure him I already had it figured out but kept my mouth shut, for once.

"Uh...well, I think that was a load of bull crap some of the guys in town started spreading. You know how boys are! Cause I never heard much about it again. Plus, once Ross got out of the pokey, they moved a few towns away, and she settled down. It wasn't until Ross got thrown in jail that second and final time that she moved back here, penniless, and told me Deanna had run off with that musician, and she was all alone in the world. But then, like I said, she left here for the diner, and I only see her occasionally now. Pity, because she sure knew how to clean...and such."

He smiled in a self-satisfied way, making me fully realize that it wasn't just cleaning he had Donna do around here. Ick. Poor Donna! I felt sorry for her.

"And you're sure about your wife? Did she know you were sweet on Adelaide?"

The color drained from his face, and he sat down hard in the chair at his desk. He swallowed a few times then shook his head as if to clear it.

"Laura? She...no. She can get surly, but she wouldn't hurt a heathen fly. My wife is a God-fearing woman! Laura would not have killed her."

If Oliver said those words in front of me one more time, I was *definitely* going to run him through a chipper-shredder.

"Damn straight I'd liked to have killed her. That hussy."

Laura stormed in with an apologetic Andrea on her heels.

"She ruined more marriages and engagements in these parts, and so help me God, I would have danced on her grave —or the very least did a jig on your porch if I'd a known she was rotting under those floorboards. Good riddance to bad rubbish. However, *we* have alibis so get the hell out of our church!"

Well, that certainly wasn't a very Christian-like thing to say!

CHAPTER 19

"*A*re you sure they both have airtight alibies?"

We were sitting on the side porch at June's, and I was disheartened with the news Andrea had imparted to me. It seemed not only did the Brewster's have an ironclad alibi for Adelaide, they also had one for Chad Barwick's murder. They were on their honeymoon the week before Adelaide went missing and were gone a full month, making it impossible to be here when she was murdered. And yes, Laura was only too happy to show Andrea photographs of the two of them in Africa, spending their first weeks as husband and wife, trying to "convert them heathens," and show them the error of their ways, I presumed. I wondered that they didn't wind up chucked at some hungry lions by those they were hoping to covert. I would have helped.

As for this past week, both of them went to visit her sister-in-law in Roswell, who just delivered another God-fearing Brewster into the world—and spent time at an Evangelical convention in Atlanta on the days Chad confronted me and the next day when I found him dead. Yes, we checked, and yes, they were not only there but were speakers at several of the planned events. In theory, they might have been able to drive all the way up here and do him in, but Brian already shared with me he pulled security footage from the hotel where they were staying, since they were on his suspect list, and it looked like they did indeed have an airtight one. They were cleared.

Ah, yes, Brian. He was waiting on me when Andrea and I returned. After the day I had, I wasn't willing to play nice and slammed my truck door, marching over to him gearing up for a fight. But he took the wind from my sails when he apologized before I could rip into him.

"I was being an ass, and I knew I was. I have no excuse, other than I got enraged thinking you'd want to be with a guy like Bubba. It made me so mad, so fast, well, I didn't give you a chance to explain," then he hurriedly continued when he saw my eyes turn to slits, "not that you needed to! I am absolutely at fault here. I should never have believed anything like that about you. I didn't really. I was enraged that he kissed you more than anything else. Forgive me?"

Maybe he caught me at a good point, or maybe it was his baby blues. I wasn't going to worry about it. He apologized, and I could be the bigger person here.

He almost ruined it when he got all "police detective" on us and scolded me and Andrea for looking into the murders. He backtracked when I hit him with my logic. Why should I? If I was the dark witch everyone said I was, wouldn't that mean I should have a bit of leeway in such things? It wasn't like this was a regular town with regular people living in it. Wasn't I supposed to be the bringer of Karma or some such?

That made Brian quiet and reflective for a minute or so, then he turned to me and made me promise I wouldn't confront anyone without letting him know where I was going or who I was seeing. I could live with that. I knew I wasn't a trained police detective, but I also knew I had power

—just no clue how to use it effectively yet. I was surprised he ceded so quickly.

"Any leads you care to share with us?"

I wasn't hoping for much but was pleasantly surprised when Brian turned to us and shared what he knew about the case so far.

"The biggest issue we have is the inside job aspect of this case. You just can't walk into the morgue and erase video feed and steal bones out of a drawer. We are talking the city here, the state medical examiner office crime lab near Atlanta, in Decatur. There just isn't any way a civilian can get in there and tamper with evidence, let alone steal entire skeletal remains! It is worrisome. As for Chad, we brought him down there as well, because of the connection to this case. He wouldn't have been allowed to be buried since he was, um, evidence as such."

"But that means a witch or an official of some sort, or an official who knows a witch, right?" Andrea asked, worrying the skin on her elbow in a nervous itch I noticed she did whenever she was thinking too long and hard on a topic that upset her. She fussed with a necklace she was wearing with a little cat charm dangling on it, making me reach up to make sure my Pisces charm was still hanging from the chain I'd slipped it on after my scare.

If Andrea was correct, that list could be endless and huge. Doctors, police officers, funeral directors, guards, anyone that worked at the crime lab, the list seemed endlessly daunting.

"No, I can't buy into that theory." Brian grimaced then shook his head in consternation. "This can't be that vast a case. Most murders happen between people who know each other and have some conflict. To broaden the suspect pool would lead to insanity. Trust me, it was someone she knew and one: upset in a crime of passion, or two: had some secret on they were afraid she'd reveal, taking their power away, or three: had money she would be imparting in a will or some such. It's usually those three things that cause someone to commit murder in the first place. Lust, power, and greed. I would know," he said this with a touch of bitter sadness in his voice. "I've seen plenty of it."

"How on Earth did one person manage to get bones, a body, files and photos out of a morgue while also managing to disable the video feed? It almost has to be a witch, and one with memory erasing skills, but we don't have anyone like that on our roles in the Council."

We sat there in silence for a few minutes until June came out to join us, sighing as she sat down in one of her rocking chairs. They were from some famous company based in Marietta called Brumby Rocking Chair Company and were highly collectable, especially ones that were manufactured before the First World War. Hers were the collectible variety, made by the Brumby family in the 1920s and lovingly restored a few years ago, so she told me, to their glossy black original finish. They were certainly comfortable chairs! I was thinking of getting a few for my own home and realized with a start that I could actually afford to buy them! What a difference a few weeks made!

"How is Beau Buford doing, Brian? Is he out of the hospital yet?" June tsk'd, still upset that someone tried to run the deputy off the road and possibly kill him.

"What was he doing when the incident happened?" I asked this because I realized with my intent focused on Adelaide and Chad, I hadn't taken the time to ask about Bubba's condition and his attack, making me feel heartless. Until I remembered his unwanted advances, then I reeled in the guilt trip a touch.

"I had given him an assignment. He was following up on a lead, and he went to go interview a suspect on my list, and he had just called in that he spoke with the man's parents, but supposedly their son wasn't at the farm that morning. Next thing I knew, Sheriff Glen received a call that someone ran the deputy off the road intentionally."

I felt my pulse hitch and quickly asked, "Would the person he was looking to interview be a Harley Jacobs? Oliver Brewster mentioned him as a possible suspect today." I refused to think of that odious man as a reverend, more like a wolf in sheep's clothing. A deranged, rabid wolf. "He said Harley might have been one of Adelaide's suitors back then."

Brian nodded yes, and my face fell, and everyone noticed. Brian quickly asked me what upset me, but I took a few minutes before I answered, collecting my thoughts.

"It's just that, well, I guess I painted this image of Adelaide in my head, and with just one day of sleuthing, I'm starting to think she may have been one of the town hussies. At least it seems that way by what several people have recounted. Maybe Nora is right, and she *was* evil." I sniffled a little as I said this, feeling as if I was betraying Adelaide for some reason.

"Now don't you fuss none regarding your aunt Adelaide, hon. She was a breathtaking witch, just coming into her powers. She was a spirited soul and enchanted many a man, not unlike you, my dear, but a hussy? No, Adelaide was no harlot, despite what some of the people in town might have said to you. Addy made *one* mistake. Some citizens in town painted her in a bad light after that, eager to spread rumors about her. It's probably one of the main reasons she left Sweet Briar…or wanted to." June proclaimed this in a fervent display of loyalty to Adelaide that made me smile.

We were treading on thin ice, because it must have been awkward for Brian to hear about all these tales knowing some involved his own father, but it didn't seem to bother him. I figured, in a way, it all happened when he was too

197

young to realize what was going on, but as the years went by, it must have been tough on him as he heard the tales. Especially since his father seemed to have a penchant for younger women!

"She certainly didn't deserve to have someone murder her and stuff her under your porch, Lily," he stated, and I ardently agreed with his declaration.

"I just wonder what Chad had to say to me and who knew he was planning to? I mean, it wasn't common knowledge that he came over here and asked me to meet him at my property. I didn't tell anyone, and I didn't let on what his reason was for stopping by. Now I wish I did."

"Maybe someone saw you? I wonder if Gordy knows something." This came from Andrea. "Weren't they like best buds or something? Some men talk."

Suddenly, his wife Sheila's reaction at the diner seemed even more suspicious in light of this.

"I need to go speak with Sheila again," I said.

"No, let me handle her." Brian looked over toward the diner, and we could tell it was fairly busy for a Monday, and he said he'd wait until it was closer to closing time. He wasn't sure where Gordy was since he didn't do trash pickups until Thursdays and Fridays, and his off time was his own.

"Wasn't Gordy the one who told everyone that Harley ran off with that Deanna Fredricks girl, then he showed up all heart broke when she left him for a musician? He, Harley, and Chad all went to school together, so it made sense they'd know each other's business." June deliberated a bit on this information. "I remember he told Sheila that it all but broke Harley's spirit when Deanna did that. Why would he take up with Adelaide if he was so lovestruck with Deanna? It makes no sense!"

Brian scratched his head. "That's what Deputy Buford was trying to get to the bottom of before his accident, although I hate calling what was an attempt on his life as such."

This he directed at me before continuing. "Beau had a rough time of it, what with his dad passing on and being in prison. I might not like him, but I can't complain about him shirking his duties as deputy. In fact, he can be a bit too enthusiastic, kind of like he is with the opposite sex. I think I'll head over to the Jacob's farm and see if I can track down Harley and have a chat. It seems too convenient that Beau was run off the road and Harley wasn't where he was supposed to be. I'll see you ladies later on today."

I watched Brian head over to his cruiser, smarting a little from that dig. I supposed he was a tad more upset about Bubba and me than he would admit to, but with his dad's history, I could understand his not being a fan of flirting games. He pulled out onto the square, and I waved back at him as he raised his hand before directing his attention back to driving. I thought about what he just revealed about Bubba and asked June and Andrea about it.

"Bubba's father...Brian mentioned he passed on. He died? In prison?"

June shook her head and worried her bottom lip with her teeth.

"Oh, that Ross Gunford. He was a no-good ne'er-do-well and after a series of petty crimes and misdemeanors got mixed up in the theft of a liquor store over in Clayton or thereabouts with some of his no-good friends. Before anyone knew what happened, the proprietor, an eighty-five-year-old war hero, was shot dead, and his employee lost an eye to a wild bullet. Ross and his buddies were the only suspects. It was a stupid robbery that went horribly wrong when they thought the old man made a move to grab a gun behind the counter. He wasn't even armed! Mores the pity, because if he did have a weapon that day, all those hoodlums would be pushing up daisies instead of rotting in a jail cell. Well, all but Ross. He went in as an accessory to murder and was serving twenty-five years when he died of throat cancer. Good riddance, I say, even if that makes me a bad person."

She paused, and I could tell she had more to say on the subject but just shook her head. Andrea took up the story in a hushed voice. "Everyone knew he beat Donna. They never got married, despite what she or some people might say, although Beau is his kid. Donna never did give him his daddy's last name, calling him Buford instead, after his Uncle Glen, our sheriff, who has been doing his best by the boy— well, man now." Andrea finished with a sigh.

"This town sure does have a bunch of skeletons in its closet." Oh, wow. I did *not* just say that!

Andrea and June burst out laughing, though—and I joined in. It certainly helped clear the air of our maudlin musings.

"Well, he certainly was a scoundrel, a thief, and an abusive man, not to mention a womanizer. He was even sniffing around Donna's baby sister, I think. Anyway, a man like that? It's a wonder Beau didn't turn out just like him. I still remember the day they arrived in town because...oh!" June's eyes got wide, and she hurriedly stood up, slamming the back of her prized rocker onto the wide plank clapboard siding.

"What's wrong?" I asked in alarm as she rushed to her back door.

"Oh, it's nothing, dear. You girls just keep visiting. I almost forgot the pie I had in the oven, and I will be a witch on a bent broomstick if I let it burn down my kitchen!"

Andrea and I laughed, shaking our heads, then decided a visit to the diner to grill Sheila might be possible if we went there in the guise of an early dinner.

* * *

WE WALKED into the diner as the lunch crowd was moving out and there was a lull before the dinner crowd came in. Donna was nowhere in sight, and a new girl, youngish in that *I'm only working here to help with college costs* way, was rushing around bussing tables. Sheila came out of the kitchen, paused when she saw us, with a slight frown, then cleared her face and came over.

Smiling in a forced way, she asked, "You ladies here for late lunch or early dinner?"

"Dinner, please!" Andrea piped up.

I chimed in with, "What's today's special?"

Joe stuck his head out of the kitchen and smiled at us. "Three days in a row! I'm starting to think one of you has a crush on me. Maybe both of you!" Then he laughed and continued, "More like you are in love with my cooking. Have the meatloaf. It's not the special today, but it's the best thing on my menu. Mashed potatoes with gravy and green beans— from my garden, mind you, none of that canned stuff here. It's my momma's recipe!"

We heartily agreed, adding two sweet teas. I was getting addicted to them by this point; the energy of one was enough to keep me going all day. When I paired it with a couple of cups of my beloved coffee, I was unstoppable!

It didn't take Sheila all that long to return to our table with two steaming plates of yummy goodness. I drooled with anticipation when I saw the platters and knew I was about to embark on culinary greatness. How Joe didn't get swept up by some big, fancy Atlanta restaurant was beyond me. His meals were gourmet perfection on a blue-collar budget.

She set our plates down and made a little squeal of joy when she spied the cat charm on Andrea's necklace.

"Isn't that just darling? I love cats. Gordy and I never

could have children of our own, so we decided we'd be the crazy cat people. I have eight." Then she dithered a bit, correcting herself, and went on, "Well, we had eight. Donna has one of our babies now. She lives next door, and one of our babies got out by accident a couple of days ago and got into her yard, and she fell in love with her. We agreed she should keep Millie. That's her name. I raised her since she was a day-old kitten."

Sheila looked sad, and I wondered why she'd let one of her babies live with Donna. She noticed my frown and rushed to explain. "I'm just being silly. Donna loves my girl, and she's all alone now that Beau moved into an apartment near the police station." Well, that explained it. I figured the two women were good friends, living next door to each other and working in the same place, and I said so.

"Oh yes, I mean, we don't have much in common, but she's a neighbor, and we get along here. We know the work-ings of this place and keep it running smoothly for Joe. Gordy built her a cat pen yesterday so Millie could go outside for a spell but not *be* outside where she could run off, you know?"

I noticed that Sheila started fidgeting when she mentioned her husband, and I went into detective mode, but first I wanted to put her at ease again, so I showed her my cat earrings. She smiled in delight, remarking at how unique they were, saying she'd love to have a pair for herself. We were halfway through our dinners and Sheila only ran off once to get us refills on our tea. When she returned, I got us back on track. Feeling slightly guilty for bringing up the murders again, knowing this little chat would suddenly take a turn into the unpleasant, I lowered my voice and asked my question.

"Sheila," I paused, waiting until I had her complete atten-tion, "what does Gordy think about Chad's murder? I heard he and Chad were good friends, along with Harley Jacobs. What do you think might have happened?"

She opened and closed her mouth a few times, just as she had the other day, but this time she didn't run off.

"I don't know what you mean asking that. Why would I know anything? Why would Gordy?"

She looked around the diner as if someone might come to her aid and take her away from our questions, only there was no one left except an older couple sharing a piece of blueberry pie. The young waitress was in attendance, in case they needed anything, and kept herself busy re-stocking the napkin holders. I was momentarily distracted with vision of blueberry goodness, covered in a dollop of fresh whipped cream, and had to stop myself from groaning a little. I was about to order a slice for myself when Sheila spoke up.

"I don't know. I mean…oh, I think Joe is calling me!"

Sheila spun around and raced into the kitchen. I was getting up to go follow her, determined to get to the bottom of her skittish behavior, when Andrea reached up and grabbed my arm, stopping me.

"Wait, cuz, look who's outside!"

I turned to look out the window and saw a man driving an old Dodge truck, more rust than white, with the words Polk's Garbage & Recycling painted on the driver door. He parked his truck and got out, but instead of coming into the diner, where I assumed he was heading, he went into the drugstore.

"Come on!" Andrea threw down enough money to cover our meal plus a hefty tip, and we ran out of the diner and hoofed it as quick as we could over to the drugstore. Before we entered, I stopped short and yanked my cousin back, stopping her forward motion.

"Ugh!" Andrea had to steady herself to keep from tipping over and barked at me, "What are you doing? I almost fell!"

"Yes, what *are* you two doing?"

Startled, the two of us looked over to where the voice asking that question was coming from, only to see our great-grandmother trotting across the street looking like a tiny bat all dressed in black, cloak flapping behind her.

"Where's the fire, girls?"

She looked back and forth as if expecting an answer then sighed when we stood there like two mute Dodo birds.

"We, um…good evening, Granny. We were just going to corner Gordy Polk in the drugstore and ask him his thoughts on Chad's murder. Among other things. Only I stopped Andrea, just now, because I thought we needed to be on the same page. We needed a plan."

"You don't have time for that." Adriana looked at us like naughty pupils who let her down after hours of intense instruction.

"Uh…we don't?"

Great, open your mouth and prove you are *a Dodo bird there, Lily.* I was trying to figure out what she meant by this when she rolled her eyes so hard, I thought she made the Earth's axis shift by two degrees.

"No, dummy, you don't. Gordy has nothing to do with this nasty business, believe me. I heard on the grapevine that your detective has been having a difficult time finding Harley Jacobs. If he'd spend less time worrying about you making out with every boy in this town and started doing police work like he's supposed to, he'd probably have this case solved already. That's the trouble with men. They don't think with their brains, they think with their—"

"Okay, Granny! Thanks for that nugget of wisdom," Andrea gulped out, giving me a look that spoke volumes on what she thought about Adriana's line of thought. "What were you saying about Harley Jacobs?"

"I wasn't saying. You stopped me before I could finish my

thought. I guess you two wusses can't handle a woman that shoots it straight, but that's not my problem. My problem is the two of you are wasting time, and Harley just showed up in town and went over to the hardware store. He's been there for about twenty minutes now, so you better hurry up and corner him! Pronto!"

Oh! Well, okay then, if she was sure Gordy was not important. I was momentarily distracted when Adriana call Brian *my* detective. But I mentally shook my head to focus on what she told us. The thought of getting *to* Harley *before* Brian could, did kind of make me excited. Competitive? Me? You betcha!

Adriana noticed the excited look on my face, nodded with satisfaction, and said, "*Vai a prenderli…*go get him, girls!"

Then she went into the diner, and I suspected Sheila was about to get round two of an interrogation; I almost felt sorry for her. Almost. *Go get her yourself, Granny!* I was sure we'd compare notes at a later date.

Hurrying across the street and past June's Emporium, we hastened into the hardware store when suddenly it was Andrea who grabbed my arm and spun me around, shushing me before I could protest.

She motioned for me to crouch down, and while I complied, I gave her an inquiring look. That's when I heard Dennis arguing with a man. I assumed it to be Harley Jacobs, as there were no other people in sight.

"I don't know why you're getting upset with me, Harley. I had nothing to do with this!" Dennis sounded agitated, but mildly so compared to Harley, who was definitely shouting, which I suspected hid the sound of our arrival, allowing us to spy on their conversation without being detected.

"I'm upset because that Lily Sweet shows up, and suddenly things that were better left buried in the past start raising their ugly heads again. And now Chad is dead, and who is going to answer for that? They go and find Adelaide under that porch, and suddenly everyone wants to talk to me. Well, I don't want to talk to no one, understand? I had nothing to do with her. My heart belonged to Deanna until she broke it."

He yelled so loudly that I heard the glass-break alarm thingamabob above their heads chirp once, as if it was worried it might have to signal a break in.

"I'm not going to rehash all those memories with nobody, not even that son of Dillon's. For all we know, *he* did Chad in himself. And don't he have cause to do so? What with his daddy hot for Adelaide and breaking his momma's heart all those years ago? Then when she disappeared, he started drinking. Then Jess left, and finally Charles. So, what does he do? He took his-self over to Ridgepole Creek and hung himself on a tree down by its bank, leaving that boy sittin' in the car until he couldn't wait no more. Next thing you know, he wandered down by the water only to see his daddy hanging there dead. Thing like that's gotta make a young'un go to a dark place. Maybe all those dark thoughts came flooding out now, and Brian decided to shut Chad up. That old fool wouldn't stop talking about Adelaide, Charlie, Jessica, and Dillon, not to mention Brian's momma. Rita is the one with blood on her hands, mark my words. She always wanted to be a dark witch. Maybe she found herself one in her boy. We don't know his mind. I had nothing to do with nothing back then."

Here he paused and held back a sob. I felt awful, like a voyeur who maybe got more than they bargained for, and I wondered how we could slip out before being spotted. My mind was reeling at what I was hearing, however, and we remained in our hiding spot.

"Don't talk about Rita that way. You know what's she's

been through. Her boy, too. Brian is a good man. He's over-come a lot in his young life."

Dennis scolded Harley Jacobs then slammed his fist down on the counter for emphasis.

"I just want to be left alone, damn it."

With that, Harley Jacobs stormed out of the hardware store, and Andrea and I let out the breaths we were holding without realizing we were doing so.

"You girls can come out now. He's gone."

We both shared a shocked expression and stood up as Dennis Carter came walking over to us.

"I could see your reflections in that mirror over there. You both looked like two foxes that got caught in a hen house by an angry rooster. I'm sorry you had to hear all that."

Andrea looked sheepish but then told Dennis we weren't upset at all and that we were doing a bit of investigating on our own. For a minute, I wasn't sure Dennis heard her since he stayed in one spot rubbing his chin. Then he pinned us both with a glare and, pointing a finger in our direction, shouted, "Forget what you heard here. Don't you two go accusing Rita of anything or you'll have to answer to me! Do I make myself clear?"

CHAPTER 20

The next evening, I was up in my room going over events of the last two days and was still a bit rattled with how upset Dennis became when discussing Rita. Andrea and I wondered if he might have been sweet on her when they were younger, but circumstances had him choosing June, and Rita stayed with Dillon Chase. That didn't make sense, though, when you considered how much Rita seemed to love her husband. What a tangled mess. I was trying to keep it all straight. My thoughts turned to what Dennis said regarding Rita wanting to be a dark witch and how it might pertain to Brian.

This morning, Andrea and I had walked to her dad's café for coffee and a treat when we ran into Stu, of all people. He agreed to join us at our table, especially when we bribed him with a French cruller. To say he was recalcitrant was putting it mildly, but after a smidge of gentle handling, we found him rather talkative in that Stu way of his.

He informed us that he had a good alibi for the time when Adelaide went missing and was upset to hear Donna had cast him in a bad light.

"Now she must have known I got called up to do some military work. I still was in the army back then. Did you two know I was in the Army?" He looked off into space, and I suspected he was reliving his glory days in service. Or maybe he just had gas.

After a few more minutes, Andrea decided to prod him. "You were saying?" she asked.

"I was sayin'? What was I sayin'? Oh, yeah. I would leave for a few months at a time. Adelaide was still alive when I left and gone when I got back…I never saw her again…not that we were ever close. I was here two weeks then had to leave again. When I got back next, I found out your momma left and then your daddy. Sad times."

Stu pulled at his bottom lip then proceeded to consume his cruller and drink down his coffee before belching loudly. Then he just sat there looking at us, like he was wondering why we were there. After a second, his eyes opened wide.

"Oh, yeah. 'Course I liked Rita, a lot…but what motive would I have to kill your aunt? I never truly believed Rita would have anything to do with me, I am older than she is. I have me a lady friend over in Clermont now. Don't look so shocked." He sniffed, offended. "Back then, she was married and," he blushed furiously when he continued telling us his tale, "well, we were sinning what with her husband still in the picture. He used to hit her. But now he's gone, passed away from cancer, poor bastard, and she and I have been seeing each other proper."

He sat there, and his mouth spread into a wide grin. Yet again, he took the time to look off into the distance and let his thoughts wander—or he lost some brain cells. Nobody could really tell.

"I had no reason to hurt Adelaide, or Chad for that matter. I moved on from Rita a long time ago. My lady friend deserves all of my heart, not a piece of it."

BETTINA M JOHNSON

Why, Stu, you old dog. Who knew he had so many layers? Maybe because it took so long to get anything out of him, nobody bothered to listen. We believed him. Although I would pass this information on to Brian to double check— just in case. I questioned whether both his sisters knew he had a sweetheart. I smiled at the thought. Good old Stu.

We considered going back and confronting Dennis Carter on his reaction the day before but instead decided to meet his son for lunch. Jake had a few cases going on at the courthouse, so it was a brief one, but it was nice to catch up with him since I hadn't seen much of him lately. He warned me to stay safe and rushed back to his office. I wondered what type of trials he saw being a witch and all. How different were they from regular folk? I had so much to learn about my new life.

Andrea and I parted ways after that. She had errands she needed to do for her dad. I decided to head home and take that long, hot bath I promised myself a few days ago. I really needed some down time. After my bath, I spent a good twenty minutes catching my great-grandmother up to speed on our investigation, comparing notes with her on a phone call. She said she had some new theories after speaking with Sheila yesterday and wanted to meet soon but didn't want to jump the gun until she had solid evidence. She informed me she would work all night on this and get with me in the morning. Did that old woman not sleep? I suddenly had visions of her hanging upside down, like a bat, in her home, working on her detecting skills, and shuddered.

Slipping on my jean jacket, for nights had finally started cooling down, I decided to go for a walk around the village green. I glanced at the clock and noted it was coming up on eleven but didn't think I'd get into too much trouble wandering around the town this late. Heh, in New York City things would just be gearing up, even on a Tuesday night.

Amused at the differences between the two places, I slipped out of my apartment, went down the stairs, then headed out the side door going in the direction of the park. I hoped the clear night air would settle my nerves.

I had just reached the sidewalk out front when I realized I hadn't been back to my house, making me search my bag to see if I had my key with me. When my hand made contact with it, I made a split-second decision to head over there instead and started out in a slow jog. I wondered if I should have told someone where I was headed, but I didn't want to disturb anyone at this late hour.

It didn't take me all that long to get there, and as I approached, my mind went to the box I had found in the desk. With all the excitement over the last few days, I totally forgot about it. This was almost enough to make me stop in my tracks and run back to my apartment to see what was inside, but then I looked at my home and knew it could wait a while longer. I fretted at my propensity for forgetting I had the box in my possession and shook my head, promising myself to make opening it a priority the next day. Right now, the lure of finding out if my mom had left other such items behind was too intriguing, willing me to take another stab at this treasure hunt of sorts.

Aunt Chiara informed me that the electricity was indeed on again, after having the account switched to my name. As I entered, I reached my hand out to flick on the switch in the foyer but paused. Knowing I wasn't doing anything wrong, yet not wanting to advertise my presence, I decided to keep it dark. I locked the front door behind me instead. I crept through the house until I entered the office again, and walked over to the desk then turned the table lamp on, filling the room with its warm glow. I sat in the leather chair and took a moment to look around.

After discussions with my family about the time I left

Sweet Briar, I discovered I was a child of three-and-three-quarter years the last time they saw me. We left town after Halloween and Thanksgiving, which meant I would have turned four in three more months. For almost four years my mother and father lived in this house with me and Aunt Adelaide. Four years, yet I could not recall the man who raised me, nor my aunt. I had no sense of ever being in this house. All that time, I played with Nora and Douglas, Lorcan and Jake, yet had no memory of them nor any of my other relatives. I couldn't recall the town or the surrounding area; nothing looked familiar.

I never questioned this in depth before, but now it was twinging in the recesses of my mind as a touch too peculiar, especially when recalling the conversation with Lorcan regarding our playdates. Why did he and Jake remember me, yet I had what appeared to be some kind of blockage, preventing me from having any memories? Well, that wasn't exactly true, since I could remember the day of the kitten incident with ease. I knew I needed to speak to my aunts or great-grandmother about this oddity.

Brushing it off as something to worry about later, I focused on the desk in front of me. I spent two hours going over the papers I found inside and on it, and while nothing out of the ordinary stood out, I was touched upon finding notes written back and forth between my parents. They weren't love notes or even endearments...but the mundane "we need to take Lily to the park next week, there's going to be fireworks," or "Lily needs a few new garments, she's growing so big," that struck a chord. Proof that I had a life before it was just me and Mom alone in the world. What on Earth had happened here to make her leave and not tell anyone? Why had my dad left, and where did he go? Why did he not come after us? Who might know more about this, and would they talk to me?

I needed to find out if there was any news regarding the missing evidence, my aunt and Chad and, well, anything really. I also wanted to compare notes with Brian and knew I needed to speak with Adriana, in the morning, as she requested.

I took out my notebook and went to write down all these things as something to find out in the morning then thought, *Well, maybe this is not so important.* I paused, shaking my head. No, it *was* important. Why did I always stop myself from questioning my past? I reached up and stroked my earrings, immediately calming down, and went to dismiss my mild paranoia as silliness, but then I stilled.

I felt something building inside me as if it was fighting against my very thoughts, forcing me to confront them instead of ignoring them. My hand, the one that had the ring on it, was tingling and felt hotter than the other. I was getting uneasy once more, my heartbeat hitching up a few beats. I went to touch my ears again when I saw a sparkle of blue light wisp out of my fingertips. Then a lightbulb went off in my head.

No. It couldn't be, could it? With trembling hands, I reached up to remove one earring but was suddenly overcome with the urge to stop and forget such nonsense. Forget. No. Again, I felt something forcing me to continue. My right hand throbbed and sparked blue, truly a battle of wills, like I had two minds fighting for dominance. I clenched my jaw and forced myself to remove one earring, then the next, my breath exploding out of me in a great whoosh when I accomplished this. I hadn't even realized I was holding it for so long.

I sat back, waiting to see if I felt different. I could hear the clock ticking in the room, counting the seconds then the minutes as I remained idle. Nothing. I didn't know what I was expecting but didn't feel the slightest bit different.

Feeling pretty foolish, and chuckling to myself for resorting to such histrionics, I happened to glance up on the shelf across the room and spied my favorite book of fairytales sitting on the shelf. I beamed at it then proceeded to open the next drawer down, continuing my search.

Then I froze.

Slowly raising my gaze to the book again, I felt my mouth go dry and my heartrate skyrocket. That's my book. No, not one I had read over and over again as a kid then packed to bring down with me on my move. That's was *my* book. One I remembered having been read to as a little girl, curled up in bed at night all tucked in, teeth and hair brushed, my reward for completing these tasks. That very book was read to me as a bedtime ritual—by my aunt Adelaide.

Rolling the chair back so quickly that I slammed into the wall behind me, I was shaking my head in denial. However hard I was fighting that memory, another one quickly replaced it, making me gasp in surprise.

"Lily, my sweet darling girl, settle down now so we can read the next chapter. Do you remember where we left off?"

"Oh, yes! That wicked lady took Ariel's voice away and she couldn't speak any more. I'm sad. Do you think she will get it back? Do you?"

"Well, we are about to find out. Shall I continue to read? Or do you want to keep asking me so many questions?"

"Read please, read! Except...well, do you think I can make magic someday like you do, so I can turn myself into a mermaid and be Ariel?"

"Oh, sweet child, you make me laugh so much. Anything is possible, Lily. I can't wait to teach you everything I know about magic, my little witch."

"Adelaide! Stop filling her head with such thoughts. She has such a vivid imagination already; you are making it worse!"

"Okay, Jess, okay...see? Naughty girl, you got me in trouble. Maybe I will be banished forever from this house, never to read to you again. Then where will that get us?"

"You girls are too much. My poor baby. Stop teasing her Adelaide or I will banish you myself."

"Okay, Charles, I'm just having a bit of fun with her, that's all. I can go and you two can take over reading duties!"

"No, stay, please! I will be good. Promise! Please read me the next chapter, please?"

I felt the tears running down my face before I realized I was crying. I remembered. I remembered them both. My aunt Adelaide and my father Charles. I recalled that night like it happened yesterday. My entire body was vibrating, and I experienced such a massive sense of loss, and betrayal, that I didn't know whether I was ever going to recover from it. How could my mother do this to me? Why would she prevent me from keeping all my memories? What spell did she put on these earrings and why?

I stood and rushed from the office into the kitchen. There was the table I remembered sitting at eating cereal and watching cartoons on the small television we used to keep on a rolling table. Looking around, I didn't see it, but I did see a chest in the corner of the den, and moving zombie-like, I propelled myself forward then sank to my knees before it. I knew what I would find in there before I even opened it. Holding my breath, I lifted the lid and was rewarded by the sight of my childhood toys.

A fabric doll I received on my third birthday that I named Amy, sporting a head of orange, curly hair made out of yarn, met my gaze. I picked her up, amazed at how small she seemed. The material was a creamy yellow with a fish on her front, the words "Save A Fish" printed under it, which matched the orange color of her hair. She was a gift from my dad when we went to Octoberfest in Helen, Georgia, and I didn't snitch on him when he let me taste his beer. My bean-bag koala, Sam, his one eye sewn back on by my mother when I managed to pull it off by accident while roughhous-ing, was there. My little plastic finger puppet dragon that I named Pee Wee, his tail showing teeth marks where I used to chew on him while watching cartoons, was tucked underneath.

I kept going through the trunk, toy after toy, memory after memory, all coming back to me in small but definite rushes. I stood, tucking my doll, bear, and dragon into my bag, and made my way into the dining room. I walked over to the china hutch and pulled off the sheet. There was my grandmother's china, my dad's mother, Rosetta. I never met her or my grandfather Antonio Junior, because they had already died in that car accident somewhere in Asia, Singa-pore, I thought. I remembered my dad telling me all about them, and how his dad, Tony, couldn't take his eyes off of the gorgeous witch he met in Sienna, Italy, when he was a transfer student in college. He came home that semester with memories of Italy and engaged to his beautiful Rosie, and they set up house here. This home came to my father upon their death.

I went into the living room and looked at the portrait of Adriana again. I remembered Christmas Day in this very room with the fireplace crackling, tree in the corner near it with the bubble lights and tinsel, glass ornaments glowing, and the record player on with holiday music. My dad would sit in the chair near the fire and read me stories about ghosts and Christmas pudding, mistletoe and sleighs. I went over to it now and curled up on it and started sobbing. I couldn't help myself; the loss of everything I knew was too profound.

* * *

I MUST HAVE DOZED off for a bit, because the next thing I knew, something jarred me awake as I sat motionless in complete darkness. My mind might have been playing tricks on me, but then the sound repeated itself. Footsteps? Maybe. A rattling sound like someone trying a doorknob. That, too, but subtly—as if someone was creeping around trying to remain undetected. The hair on my arms and the back of my neck bristled as fear coursed through my body. I felt my adrenaline kick in.

What could I do? Then I remembered my magic. Untrained though I was, it wasn't as if I was helpless; I hoped. I stood up and quietly crept toward the noise, which, upon reflection, seemed to come from the office—and froze. I left the light on in there. That meant someone was in the house with me! Looking around for something to use as a weapon, I was startled when I saw a shadow cross the front porch, pause at the front door, and try the knob. I thanked the heavens above that I had locked it when I arrived, so I deduced whoever it was remained out and not inside with me as I thought. But they were attempting to enter, it seemed. The shadow went back the way it came, and I moved to follow through my home when a strange noise made me pause. Was that a walkie-talkie or a police radio? I heard another soft scratchy broadcast, but whoever was out there had the receiver turned down low, so it was difficult to discern what was being said.

Smiling with relief, I figured it was probably Sheriff Glen or, even better, Brian, come to investigate why the light was on in one of the rooms, and I went to the front door to let them know it was only me. I opened the door and walked around to the side porch, which was on the same side as the office. This was unfortunate, because not only was the hole currently not repaired, I still got the willies from being too near it. Calling out to whomever it was, I tittered a bit and said, "Hey, guys, it's only me, Lily. I just came by go through some things and take inventory."

No one was standing there, as I presumed, which I thought curious, and I wondered if they were now coming around the other side of the property. Feeling like I was playing a game of cat and mouse, I was tempted to call out again so as not to alarm my visitor. About to head the other way, I heard a noise behind me. Before I could turn and look, I felt a bone-crushing explosion on the back of my skull and felt myself pitching forward into darkness.

* * *

WHY WERE those lousy birds singing when it was still dark out? I mean, really! Couldn't they wait for the sun to be up at least? My head was foggy, and I felt odd, and I realized my room smelled musty. How could that be? June changed my sheets just yesterday, and it always smelled of roses from all the potpourri sachets she had everywhere. Ugh. Why was the bed so hard? I went to shift, but an incredible pain shot through my body, and I curled into a fetal position. That's when I discovered I was lying on dirt. What the heck? I went to sit up and bashed my head onto something sharp, causing me to scream out in pain. I felt blood spurt from my temple and gritted my teeth, trying to remain focused and not pass out. I suddenly had an unrealistic fear that I was buried alive and inside a coffin, but no, why would I feel the dirt?

I sat there crouched down, feeling around in the dark, my brain desperate to remember the last thing that happened to explain my circumstance. I put my hand to my temple to stave off the flow of blood and pulled a long splinter out of it. Ouch! I slowly opened my eyes, realizing as I did, that I could make out soft rays of sunshine peeking through the cracks of whatever was above me. Looking up, I saw a rather large opening and what looked like a roof and a sliver of sky. The sun was out, which explained the light. A hole? Above me and *oh my God*! I was in the hole! I was in the same lousy place in my porch that not only had Chad gotten stuck in but where I discovered Aunt Adelaide's skeleton.

Even worse, I tasted what had to be dirt in my mouth and gagged at the prospect of ingesting the very ground where a body had slowly decayed for the last twenty years! Oh, this was *not* happening to me! Yuck! Revulsion and fear were competing with pain and anger. You bet I was mad. Some asshat knocked me out, probably trying to kill me, and was more than likely laughing at the irony of where my bruised body landed. I was so going to lose it on this jerk when I could manage to get myself out of my current predicament.

I methodically and deliberately crawled under the opening and just as gently stood up. Hands reaching either side of the gap in the floorboards, I slowly pulled myself out then rolled away from it and leaned against the house. Glancing around, I gathered too late that I was in the same spot the very dead Chad Barwick was propped when I found him.

Bloody hell.

I gingerly stood and managed to hobble around to the front door when I collided into someone's crotch. What? I was bent in half and in extreme pain here. You would have done the same thing. My fight or flight kicked in, and I screamed and flailed out. At the same time, I heard a man groaning and a tremendous crash as he fell to the ground. Oops, must have been a direct hit. Sorry, not sorry.

I was just rearing back to kick out when I glanced down and saw Jake lying in a ball protecting his, ahem, um, protecting the family jewels from further attack. He was writhing around, albeit slowly, but managed to look up at me, his eyes going wide. Great, I must look like the *Creature from the Black Lagoon*.

"Oh my God. What the hell happened to you?"

Yeah, buddy, that's what I'd like to know.

CHAPTER 21

*I*t was one thing to be fussed over and cared for when hurt, but this was borderline smothering. I was on the sofa at Eileen and Henry Reid's place. Jake carried me there since he literally ran into Henry rushing over from his yard when he heard the commotion. No…really.

We had a slapstick comedy moment. Jake, holding me in his arms, decided I was too delicate to walk, and hobbling around the side of the house as fast as he could, literally slammed into Henry as he was heading our way at top speed. I screamed from the pain of being squished between two men and felt myself being unceremoniously dropped onto the ground.

I took Jake down with me; Henry was already there. That's when we noticed the impact had knocked his dentures clear out of his mouth.

Eileen screamed from her back porch, which sent Lorcan flying out of the house and over to us in record speed. He even came to a sliding halt, kicking dust and dirt up and sending gravel pellets everywhere.

Then the testosterone moment began in earnest. Jake, still

sore from my stellar head-butting skills to his groin, groaned loudly when reattempting to lift my battered body. Lorcan, seeing this display of "weakness," insisted he should be the one to carry me, and the two of them started arguing. This posturing went back and forth for what seemed like hours, which made me start crying. They were so in each other's faces, they failed to notice my distress, putting them high on my poop list. Something else unobserved was no one bothering to help poor Henry retrieve his teeth, which he just wiped off with a little spit cleaning and reinserted. Eileen screamed again, this time at Henry.

We managed to get settled in the Reid's family room, where I finally got the attention I needed. My happiness was short lived. Eileen believed I needed professional care, so against my wishes, the EMT was called. It took Shirley Jones less than three minutes to arrive, which had me suspecting the neighbors, hearing the commotion, had already called for assistance. Sheriff Glen was on her heels, proving my point, and was trying to interview everyone but was having little luck doing so. Lorcan was pacing the room, sending out curse word after curse word, while his mom reprimanded him, as she began fluffing pillows around my head.

Things got dicey when Aunt Iona showed up. I wasn't sure who called her, but she came flying in the door with a huge carpetbag filled with witchy stuff. Shirley, who was trying to tend to me with traditional methods, had a run in with Aunt Iona, who was trying to get me to drink some awful concoction that I was sure a junior witch flunked at making in potions class. Henry and Jake were alternating shouting into their phones, but I couldn't make out who they were speaking to.

I thought perhaps it was Brian, and then I recalled last night and shot off the sofa, much to the alarm of everyone present. The police! No way. I remembered just before being conked on the noggin hearing a police radio. I also thought of what we surmised be an inside job at the morgue, then my thoughts became even more disturbing when I recollected Dennis Carter's reaction over Rita Chase and her son. Brian. Her son Brian, the police detective, who discovered the body of his father hanging in a tree by the creek because of my aunt.

With Glen Buford sweet on his future wife back in the day, leaving him out as a prime suspect, and his nephew, Beau "Bubba" Buford the victim of an attack, making him highly unlikely to be involved in Chad's murder, it left only one police officer that I knew had any ties to the events from the past. Brian Chase. I was confident the sound I heard last night was a police radio!

"No, dear, sit. Come back here. You shouldn't be up!" Eileen led me back gently toward the sofa. I was suddenly feeling dizzy. A heavy fog-like wooziness was taking over, and I tried to fight it. What was *in* that brew Aunt Iona gave me? Or was it the shot Shirley managed to sneak while she wasn't looking? Oh my gosh, what bad timing!

"No...I...Brian."

Aunt Iona clucked and patted me on the shoulder.

"Yes, yes, we will call him over, but you need to relax before he gets here. A few hours one way or the other won't matter much. He will sit right by your side until you awaken, I'm sure." Smiling at me, she tucked an afghan around my shoulders, helping me to lay back on a pillow.

Sit with me?! Oh my God, they were sending me off to la la land and inviting a murderer to stand watch over me. How nice. It wasn't like I could make them comprehend the danger that this would put me in when my tongue felt numb and double its size. I had to try once again.

"No...Brian...help."

"Yes, dear. Brian will find out who did this to you. Never you worry about that."

Aunt Iona was trying to kill me. Okay, she didn't *know* my doom was arriving in the form of a hot police detective with wild black hair and a perfect five o'clock shadow—but coming he was. The bastard. He flirted with me, kissed me even. If I wasn't so bruised and stoned off my rocker, I'd give him a piece of my mind. *After* I zapped him to the Almighty and back. How *could* he?

The last thing I remembered was Lorcan and Jake standing side by side, staring at me, concern dripping off them as my eyelids shut for the last time. Or so I thought.

* * *

I WOKE up in my room. Birds were chirping, and the sun was just peeking up over the town square. I could hear a lawn mower whirring in the distance and felt a cool breeze from the window, which was opened a crack. The curtains fluttered as the smell of coffee and some baked goods reached my nose. Blinking slowly, the first thing I realized was my apparent death hadn't occurred yet; the second thing to hit me was somehow I had managed to get home to June's, not having been accosted by my attacker, and was safe for the moment. Breathing in deeply, I only winced slightly from pain that must still be dulled because I was convinced I bruised a rib. I let it out in a sigh of relief and swung my legs off the bed, standing up. Okay, not too bad. I managed to creep into the bathroom and look at my face in the mirror. Not a good idea.

I looked like a stitched-up doll. No, I looked like Sally from *Nightmare Before Christmas*, only worse. The cut on my temple was angry and bruised, crusted over with a scab. My hair was matted. I was still in the jeans from yesterday, but someone, June maybe, had put me in a new top. My eye had a good-sized shiner starting, and they were bloodshot enough to make any junkie out there jealous. Dislike.

I slipped on my Keds when the third thing to hit me made my blood run cold. A motorcycle was approaching fast, and what's worse, I recognized whose it was. Brian! He was coming to finish me off! I hobbled over to the window just in time to see June pulling out of the driveway in her car, waving to Brian, who waved back. He then turned and spied me peering out my window at him. Instead of trying to pretend by smiling, he scowled at me, and that's when I knew I was right.

Backing away from the window, I grabbed my purse, my keys, and a paperweight on the desk by my bed. What? It was a hand-painted rock! More pet rock then paperweight, but it would make a decent weapon! What else was I supposed to reach for, a bat? Oh! Jake's bat! I pulled it off the wall in my room, noting it had a nice weight to it. Not waiting another second, I ran, as best I could, out of my apartment and down the stairs, flying into the shop's kitchen to look for a good hiding place.

Too late to find a perfect spot, I heard Brian enter, so I quietly placed my frame up against the wall behind the kitchen door. I waited for him to go up the stairs to my apartment. And waited. Nothing. I listened carefully, and I could hear him breathing on the other side of the door. Did he suspect I ran, figuring out it was him yesterday and already out of his menacing grasp? Would he look in here? I hoped so. I was ready to bash his brains out, the big meanie. That awful, bad, boyfriend, biker cop, meanie.

"Lily? You up there, still?"

Yeah right, bucko. Like I'm about to answer you and make it easy. Not.

A few more seconds passed, then I heard him climbing

the stairs. I had a few choices here. I could run like a madwoman out the back door to my truck, but he might be down the stairs quicker than I could make my escape. I could head out the front but wasn't sure I could unlock the door in time and reach the street where I was sure help could be flagged down. Or, and this one gave me some perverse pleasure upon contemplation, I could stay right where I was and use the bat like a pro-baseball player, knocking Brian's head clear off his shoulders then doing a victory dance over his dead body.

Yeah, I could do that!

I softly moved into position, placing my purse on the table June used to toss her keys and mail on. Raising the bat over my head, I stood like a rookie batter at the plate in his first World Series appearance, hoping for a home run. Or in my case, a solid connection to the head of my quarry. I waited patiently, visions of parades and the key to the city being bestowed on me for capturing the town psychopath, when I heard someone clearing their throat on the other side of the room.

"What do you think you're doing?"

Brian was standing at the entrance to the store from the kitchenette, and belatedly I remembered my *own* kitchen upstairs, complete with the back staircase that led to the store front. I felt betrayed by my own apartment and wanted to kick myself for being such a fool for not remembering its existence. So, I did what any dark witch heroine would do.

I screamed and threw the bat at Brian's head, hearing a satisfying *bonk* as it made contact.

Not waiting around to see if he'd congratulate me for my accuracy, I hightailed it out the back door and reached my truck, only realizing too late that I had left my bag inside.

"Stupid, stupid, stupid, idiot!" I remanded myself and swung my head all around, looking for an escape route.

Racing to the back of the building, figuring Brian would assume I'd head straight to the square where people might be out and about, I tore over to the rickety fence lining the property and squeezed through to the alley beyond. I tore up the street toward Main and couldn't believe my eyes when I saw my unlikely hero of sorts. Bubba was walking toward me, looking a bit battered himself, and stopped short when he noticed me approaching.

"Bubba! Help! I'm being chased by Brian, um, Chase!" That sounded idiotic, even to my ears. "Really…I think I have proof he killed Chad and probably knows who killed my aunt all those years back. Please. It must have been his mother, Rita. Help me. Hurry!"

Instead of running toward the shop and confronting Brian, Bubba grabbed my shoulders and tried to calm me down.

"Okay, darlin,' you sure about that? Dang, girl, but you are messed up good." Leading me in the opposite direction toward Main Street, he continued tugging my arm. "Let's go this way. My momma is right there in her car, see? We can get in and drive over to the police department and get Sheriff Buford."

Well, fine, be that way. Then again, I could see why Bubba wouldn't want to confront the detective all by himself. Brian was lean, mean, and looked like he could bench press one hundred and fifty pounds without breaking much of a sweat. Bubba, in comparison, looked like he *weighed* one hundred and fifty pounds more than he should. Yeah, maybe running was the smartest course of action.

We headed to Donna's car, which looked like it had seen better days, a large white scratch up one side met a mangled front end, as it idled in the street. She looked beyond confused when I gushed, "Thank you," and scrambled in. Bubba followed me into the back as she tore away from the curb and peeled up Main Street toward the diner. Turning left, she followed the square, but instead of continuing to the police station, she made a sharp right heading north and flew past the inn and Catholic Church. Why were we heading north out of the town toward the state border?

"Where are we going? Isn't Sheriff Glen at the station? Is he where we're heading?" I looked at Donna through the rearview mirror and saw her eyes dancing with mirth. "Um, I just told Bubba that I discovered Brian Chase might be the murderer." But even as the words left my mouth, I realized I was looking into the eyes of a mad woman and sitting next to the crazy lady's son. Especially when he started laughing in a very menacing and familiar way. I might have whimpered a little when he roughly pushed me down on the seat. Looking up into his grey eyes, the memory of that same hyena-like laugh made all the blood in my body run cold. Oh, hell no, it was not.

"What's the matter, Lily? You gonna cry like a little baby? You gonna cry baby tears, little girl?"

Okay, so it was.

My eyes locked onto his grey ones, oh so familiar to me now. How in all the world did I manage to not only reconnect with the mean boy from my past but have his odiously vile mother be as sick and demented as he was? Then I realized how bad a situation I was in, locked away in a speeding car and heading out of town away from anyone who might know where I was.

Brian. I thought of what I did to him and wondered if I injured him badly as a small sob lodged in my throat. How could I have gotten it so terribly wrong? I refused to show how distressed I was. I didn't want to give these two the satisfaction. Instead, I didn't what any hostage would do. I began to talk.

"You killed Chad."

"No, I didn't."

"Yes, you did, Bubba. Who else could it be?"

Guffawing out loud then winding it down into that annoying hyena chuckle, he looked up front toward Donna and enthusiastically ranted, "She don't know much, does she, Momma? Some dark witch she is."

He looked at me and continued, "I was at the station with the sheriff looking over the notes on the skeleton. It was Momma here who done ol' Chad in. Then a few days later I took any suspicion off me by having my little "accident."

They were smiling smugly as I sat there, mouth agape. The deviousness of their actions made me think I probably didn't have a chance in hell of getting out of this alive. Why would anyone suspect Bubba when he was conveniently "attacked" by some unknown villain and forced off the road? I mean, he looked as if he ran into a brick wall.

"You truly are stupid for a witch, that's for sure." This from Donna, who snarled at me with such hatred that I recoiled into my seat and started shaking. "Well, you don't have to fret much longer. We have plans for you, honey."

Focusing her attention back on the road, she continued to speed away from town, leaving Bubba to lean toward me, his hand suddenly rubbing up and down my thigh.

"Yeah, listen to Momma. We have plans for you, darlin'. Momma always has the best-laid plans. But I'm sure she'd give us some alone time before she kills you. Lily Sweet, soon as you showed up in town, I thought to myself, *now that there is a gal I'd like to get to know.* Never saw someone pretty as you. I am going to enjoy getting to know you better, even if it's just for an hour or two."

Could it be this joker had no idea I was the little girl from so long ago? I pushed him off me and sat up, looking at Donna through the mirror again. She gave me a little wink then laughed so hard, a confused Bubba, who didn't get the inside joke we just shared, couldn't help himself from guffawing along with her.

"You people are mental."

Instead of giving me a response, Bubba hauled off and punched me, hard, and for the third time in twenty-four hours, my world went black.

* * *

I WOKE UP, head yet again throbbing, and realized I was tossed over Bubba's shoulder as we trudged through woods on a well-worn path. The disgusting pig was fondling my rear end as he walked behind his mother, and I swore right there I would beat the living stuffing out of him before I became his victim. I made sure my body stayed relaxed, because I didn't want to give away that I was conscious, and waited for an opportune time to make my move. What that move would be I had yet to work out.

I felt Bubba shift my weight, grunting a little. I told myself it was from the extra weight *he* was towing around on his person, rather than any extra burden my petite frame caused him. I felt his sweat coming through his shirt and off his skin, and I wanted to squirm in disgust but knew I had to continue with my guise until a prime moment came my way. I wondered if my newfound magic would aid me or let me down when I needed it most. I tried to call it up from my depths but didn't feel anything except Bubba's shoulder digging into my gut.

We paused, and I was shifted again before we moved forward and up some stairs onto a covered porch. Bubba accidentally whacked my head into an old ice cooler on the front porch, yet I remained quiet and managed not to tense up, despite the pain. I kept my eyes shut into slits and could just make out that we were deep in the woods somewhere, at a run-down cabin. Unlocking the door, I heard Donna tell Bubba to toss me in the spare bedroom and use a rope to hog-tie me. Hog-tie? Oh, this was not going to be pleasant.

He hitched me up once again and clumsily made his way toward a small room.

"Not that one, you damn fool. That's where them bones and stuff is at. Take her to the other."

Any doubts I entertained dissolved at Donna's comment. I wondered where they stuck Chad Barwick. On further contemplation, recalling the freezer on the porch, I surmised I had that answer.

I felt nothing but dread when he kicked the door closed behind him, yelling for Donna to take her time making supper while he got reacquainted with me. She just cackled manically in response. The lunatic.

Tossing me onto the bed, I heard the mattress protest under Bubba's weight as he plunked down on it and wiped his brow. I managed to take a peek and almost recoiled in horror as the room was riddled with all manner of taxidermy; little pathetic eyes were staring at me as if they sympathized with my current situation. I also smelled an unfamiliar scent and noticed bottles of developer on the table beside the bed and an older model camera sitting near them. That explained the photograph taken of me near the diner. I quickly shut them again when I heard Bubba kick off his shoes then felt his weight above me and could smell his breath.

"You ain't foolin' me, darlin'. I know you're awake. Damn shame I had to do that to your face, but sometimes a little pain makes Bubba a happy man, especially when he's the one doling it out." He laughed and shifted his weight, using one hand to stroke my face then give it a little smack. "Open your eyes, witch."

His words made my blood run cold. I realized in that

moment that his kind of evil was the kind I needed to rid the world of. I sensed the stirrings of my own dark magic, coiling inside me, aware, and working its way up. The sensation of my power gave me confidence, and I opened my eyes, slowly giving Bubba a lazy, seductive smile.

"Hey there, big boy."

That seemed to be the last thing he expected.

His eyes widened, and I saw him react with a sharp intake of breath, but then his eyes squinted, and he backed away from me a touch.

"You don't fool me. You tricked me into thinking you liked me once, but I'm not stupid. You can't fool me again."

I opened my eyes wide and pouted a little, looking deep into his nasty grey eyes. I wondered if mine had gone from cognac to black yet and hoped it wouldn't hamper my ploy if they did.

"Fooled you? How did I fool you, Bubba? Last time we were together, you kissed me goodbye, then I never heard from you again. Of course, I now know your accident wasn't a *real* accident, but when I heard about it, I tried to see you in the hospital. No one would let me in to be with you, seeing as we aren't related or anything—yet. If you were out, why didn't you contact me?"

I could see the big idiot chewing my words around his puny mind, suspicion mixed with a glimmer of hope. *Ugh.*

"Don't try and trick me, witch. You know we killed Chad. Why would you still want me if you thought we did that, and worse? Dang, girl. I was the one that bashed you in the head, knocking into the hole in your porch! Pretty easy for us to sneak around your property and hide, what with all those overgrown bushes and limbs. Don't tell me you'd forgive me after doin' all that stuff."

I made note to trim everything back and have some landscaping done at my home—if I ever got away from these two.

He stayed firm in his mistrust of me, but I felt his breath catch, then speed up, as he watched me slowly lick my lips and smile.

"Bubba, you don't know much about me, and how could you? After all, you don't know me, and you don't fathom just how evil and dark a witch I really am."

I reached up slowly and wrapped my arms around his neck with my mouth slightly open then whispered, "Why don't you kiss me again, Bubba, and find out?"

I could see he wanted to, but still he resisted my wiles and stubbornly continued to question my motives. Ugh, come on, lug nut.

"What about your family, your new friends here in town? What about them? You sure seem to be happy to be among all of them, making such a big deal about you returning and all." He swallowed, loudly, and I knew my fingers, teasing his neck, were having an effect on him.

"Oh, Bubba. Silly man. I hate my *family.* My momma told me all manner of nasty things about them, and I grew to loathe everything and anything to do with the lot. I just came back to sell that house and all its contents and see what more I could get from them before I went back to New York. Or set out somewhere exotic. My momma left me rather well off. I could go anywhere I wanted in the world—and take you with me."

I raised myself up and lightly kissed his lips. The only thing stopping me from hurling in his piggish face was the evil darkness surging out of me and starting to swirling around us. How he didn't sense it was beyond me, but I knew in that instant his will broke, and he chose to believe me.

"I'm going to have you, witch. I'm going to make you beg me to stop then laugh when you ask for more. I'll make you tell Bubba you're sorry for being such a bad, bad girl."

Clamping down on my mouth, he started to return my

kiss when I brought my right hand down to his chest, stopping right above his heart. I broke away from his feeble attempt at kissing and smiled.

"I've been waiting for this my entire life, Bubba. I swore all those years ago I would *never* apologize to someone as disgusting as you. You're a pathetic bully without a spine, who enjoys hurting small animals. But that makes you weak. Remember that, remember that you got bested by the little girl you tried to bully and scare, and may that be the last thing you remember in this lifetime."

His eyes widened as recognition filled his eyes, and he tried to move off me. But that's when I let every bit of magic I pulled out of my core into him. His body tensed, and he bucked backward as my power flew deep and hit its mark, sending him back onto the mattress. I didn't let up until I smelled the bed smoking from the jolt I was forcing through his heart. It didn't take very long at all, and I sensed nothing but satisfaction coursing through my body as his eyes lost all life.

Sometimes a little wicked *did* make everything good. Or in my case, the darkness in me extinguished the evil in my nemesis, forever. I felt justified in removing this pathetic excuse of a life, and it felt awesome. Karma was indeed— well, *you* know!

I sat back, exhausted, but satisfied that I had saved myself from the horrors of Bubba, still feeling some small remorse for embracing my dark magic. Rationally, I knew it would have been me or him, and I was saving my life. As I came down off my magic high, I became rather dizzy with having spent so much of it at one time. So much so that I didn't hear the door open behind me or feel the frying pan slam into the back of my head until it was too late. Not again. Yes again... enter darkness.

CHAPTER 22

his time I woke up and knew several hours had gone by. The sun was still up, but I could tell it was late afternoon, approaching dusk, with shadows low in the small cabin. I found myself tethered by a heavy rope to a wooden chair and sitting near the kitchen table while Donna sat nearby, gorging on the meal she had prepared earlier. I was sure I killed Bubba. I couldn't believe this woman, cool as a cucumber, sitting here dining with his body in the next room. But heck, what's one more, even if it was your son?

"Yeah, you killed him all right. Did me a favor, though, didn't ya? He slipped up bashing you like that last night, not waiting for my orders...but now I can pin this all on him and walk away, the poor distraught momma."

I knew my head took a bunch of whacks as of late, but I still wanted to ask her if she felt no remorse over me killing her child, overgrown swine that he was.

"Don't you start tossing questions at me, you little witch!" Spittle flew from her mouth, and a wild look was back in her eyes again. Bubba may have been a mean bully, but this chick was unhinged. Lovely.

"I'll do the talking, thank you very much. So, you want to know the who, what, when, where, why, and how of it, don't you? Oh, come on! You've been trying to figure this out with that mooning cousin of yours. Pathetic little cur. Following you around like a puppy and hoping you'd become best friends. She makes me sick. All your Dolce and Croy relations make me sick. Especially your matriarch, Adriana."

This she spat out with venom. Donna picked up her plate and threw it into the sink where it shattered then leaned over and smacked me, hard, across the face. Ow! That stung. I was getting tired of all this brutality to my person. Instead of making me recoil in fear, I surged toward her, straining my cords.

"Oh, feisty one, aren't ya? Well, it ain't gonna do you any good. I know you're new at this magic stuff, though you used the kind of magic any regular woman knows how to use to her best abilities to fool a man. Bubba was an idiot. I'm not. That boy didn't even recognize you! Of course, I never did let him in on my scheming. He was just the brawn to my brains."

She got up and moved her chair across from mine, straddling it.

"So, you think you have some of this figured out, but I'm sure you don't have all of it, am I right?"

"You killed Adelaide because she messed with your husband Ross, didn't she?"

Donna stared at me a long moment then threw her head back and cackled like a rabid chicken.

"Girl, I thought you had some brains in your head. You believe all those rumors I spread around town about Adelaide? She was no slut. Oh, she made one mistake with Dillon Chase, whose fiancé was fixing to forgive them both. That's when I put the suggestion in her head that the girl was a laughin' at her. When in reality, the sniveling 'harlot' was crying in shame. After that, what with the menfolk wanting her, I let the rumors take wing. Each and every one of them was an easy sell. But no—that girl had eyes for only one man. Charles Sweet."

My expression of shock had her slap her knee with jubilation.

"And she couldn't have him, now could she? Not with him and Jessica the ones to be married! Aw, look at you! You had no clue about any of this. Well, doll, you just sit back and listen to this little tale of mine."

She reached over to the table and lit a cigarette, taking a long drag before she settled in to continue her story.

"Adelaide Croy was the prettiest girl in this town. You look more like her in some ways than you do Jessica, but in truth you are all Charlie Sweet. Spittin' image of Adriana, aren't you? Anyway, she could have any man in town exceptin' the one she had a crush on since first grade. That's when she walked to school with her big sister Jess, and they met up with a boy named Charlie. He and Jessica had been pals since kindergarten, but it was starting to blossom into something else by the time they were pre-teens…all those ragin' twelve-year-old hormones and nothing to be done about it. She just tagged along and daydreamed about a boy that would one day become her brother-in-law. Kinda sucks, huh?"

Donna nodded her head in a gratified way then glared at me again.

"Well, they all played together and when they were older would run off exploring and such. When Addy got older, about sixteen I guess, she must have got tired of watching her big sister canoodling with Charlie, so she set her sights on Dillon Chase, our sheriff. He favored your daddy—did you know that? He must have some Latin blood in him. Anyway, I don't know if she seduced him in the normal way or used a spell, but he jumped at the chance to be with her. When she realized a close second could never replace her true love, she became despondent, and your daddy tried his best to pull her out of depression. She was a bit wild after that, but not a slut, no, not that. She took up with old Chad again, but he was already drinking heavy, even in his youth, and men like Dillon, well, our sheriff didn't want to see her hurt, especially not by his deputy, so he tried to step in, and it caused a ruckus. 'Course, a little whisper here and there made folks think it was a lover's triangle. Heh, I am good at whispering the rumors."

Donna had a self-satisfied smile on her face that I was itching to wipe off, and my mind kept trying to figure out ways I could escape to do just that.

"Didn't surprise many folks around here when they took off not long after that, only I remember Jess didn't want to leave at all. But eventually, they did and then came home from that journey with you in tow and Jess and Charles married in Las Vegas. Now how could Adelaide remain here very long after? She lasted, what, three and a half or four years before she went through with her threats and ran off to Vegas to be a showgirl?"

She shook her head, pleased with herself, then continued her tale.

"Only person she ever told was Chad Barwick, and he swore with his life he'd never tell a soul that she was a-goin', and that's why he had to die. That, and the fact that he saw me get her onto a Greyhound bus then cast a mighty powerful forget and erase spell. That's my specialty, only I was smart enough to never register as a witch, so no one knows I am. Hell, any time someone suspects, I cast a forget spell and voila! Gone. It's taxing, though. Those are draining spells, and it's difficult for me to achieve one then get on with my day, you know?"

What? I was supposed to show her sympathy or something here? I think not. She must have read that on my face and gave me a little sneer.

"Beau gave me his passkey when we met at the morgue. He gave the sheriff a sleeping draught and when poor old Glen woke up hours later, he found Beau snoring right along with him, so he figured they both nodded off. But Beau was with me and helped carry the evidence from the morgue. It was easy, what with my forget and erase spells going off left and right, and since everyone there knew and trusted the fine deputy! Beau drove back because I was done in. All we had to do then was hightail it back here to stash the evidence. Nobody knows my Ross left me this run-down place in his will. I never made anything of it, because it's the perfect spot to hide things when I need to. After drinking one of your aunt Iona's restorative potions, and ain't that irony, having a Croy help me in my time of need, I took Beau back to the police station, with Glen none the wiser.

Early last Sunday, to remove any possible suspicion off Beau, I met him on the highway on his way back from interviewing suspects, and rammed his car, then we pushed it into the ravine. I even bashed his head and torso with a crowbar to make it look authentic, then he woozily got behind the wheel and I hightailed it up the ravine and called his accident in from that old payphone just inside the town limits, making sure not to leave fingerprints. I was back in Sweet Briar and started work that morning, minus my car, with no one being the wiser. I left it in my garage and begged Sheila for a lift, telling her I had a dead battery."

Grinning maniacally at me, she turned shrewd and scratched her chin before continuing.

"Well, maybe Sheila suspects, but I have that covered. Got me one of her precious kitty cats, now don't I? I had already done Chad in, so the second part was easy. How did I know about Chad? Oh, I saw him confront you that day, right from the diner windows, and I knew he was going to tell you about Adelaide. I waited the next day, taking off of work. I pretended I needed time to go visit the Brewster's, I used to clean for them, but instead I started tailing Chad. Didn't even need to bother, because by seven thirty that morning, when I followed him to your house, I knew I could kill him, then actually go see the good reverend. I'm sure he'd fudge the timeline if I need an alibi. I know things about that man that he'd sell his soul to keep quiet. Killing Chad was easy. I even used his own knife on him! Last word he ever said was 'Adelaide,' the fool."

I opened and closed my mouth then chanced asking one question.

"She's alive?"

"Who, Addy? Well, of course she's alive or should be. Didn't I just tell you she ran off?"

I tried to process this but then remembered the skeleton under my porch.

"But the remains at my place…they were female, and…"

"And nobody suspected they'd be my dear departed sister Deanna's remains. That's why I had to steal them, her dental records. That slut had the nerve to sleep with my Ross. He might not have been the finest catch in this damn town, but he was *my* man. Even if he did try to calm me down saying he could easily have us both and I should share him. Nuh-uh, we done had a kid! She crossed the line when she messed around with him." *Strange sense of propriety there, sister.*

"But why not punish *him*? After all, he messed right on back with Deanna. Why just—oh my gosh, you killed your sister and put her under my porch!"

Donna reached up and slapped me hard across the face again. This time the ash from her cigarette fell on my lap, burning me before it went out.

"Now look what you've done."

She lit another cigarette and sat back with a smug look on her face then glowered. "'Course I was mad at him. Who do you think called the cops and gave them a tip on who done the robbery? And yeah, I done Deanna, too. Bashed her brains in and pulled up the floorboards of your porch, tossing her under there after your momma did a runner with you and your daddy followed. Had to wait a few months until everyone gave up on the idea they'd be back and closed up the house. But my freezer here came in handy. Used to keep it in the spare room. I had her stashed in here, right back there where Beau is lying dead, but knew I needed to get rid of her before someone came along and found her. Best spot in the world, once your family was all gone."

She could see I had more questions and continued her vile tale, not waiting for me to speak up.

"It started out as a lark. I wasn't intending to keep at it until I saw it was working and Addy left town. You know it was me that used to call Jessica and keep her paranoid and would whisper in her ear that she had to run, or 'they' would find you, right? Run she did with Charles not far behind her. I wanted your daddy, see? Tried to tempt him, but he wouldn't have any part of it. Only had eyes for his *girl*. Made me sick when I found out how much he loved her. I started sending notes from clear over in Hiawassee where we moved. They never could figure out who was sending them. I made out some bad people had Adelaide and were torturing her. I used to clean house for that Gloria Stillwell when she just started out doing hair at her place. Adelaide used to go there all the time, and I never did throw out none of it. I kept all of it. Came in handy when I sent it to your daddy telling him to try and find her before her locks of hair would be followed by body parts."

She smiled, remembering the horrible things she did to

my family, and puffed smoke in my direction as she turned my way again.

"Before he left, though, that was my best work. See, I started sending notes to Jessica that 'we' were coming for baby Lily. That 'we' planned to do horrible experiments on her because she showed signs of being a strong dark witch and that no matter what they did, we'd be able to find her—you—and take you away forever. Your daddy, he went a bit mental toward the end and sent Jessica away with you, giving her those black kitten earrings you've been wearing to block your magic—and block any witch in this town from being able to trace you. Guess who he got them from? Good enough to take those from me when I offered to help, with my skills. It was your own daddy that made sure you'd never be found and lose your memories! How do you like that? And you have probably been blaming Jessica! Of course, he was supposed to go fetch you if he succeeded in finding Adelaide and bring you all home safe. When he never came back, well, I guess Jessica chose to stay away in hiding all these years, until cancer finally rid the world of one more Croy, doing us all a favor."

I was crying by this point. I couldn't help it. Such evil things done to my family, and for what? Jealousy? Revenge? Seriously?

"He didn't do that to me...you did. Why did you hate my mother so much? My aunt? Why did you destroy my family?"

Her face became so red and she screamed so loudly that her vocal cords stretched to the breaking point. "Because your daddy told me he could never love someone like me. Someone with weak magic. He told me my sister might be a slut, but I was a slut hiding my witch ability, and his *family dynasty* had to continue with strong witch blood. He tried to make it sound like he only had eyes for one girl, but what man can do that? I begged him, told him I'd register with the

Council, but he shook his head, saying I was delusional and that it didn't matter about me hiding my talent. It was all about my *personality* and me sleepin' around. Well, who would care so much about something like that? So, I knew he was using it as an excuse. You see, he owed me and kept my secret, because I kept one of his after I found out—so we were in a sort of uneasy truce."

With that last statement, she leaned forward and put her cigarette out on my shoulder, the burning pain dulled by the ache in my heart, for the loss of my family due to this sick, wretched woman.

"But my father, he's still out there. He never discovered where Addy went. You said she left to try becoming a show girl out west."

"The last thing I forced my dear little sister Deanna to do for me was a strong charm spell. Deanna might not be a strong witch, but she sure knew how to make love potions… lust, really. The stupid girl thought I would step aside and let her have my Ross and our new pretty house in Hiawassee and leave my boy with no daddy or home. He started making good money running drugs out that way, and she wanted a better life, so she agreed to do this last thing for me in a deal. Deanna made one for Charlie and one for Addy, turning them into lustful horn dawgs. Little did she know, once she cast those spells, I was planning on bashing her head in with a crowbar. I beat her head in until I couldn't recognize her no more."

Yeah, this psycho was the definition of pure evil. I got it now, a tad too late, it seemed. Donna started laughing hysterically again, letting me see how far gone she truly was.

"The spell made Adelaide and Charles forget who they were once they left the town border. She ran out west or down farther south looking for excitement and fame. She got off easy, to tell you the truth. More than likely became a porn star in California with that much lust juice in her! I put Charlie on her trail but also made him forget you and Jessica. Who knows? Maybe he found Addy and killed her then did himself in."

I looked in confused horror at Donna, because with a lust spell…well. But she cleared it up for me, causing me to become sick to my stomach.

"Oh, yeah, that was the final part of the spell Deanna cast on him. See, she could do powerful love spells but also had even stronger reversals. The minute he started out on his journey to find Addy, Deanna hit him with it. If he ever found her, lust turned into anger. He either found her, and turned her into a sex slave, or more likely he found her and killed her in a lust filled rage."

I'd never in my life experienced such depths of malevolence and now understood the difference my family tried to impart between being a dark witch versus fighting true evil with dark magic. I vowed if I ever got myself out of this situation, I'd start my lessons with my great-grandmother in earnest. I didn't have to like it, but I'd do it. It wasn't looking good for me, though.

Suddenly, Donna stood up and pushed my chair over, knocking me backward so I was facing the ceiling. She stood over me, but there wasn't much I could do with my legs, arms, and chest fastened securely to the chair.

"Don't worry, hon. I won't make this too painful." She walked over the other side of the kitchen, and I heard metal scraping along the floor. Still staring upward, I could barely turn my head in her direction because the pain in my temple was making it difficult. I was shaking with dread and fear.

"Now, keep your eyes open or close them tight. It doesn't matter much to me, sweetie! Nighty night, toots."

That's when I saw her raise a giant crowbar high over her head and start a downward motion. I closed my eyes, tight.

Oh, come on! You would, too. Don't tell me you'd have the hutzpah to stare Death in the face! Even if Death looked like a middle-aged, deranged, beehive haircut–wearing, one. You *would* not.

I tensed, waiting for the first, and more than likely fatal, blow, when a loud explosion rocked the room, rendering me all but deaf.

"Take that, you lousy bitch."

My ears were ringing, and my mouth couldn't even form the scream I heard myself making in my head. I judiciously turned in the direction of the voice and couldn't believe my eyes when I did.

My itty-bitty great-grandmother was standing there, dressed like a ninja, with blue sparks snapping and trickling out of her fingertips…and behind her, Susanne Washington was holding a smoking shotgun and nodding in a self-satisfied way.

"You got her with your magic, Miss Adriana, and it looks like I hit her with my buckshot. Two old biddies, we did that unholy woman in."

"Praise Jesus," said Granny.

I passed out.

CHAPTER 23

wo blissfully quiet weeks had passed since my horrible ordeal and brief hospital stay. The wounds on my face and body were healing nicely. The wound in my heart? Not so much. I received so many cards and gifts that I was overwhelmed by all the love I was shown. Brian sent a big bouquet of roses, Jake sent a small mug with assorted teas and a "get well" balloon, and Lorcan sent me a bag of black jellybeans, Jelly Belly, which had me laughing so hard I pulled a stitch out. He *had* noticed my obsession, it seemed! Andrea sent me a gift tin of assorted treats from the bakery, which would go well with my new mug and the tea. Family and friends alike all made sure to pamper me.

When I finally got out of the hospital to continue my convalescing at home, I made peace with Brian, who seemed a little hurt that I suspected him. Under the circumstances, he understood completely...or so he said. We hadn't gone out on any dates or ridden his bike or made out like wanton bunny rabbits, not that I could yet, so yeah, I kind of wondered where we stood.

Jake, my hero for rushing me to Eileen and Henry's place,

246

forgave me for ramming my noggin into his man parts, which was big of him. He visited me while I convalesced, letting me know what was going on with the trial. Yeah, the Witch Council did things a bit differently than regular folk, and I didn't envy Donna her comeuppance.

Oh, yeah—she lived. Great-grandmother blasted her, but it went askew since Adriana's eyesight wasn't what it once was. And Susanne? Well, she was never a good shot, anyway. She might have thought she'd sent Donna to visit old Beelzebub, but the buckshot hit her in the foot, which dropped her to the ground, making her unable to flee. Not that she would have gotten very far. Brian rushed in just after I fainted and saved the day, apparently. It seemed he started suspecting Bubba when he showed up for work the morning after he accosted me and didn't have his passkey on him, saying he lost it—or gave it to someone to use. I supposed Donna forgot to give it back to him.

I informed my aunts Iona and Chiara that I regained some of my memories and told everyone what Donna did and said. It wasn't easy reliving all that, and the Council, with Aunt Chiara at the helm, started things moving to try and find my dad and Aunt Adelaide, if they were both still alive. I chose to believe in hope, and waited daily for any news. My great-grandmother destroyed my kitten earrings, promising me another pair clean of any cloaking charms. She also asserted those in the Council look for traces of magic leading out of town, convinced that Donna and Deanna put the same kind of cloaking spell she used for my earrings on my dad and aunt as well, despite Donna insisting she didn't. It wasn't like her word could be trusted. This meant they wouldn't be found if searched for, but if the witches doing the search knew one was used, they might be able to reverse it. Which made sense, since in all these years they were never found. I didn't want to consider any alternative theories.

Rita came to visit me while I was bedridden, bringing me a soothing tisane from her shop. It tasted like mulberry and made me stupid drowsy but allowed me to sleep soundly, banishing any bad dreams which I suffered from for the first two nights back home. She was followed by Eileen and Henry Reid, who brought three casseroles, stuffing them in my tiny freezer, then fussed over me for a while. I wouldn't need to scrounge for food for weeks!

Gloria Stillwell showed up and offered to trim my hair, giving my long locks a stylish layered look, which helped hide some of the stitches I sported for a bit. She was indeed a talented hairdresser, and I vowed to return to her shop when I next needed my hair done.

June and Dennis fretted over me, both wanting me to move into Jake's old bedroom over the hardware store where they resided, but I insisted I was fine right where I was, thanking them both. June was a guilty mess for a while. She had stopped herself from finishing her story about Donna and Bubba, pretending her pie was burning in the oven—all because she didn't want to say they had arrived back in town the same day my mom and I left. Not wanting to bring it up in front of me. Had she, well, it certainly would have made *me* realize who the culprit was. With that information, I would have known Bubba was the mean boy earlier, sending me after them and not Brian. I told June not to let it wear on her. Then I told husband and wife both to stop worrying so much, and I was perfectly happy and had all I needed.

It didn't stop them from allowing Donald and Doreen Murphy to stop by with an endless supply of hot soup and sweet tea. Doreen told me to stop by the motel any time for a visit and more goodies when I felt up to it. Donald, winking at me, even made sure to lock the door on his way out.

Shirley Jones drove me home from the hospital with her brother Stu, since they were heading this way, and she wanted to make sure I wasn't showing any signs of a concussion, her EMT skills notwithstanding, since she was the one who patched me up and did my stitches to stop all the bleeding when they found me. Stu whittled me a wooden Ford keychain, just about an exact replica of my truck with the name George carved on it. I had no idea he was so talented and was very touched he took the time to make it. I kissed him on the cheek, telling him what a fine artist he was; I never saw a man blush so deeply as good old Stu.

Sheila came by with my lunch daily, compliments of Joe. His diner food was one of the reasons I was healing so fast, I was sure of it.

Andrea stayed over several nights, never far from my side, snoring away on her sleeping bag. Her dad, Stephen, would bring me treats from his bakery every morning. It was good having an uncle who baked earth-shattering delights married into my family! I was getting fat from all the strudel I was consuming.

Susanne had her church ladies knit me a throw and proudly delivered it one day. Sitting on the porch now, I wrapped myself in it, thinking about her parting words the day she delivered it.

"Honey child, the Good Lord works in mysterious ways. I just happened to be on my way out of June's Emporium and had just pulled away from the curb when Sheila from Joe's Diner flagged me down. She saw you looking all agitated with Beau, and when you got shoved in the back seat of that car, with Donna driving like a mad woman? Well, Sheila said she couldn't keep quiet anymore. Sent me on a car chase, she did. I followed discreetly, and when I saw they were heading north, out of town, toward my church, I called your granny. She didn't need any convincing because just that day she cornered Brian and told him it was more than likely Donna who was behind it all. She got Sheila to confess something and put two and two together, or so she says. She also found out Ross owned that rundown cabin property, and it all clicked into place for her. Brian was heading over to your apartment to guard you when you bashed him over the head, knocking him out instead, until he came to and Sheila told him what she had me doing."

I got dizzy with all this coming at me but couldn't bear to stop Susanne from her fascinating report.

"Adriana and I met near the entrance to the rental cabins. Everyone was singing loudly that day, in my congregation, praising Jesus, when I snuck in and grabbed my daddy's shotgun. Bless his heart, and may he rest in peace, he always did keep that thing loaded in case some bad folk would decide to come calling. Looks like the Good Lord put me in the right place at the right time, and I was able to send that evil woman to the Devil where she belongs! Or at least the prison hospital. You rest now, child, and feel better soon."

I planned on bringing Susanne and her entire church group some of Uncle Stephens baked goodies the first Sunday I was given a clean bill of health.

Sheila stopped by right after Susanne left, clearing up her role in all of this. She noticed the damage on Donna's car, yet it was smooth as a baby's bottom the day before Bubba's "accident." She also heard her talking out loud to herself the day she saw Chad Barwick come up to me outside on the side deck. Apparently, she spied us from the diner then mumbled something along the lines of, "I should have gotten rid of him back when I did Deanna a turn." Putting two and two together, Sheila knew Donna had to be guilty of something horrible. She planned on telling, but Donna had Millie, her cat. That was Donna's security blanket—knowing she could use the cat as a threat. We surmised Donna must have noticed Sheila eavesdropping, and the risk to her precious cat was more than the poor woman could handle. She apologized profusely for not telling someone sooner, but I understood. I really did. I would have chosen to save my kitten, too, if I had the choice. I was glad Millie was back where she belonged.

Even Nora and Douglas showed up, although Nora had asserted, "You are probably enjoying all the attention, and I hope you had enough drama," hoping I wouldn't want to stay in Sweet Briar. When I informed her I planned on renovating the house and moving in once I felt up to it, she put on a pout and managed a polite, "How nice for you." Douglas just said, "Cool," and shrugged in that laissez-faire way he had about him. Sigh. Cousins. Gotta love them, I guess.

My great-grandmother Adriana waltzed in all smug, like she solved the case of the century and saved the day all by herself. While the jury was still out whether or not she really did pin Donna as the murderess, she had come ready to do battle. I had to concede her that. Imagine my surprise when she sat on my bed and gave me a gentle kiss on my bruised temple.

"Be well, little one, *stammi bene*. We have much work to do whipping you into witchy shape when you are ready. I have to make sure you are all healed up before I start smacking you around again, *cara mia*." Aw, I knew she liked me. I think. I made note to pick up an English-Italian dictionary.

The one person I didn't see much of was Lorcan, which was why I was surprised to see him coming up the driveway this morning. It was chilly, now well into October, but still not at the level I knew the Catskills was experiencing. There the leaves were at peak color, while here just a few maples and some other unidentifiable varieties were going golden and orange. Much of the rest of town remained green, with mild days and chilly nights. I was sitting there enjoying the comfort of my throw when he walked up the steps and sat down next to me in one of the Brumby rockers.

"You know, I might think you've been trying to avoid me, if I didn't know any better."

Lorcan smiled at me to take the sting out of his words and show me he was teasing.

"My life has been moving pretty fast lately. I'm as sorry as you are that I've been otherwise occupied." I shook my head then winced as a remnant pain let me know it was still there and my temple still tender.

"Life moves pretty fast. If you don't stop and look around once in a while, you could miss it," Lorcan stated, looking at my truck, nodding a bit, pleased with his proclamation.

I laughed out loud. "Nice one, but *way* too easy. Matthew Broderick, *Ferris Bueller's Day Off*, 1986."

"Touché." Lorcan held his hands out in front of him, examining his nails. "But you know, I just heard from Shirley, and our resident EMT told me there was no reason you couldn't take a short ride with me, just over to my shop. I still never got to show you that thing I told you about."

Jumping up, I all but tossed the wrap on the ground but saved it at the last minute, placing it on the rocker I had just vacated.

"You're on! And this time, no one and nothing is going to stop me from seeing it. Let's go."

"Yes, we can go, but first go poke your head in the shop and let June know where you are heading so she doesn't have a heart attack wondering where you ran off to."

Not wanting to waste another moment, I rushed in to tell June my plans then met Lorcan out front. He helped me up into his big Chevy truck, and I bounced a little in anticipation. Lorcan chuckled at my antics, I could tell he was excited to show me this mysterious thing. I couldn't blame him—he had been trying since my third day in town, only to be thwarted at every turn. Now I was finally going to see it!

We made the short drive over to his shop just off the

square, but he stopped me before I could get out, running around to my side and helping me down so I wouldn't feel any pain. He took my hand and walked me past his place, which had me wrinkling my forehead. I assumed whatever it was would be in his shop. We stopped at a building next door, at a rusty old garage-style door. The structure was covered in a local ivy I found out was called kudzu and was purported to have "swallowed the South." I wasn't that impressed upon first glance. You had to turn down this small alley that sported a few parking spaces and the garage door opened toward the side of Lorcan's shop—or would if it didn't look to be rusted shut.

Lorcan leaned down and opened the door. It protested, groaning and creaking the entire way up, but open it did. We walked into the spacious room, which was dusty and empty, when he turned to me and went, "Ta da!"

Ta what? I turned slowly, noting the huge windows that were facing east but covered in those nasty vines, blocking the view. Then I spied a small kitchen area with industrial sinks and a massive fridge that I was sure didn't run. The floor was concrete and had four drains in each quadrant as if it was once split into four equal-sized areas. It had high ceilings, and I saw that a wooden staircase went up to a second-floor open loft. There were a few open doors up there; one led to a half bath, and one to what I assumed was a closet. Looking back toward the kitchen area, I noted another door, which I could see was a larger bathroom, then looked beyond that to the floor-to-ceiling shelves lining the back wall.

I turned to him inquisitively, and he smiled down at me then slowly spun me around to face the windows once again.

Standing close behind me he whispered, "Imagine those windows without all those vines blocking them, on both levels. Then think of what the light would be like in here." He tilted my head up toward the ceiling center. "And that is a massive skylight, also covered by kudzu vines. Just imagine all of them gone and this place cleaned out and ready."

"Ready for what?" I turned to face Lorcan and watched his deep brown eyes crinkle in the same way his dad Henry's crinkled when they were happy.

"Ready for you. This is your art studio, Lily, if you want it."

I was shocked into silence, which for me was saying a lot. I looked at Lorcan then slowly took in the space one more time until I was facing him again. Reaching up, I gave him the biggest hug I had ever given anyone in my entire life.

"I would love it...but..." Reaching down to touch my lips, Lorcan shushed me then grinned, his entire face transforming to the little boy I could now just barely remember if I tried hard enough.

"This was part of the garage my granddaddy, Malcolm, left me, along with my truck, only I never needed the room. It has been sitting here for decades just waiting for someone to need it. To love it. It's yours, Lily. It will make a great studio for you. And you can't beat the location."

I decided right then and there not to worry about it another minute. I would figure out how to pay for it and hoped whatever Lorcan decided my rent would be was something I could handle. I felt like shouting and was about to burst with joy. Instead, I turned to Lorcan again.

"I can take my found things here and create. Oh, Lorcan—yes. Yes, yes, yes, yes, *yes*! I'll take it!"

"I'm glad, Tink. Let's shake on it." We shook on it then laughed, and my toes curled when he instantly understood my reference. I think I may have just named my studio: *Found Things*.

Despite all the horrible trials that I went through since I arrived in Sweet Briar, I knew at this moment I was truly home. Oh, I still had to get to the bottom of the Jake and Lorcan drama that involved Nora.

I wondered at Dennis Carter and his overenthusiastic defense of Rita Chase—what was their story, and would I ever find out, and did I need to? My thoughts then turned to Aunt Adelaide and my poor father. Carlo Sweet, Charles, my dad Charlie. My dad. Were they still alive, and would the Witch Council be able to track them down?

Lastly, I thought of the coming chaos that Aunt Chiara spoke of. When I worried her about it a few nights ago, she brushed it off and declared most of it was hearsay and premonitions, and we had plenty of time, but I knew I needed to find out if there truly was a threat looming over this wonderful town I would now call home.

I still wasn't quite sure I could totally embrace being a dark witch—I had the occasional nightmare where Bubba would show up and try to kiss me, only I turned into the Grim Reaper, killing him again and again. Yeah. See why I'm so reluctant to embrace anything that hints at darkness? Yet, despite it all, I figured I could be a little wicked when the need arose.

* * *

A FEW DAYS LATER, after shooing Andrea away, promising to show her my new studio the next morning, I went to my window and looked out with a smile on my face and wonder in my heart. It had been a busy weekend, and I was reflecting on it all.

The town had a small ceremony and burial for Chad Barwick—and another for Deanna Fredricks earlier that week. There were no relatives left to speak of, so the entire town turned out.

This past weekend, a handful of my Croy relatives, along

with a few Dolce ones, and close friends, had a more private ceremony. We celebrated the life of Jessica Croy Sweet. My family interred her cremains in the small graveyard surrounding the Catholic Church where she had been a member. Then we all went back to Aunt Iona's place for a celebratory meal that gave me a small sense of closure.

Walking over to my bed, I began talking to myself.

"Lily Sweet, you have a family. You have friends. You have a new town to get to know and love. A house of your own to fix up and live in—and a wonderful new art studio to go create your art in. You have some cute men making eyes at you. You have a home! What more could you ask for?"

Laughing a little, I plopped down onto the bed, ignore the niggling pain, too excited about my new life to let it shadow my happy mood. Then my thoughts went to Adelaide and my dad again, and I quickly sobered. Were they out there, alive somewhere still, without their memories, as I had lost mine? I thought of my mother Jessica and the sacrifice she made to keep me hidden. I now knew the evil she feared indeed existed, her paranoia justified. If only she and my dad knew it was one deranged woman and not a group after me. I wondered how different our lives would be had Donna Fredricks not come into it.

Donna was locked away in the Witch prison that I learned was vastly different from any regular human one. For one thing, it was heavily warded, and I was told I need not worry that she'd ever see the light of day again. Hopefully, Jake would make sure of that, especially with everyone's testimony and Brian diligently putting all the evidence back where it belonged. Once the trial is over, and she received a life sentence, I was sure I'd sleep better.

Brian. Yeah. I wondered where that was going. He stopped by tonight to check in on me and, when he left, brushed my lips with a soft kiss that made my toes curl and my heart go a-flutter. His baby blue eyes twinkled down at my molten brown ones, and his perfect hair, mussed in a way that other men had to pay hundreds of dollars for, to achieve the same effect, made me smile. I called him on that kiss, saying he didn't have the right to do such things if he was going to go around accusing me of being a loose woman. He came back with, "You spark potent magic, have a wicked slap and possess excellent throwing skills; my head is still rattled from that thumping you gave me, I think we're even, my sweet." Aw, he knew just what to tell a witch.

Then there was Jake and Lorcan, the other two men in my life. I had so many emotions to consider that I decided maybe I needed time to think things through before I went any further with Brian. Especially since there was Steve Junior to think about. Who, you ask, is Steve junior? Uncle Stephen's son from his first marriage, that's who.

Uncle Stephen was a widower when he met Aunt Chiara, and when they decided to marry, he came with a son in tow, now Aunt Chiara's stepson. Not related by blood and way easy on the eyes, I chastised Andrea from keeping her older half-brother hidden away from me until recently. Tall, blonde, with light chocolate brown eyes, Steve and I hit it off fabulously at the small gathering at Aunt Iona's house. I couldn't help but notice the scowls on Brian, Jake, and Lorcan's faces every time the new man, who held my attention, said something to make me laugh. This could get interesting.

What? A girl had to have options! Or at the very least, have a way to keep her suitors on their toes! Let me enjoy my fun. I had no plans to step in my dear aunt Addy's role as town's very own Scarlet O'Hara, but I deserved some time to enjoy the chase, after the life I had lived up until now. Especially now that I was home sweet home!

Poor Molly was devastated when I called her to say that,

yes indeed, I was here to stay. She promised to come visit, one of these days.

I reached up and touched the Pisces charm that I still wore around my neck. I found out at that same party that it was a gift from my father to me when I was born. Looking at the mantle where my childhood toys, Sam, Amy, and Pee Wee temporarily resided until I moved into my house, I couldn't help but get choked up with all the memories that would sneak in when I least expected. I knew it would take a long time to heal. But I had that time, didn't I? I was about to reach over and turn off my lamp when I recalled the wooden chest! Oh my gosh!

I hopped out of bed and ran to the closet where I'd hung the big bag Andrea brought back from my place the day we got caught sneaking around by Bubba; may he rot in pieces.

Pulling the ornate wooden box out of the sack, I sat on the floor and began to inspect it. As I noted that day, it had designs engraved deeply and by a very talented artist. It was exquisite! Then I noticed there was no apparent way to open it up. No latch, no keyhole, no secret lever. Nothing. Would you look at that? I shook it and could just barely hear something rattling around in there, but mostly it was a solid block of nothing, except I could see where it should open—if only I could figure out how.

Great. Another puzzle. I ran my nails around the horizontal line that circled the entire piece. Groaning in frustration, it remained firmly shut. Think. Think, think, think. There had to be some secret way to unblock this seal. And no, I was not about to toss it out the window onto the concrete below. Oh, I thought about it, for a second or two. But no, I wouldn't resort to breaking it if I could help it. Something told me that would be a mistake. For I could feel a pulse of energy emanating from deep inside. Yeah, my witchy senses were manifesting in me faster than the boobs I grew at puberty. Go figure?

I sighed heavily and was about to give up when I noticed tiny writing at the base. I jumped up once again and ran over to the small desk that shared a space with my dresser. Remembering I'd seen a small magnifying glass in the top drawer, I grabbed it and sat down on the floor near the light once more and began to read:

"Only she who owns this box can ask for what it holds be revealed. Polite words, a token placed, followed by her life's motto, shall open that which she seeks."

She? Well that must mean me. Polite words? Hmm…okay, here goes nothing:

"Wooden box, open for me—please?"

I felt a slight vibration, then nothing.

Polite words. Well, I did say please. Token. Life's motto? I groaned and rolled over onto my side, holding the box out as I landed on my back. I put my feet up onto my bed and stared at the chest. I could almost swear it was looking back at me, aware. Watching and waiting for my next words.

I looked at it again then sat up slowly and marveled at the small Pisces symbol I failed to notice until now. Right there on the top, just under a large flower that was carved front and center. No way—could it be? I removed my necklace and slipped the charm off of it, onto my hand, then placed it on the box. It was a perfect fit. I tried again:

"Wooden box, open for me—please?"

I felt a slightly stronger vibration, then nothing.

This was all well and good, but I seemed to still need my life's motto and—oh! Duh!

Scrambling over to my bedside table. I opened the drawer and hurriedly removed the letter my mother left behind for me and rushed back to sit once more on the floor, cradling the box in my lap. One more deep breath, I again opened my mouth and spoke the words:

"Wooden box, open for me please? Sometimes a little Wicked makes everything good."

Click, the wooden box popped open in my hands. Trembling, I lifted the lid entirely and frowned as I took note of its contents. Inside the box was a tiny collar that looked like it belonged to a cat. It was green with a little charm attached to it that spelled the word Wicked. The next item was a shiny black dagger, very thin and long, almost as long as the box, and I observed, with a start, that it had what looked to be dried blood on it. The last item in the wooden box was a rolled-up parchment. When I unfurled it, I found a crude hand-drawn map of sorts on one side. Turning it over, I found a message, beautifully handwritten in cursive, which said only three words:

"Lily. Find Me."

Unbelievable longing coursed through my body, and looking out the window, up to the moonlit sky, I opened my mouth to answer.

"I *will* find you. I promise."

* * *

THANK YOU FOR READING! I hope you loved meeting Lily, Adriana, and the rest of the characters. The next book in the Lily Sweet Mysteries is Witch Way is Up?. Find out who or what send that cryptic message to Lily and if she will ever fully embrace being a dark witch. Or will she be too distracted embracing one of the men she seemed to enchant?

CLICK HERE TO READ WITCH WAY IS UP? NOW>

And if you enjoyed Home Sweet Witch, you'll love the quirky, sometimes funny, sometimes dark, but always magical paranormal gang of monster-hunting antique appraisers. A Tale of Two Sisters, the tie-in series to my Lily Sweet World, highlights Lily's cousins Maggie and Ellie Fortune and is FREE on Kindle Unlimited!

"I am loving the snark in this book."

- S. Keller, BookBub author reviews.

I'd appreciate your help in spreading the word, including telling friends and family. Reviews help readers find books! Please leave a review on your favorite book site.

You can also join my Facebook Group: Author Bettina M. Johnson's Team Wicked for exclusive giveaways and sneak peek of future books—and just plain silliness!

SIGN UP FOR BETTINA M. JOHNSON'S NEWS-LETTER: http://eepurl.com/gZKo51

Continue on for a short excerpt from Witch Way is Up?...

Witch Way is Up?

"I HATE YOU! You stupid, dumb, plant—argh!"

Never underestimate the tenacity of the kudzu vine. The doggedness of this invasive species of plant from Japan, introduced to the United States in the late eighteen-hundreds, is legendary. Some joker convinced Southern farmers at the Centennial Exposition in Philadelphia that using this vine as a preventative measure to soil erosion, and as a food source for their animals, would be a stellar idea. It was a bad idea. A very, *unbelievably bad* idea.

"I can't believe I am going to be bested by a lousy weed that grows a foot a day. This is ridiculous! How is anyone supposed to win against this beast? I saw a large mound at the end of my street that I assumed was solid earth, but Donald Murray informed me it was Mr. Peterson's old shed. The vines *ate* it!"

Lorcan Reid, my friend, and landlord—he's letting me use an empty warehouse he owns next door to his mechanic shop for my art studio—just stood there laughing at me. He wasn't doing it out loud, mind you, his back was turned away from me, but I could see his mirth in the way his shoulders were shaking. That, and the fact that I noticed redness creeping up his neck to his ears as he struggled to hold it all in.

"It's *not* funny!"

I stomped my foot for emphasis, which was just too much for him to take, I supposed, because he guffawed, bending over, hands on his knees from the effort. I was not joining him in his merriment. Wheezing in between replying to me, Lorcan managed to straighten up, but not stop the flow of happy tears from running down his face.

The snot.

"That explains what happened to old Mr. Peterson, then." He barked out another laugh, trying to contain himself.

This was getting old.

"Oh, please! Nice try, mister. He moved to Boca Raton to be with his daughter and grandkids. Stop trying to trick me. I know better than falling for your shenanigans even though I've barely been here for two months."

Turning away from Lorcan, I sniffed, insulted, and let him know it by making a "hmph" sound, then trudged over to my worktable to try a more significant sized lopper. Dennis Carter, over at the hardware store, told me it was the biggest one they carried. I suspected he was only saying this to try and prevent my early demise. You see, I had already managed to drop the smaller one I owned on my noggin. It narrowly missed snipping my nose off in the process. However, it did give me a fat lip, and I spent a week looking like Billy Idol sneering into the camera in one of his videos from the eighties.

"Why don't you wait until this weekend, and I can round up a few guys to help me tackle it for you? You are so stubborn."

I know he means well, but I have been patiently waiting for him and his buddies to do just that for two weeks now, ever since I told him I'd rent the place on the day he surprised me with his offer. Lorcan Reid, an exceptional mechanic and all-around nice guy, brought me here while still recuperating from a nasty incident that laid me out in the hospital for a couple of days a few weeks ago. I barely managed to survive with my life, having tussled with a psychotic woman and her deranged son. The son I managed to zap to Kingdom Come, but his mom walloped me on the back of my head, hog-tied me and if it wasn't for my great-grandmother using her witchy powers and a church lady friend bearing a shotgun, I might not be here telling my tale right now.

Oh, yes, the witchy stuff. My name is Lily Sweet, and I am a witch.

* * *

SOCIAL MEDIA LINKS

I write in my own style that may not be everyone's cup of tea —so if you enjoy my characters and humor, my plots, how the storyline is developing, etc. and are eagerly anticipating the next in the series, be aware that I am just as excited as you are—I've found someone who thinks my story ideas are neat! That is thrilling for any writer to know (or it should be). THANK YOU!

Visit my official website to receive updates, find out about special offers and new releases, or read my blog about writing and farm life - complete with photos - you might even catch me mowing my ten acres (seriously): http://www.bettinamjohnson.net

For more information or to contact me:
author@bettinamjohnson.net

For even more (if you just can't enough of me) follow my
Social Media Links

Mailing List - https://bit.ly/2BvQXmP
BookBub - https://bit.ly/2Epejwj
Goodreads - https://bit.ly/3aTejQW
Author Page - Amazon - https://amzn.to/3lj7L2L
Instagram - https://bit.ly/2QpZa01
TikTok - https://bit.ly/2PQa6Hg
MeWe - https://bit.ly/36A2RcM
Facebook - https://bit.ly/3gOaFZY
Twitter: https://bit.ly/3jahMgY
YouTube - https://bit.ly/2Stvy2X

ABOUT THE AUTHOR

I always knew I wanted to write. As a kid, way before the technology age had hit, I'd be stuck in the car with the folks as we drove from our home on Staten Island, NY, where I was born and raised, to our family property in the Catskill Mountains. To drive away boredom, I would sit, staring out the window, and create adventures of daring thieves riding horseback along the road, trying to escape the law. Other times I'd imagine a wild girl riding her unicorn into battle (I had a vivid imagination - we didn't have video games yet!).

As the years passed, I'd start writing a book, then stop, then start again only to let life get in the way, until one day I had an epiphany—a kick in the pants moment. If I waited any longer, all those wonderful characters in my head would never have their stories told, and that made me sad. So, I treated writing as my career. Once I started, it became apparent nothing would ever stop me again. YOU, dear reader, are stuck with me until I go off to that great library in the sky...or wherever writers go when they crumble to dust in front of their typewriters (or laptops...whatever!).

I live in the North Georgia mountains on what I like to call a farm, with my husband and almost adult kids, a Cairn Terrier, a bunch of cats, and fish. Occasionally other critters show up to keep things exciting.

BOOKS BY BETTINA M. JOHNSON

The Lily Sweet Mysteries:

Home Sweet Witch

Witch Way is Up?

How To Train Your Witch (Coming soon!)

* * *

The Fortune-Telling Twins Mysteries:

A Tale of Two Sisters

Double Toil and Trouble (Coming Soon)

www.ingramcontent.com/pod-product-compliance
Lightning Source LLC
Chambersburg PA
CBHW031611240626
47153CB00002B/709